THE
FRENCH
WIDOW

ALSO BY MARK PRYOR

The Bookseller
The Crypt Thief
The Blood Promise
The Button Man
The Reluctant Matador
The Paris Librarian
The Sorbonne Affair
The Book Artist
Hollow Man
Dominic

A Hugo Marston Novel

THE
FRENCH
WIDOW

MARK PRYOR

SEVENTH
STREET
BOOKS®

Published 2020 by Seventh Street Books®

Cover image © Shutterstock
Cover design by Jennifer Do
Cover design © Start Science Fiction

This is a work of fiction. Characters, organizations, products, locales, and events portrayed in this novel either are products of the author's imagination or are used fictitiously.

Trademarked names appear throughout this book. Start Science Fiction recognizes all registered trademarks, trademarks, and service marks mentioned in the text.

Inquiries should be addressed to
Start Science Fiction
221 River Street
9th Floor
Hoboken, New Jersey 07030
PHONE: 212-431-5455
WWW.SEVENTHSTREETBOOKS.COM
10 9 8 7 6 5 4 3 2

ISBN 978-1-64506-023-9 (paperback)
ISBN 978-1-64506-030-7 (Ebook)

Printed in the United States of America

This book is for Romano,
the newest member of the Pryor family.

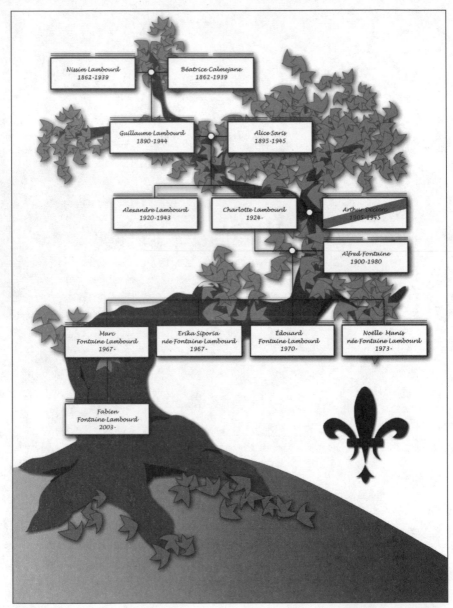

Illustration by James Ziskin

CHAPTER ONE
THE KILLER

The outskirts of Paris glide past my train window, filling it with concrete apartment blocks and warehouses interspersed with streets of cramped, brick row houses. Streaks of rain cut jagged paths through the grime and I wish they wouldn't, because I don't like to see this part of the city. Not just because it's ugly.

The city's heartbeat is the River Seine, which brings tourists, products, services, everything you need to live, it brings it all to and through the very center of the city. Tourists, too. And lovers foreign and domestic, all are drawn to the water like mosquitoes to a stagnant pond, they hold hands and gaze at the river, hang those stupid padlocks of love on its bridges. There's not a romance born or experienced in this city that hasn't involved a picnic by the river, or a soulful gaze over its sparkling waters at night.

On the flip side, fifty bodies are dragged out of the River Seine every year, in Paris alone. One a week. How many float through unnoticed, or sink to the bottom, never to be seen again? How many people are chopped into pieces and devoured by fish before they can be found and pieced back together? Probably not too many of the latter, but my point stands: the River Seine is death soup, it's body broth. Well, it's cold in there so maybe it's ghastly gazpacho, but you get the point.

If you don't, let me repeat: things are not what they seem. The same way people aren't. And as I cruise into the city center to take up my old room in my beautiful old house for a week, these graffiti-spattered warehouses and trash-filled alleys cut a little close to the bone. You'd never guess by looking at me that I'm planning something awful. Evil even. But I am, and the wheels have been turning for a while.

Is it better or worse when you do it to your own family as opposed to a stranger, I wonder? If they deserve it, like in my case, then it has to be better. Strangers never deserve anything because, well, they're strangers.

I checked my Rolex, a gold beauty that my father left me before he popped his clogs. I was impatient to be at the station, but then patience has never been a virtue for me. A momentary reflection in the window showed a few hairs out of place so I pulled the comb from my jacket pocket and rectified the mess, and then spent a few seconds staring at the woman three rows ahead of me, but facing me across her table, just to make her uncomfortable. I don't do well when I'm bored.

Fifteen minutes later a limousine driver waited with my name on his iPad, and I gave him a frown because they used to hold pieces of paper with my name on it, which I preferred. I dropped my bags at his feet and let him figure out what to do with his iPad and two heavy suitcases as I walked out to the car.

"In town for long?" he asked, once he'd buckled himself into his seat.

"A week. Family reunion, of sorts."

"Those can be fun, or . . ."

"Fucking awful," I said with a smile, watching his eyes in the rear-view mirror.

"Well, I didn't want to say that, but . . . yes."

"This one will be fun, I think."

He looked down, and then back at me. "The address I have, it's Château Lambourd. Is that right?" He sounded perplexed, and I knew why.

"Yes, that's right."

"Oh. I thought it was a museum now, just open to visitors. I live a few streets away, you see."

"A museum, yes. But every year we have a family gathering and a party for Bastille Day."

"So, does that mean you're . . ."

"Yes, part of the Lambourd family." This was beginning to get tiresome.

His head nodded for longer than it should, and then he said, "Do you mind if I ask, is the legend true?"

I sighed loudly. "A legend is a story popularly regarded as historical but generally not authenticated. The story of my family is not a legend, it's . . . a story."

"A true one?"

I gave him an enigmatic smile, having learned that people loved to hang on to a little mystery in their lives. I didn't want to dispel the romance around the myth of my family by making it real for him, cementing its truthfulness so he could do the same for anyone he cared to tell.

Thing being, the story is true. And it's a good one.

CHAPTER TWO

Hugo Marston sat in his office with both feet on the desk, admiring the tops of his oldest pair of Tony Lama boots. He'd bought them in Fort Worth two decades previously, and they were in that delightful stage between new and decrepit, a stage that would last another ten years at least. They'd seen so much wear and so many buffings that they seemed to gleam from within, the cracks and creases adding character in the same way that wrinkles change the face of an aging, but still beautiful, movie star.

Hugo's secretary, Emma, appeared in the open doorway with a mug of coffee in her hand.

"You made me a second cup?" he asked.

"What? No, this is mine."

"Tease."

"Did you hear from the ambassador this morning?"

"No. Something going on?"

"He's trying to decide whether to go to a party on Bastille night."

"I doubt he'd ask my advice on that," Hugo said.

Emma smiled. "Right. Because if it involves you having to go, too, your advice would be against attending."

"Precisely."

"You don't even want to know where the party is?"

"I do not."

"Not even a little curious?" Emma pressed.

"No, and I'll tell you why. No matter how impressive the building, whether it's a château or the finest hotel, once you're inside it's the same thing. Rich people in expensive clothes guzzling champagne and trying not to make it obvious how many canapés they're stuffing into their wealthy gullets."

"Hugo, be nice."

"And as the evening progresses, the same one or two people will consume just a little too much bubbly and start acting crazy until their significant other drags them out to the Mercedes and drives them home. And that's happening at an embassy party, a fashion after-party, and a Christmas party. Especially a Bastille Day party."

"You're like the Grinch, you know that?"

"Not at all," Hugo said. "Those people are welcome to get their fun that way, I wouldn't stop them."

"You just don't want to see it."

"Correct."

"Well, then. I'll be sure and tell the ambassador *not* to ask your opinion." She turned to go, looking over her shoulder to say, "Although this party's at Château Lambourd."

"Lambourd . . ." Hugo swung his boots off the desk. "Why do I know that name?"

"Because of that book I keep telling you to read. If you'd put down your mystery novels for a moment and read some Paris history, you'd know all about it."

"Right, right, the Jewish family. The place is a museum."

Emma sighed and turned back to Hugo, hesitating a moment before walking into his office and settling into a chair opposite him.

"Yes," she said. "Most of the year it's a museum. But that's not the interesting thing."

"Tell me."

"You mean, *remind* you."

"Yeah, that." Hugo gave her his most innocent smile.

"I think it was around 1890 when it all started."

"I do enjoy story time," Hugo said. He swung his boots back onto the desk, but Emma swatted them back down.

"That's rude when you have a guest in here."

"You're an employee, not a guest."

"That's rude, too."

"I was just trying to get comfortable."

"Do you want to hear this story or not?" she asked.

"Is there murder and intrigue in it?"

"Oh, yes." Emma smiled. "Aplenty."

"Then by all means, proceed. Please."

"It was in 1890 that Nissim Lambourd moved here from Algeria, where he'd made his fortune selling silks and other cloths. He bought land beside Parc Monceau and designed Château Lambourd himself, with help from an architect friend. He lived there with his wife, Beatrice, and their son, Guillaume. Eventually, Guillaume inherited the place when his parents died, and had two children with his wife, whose name I forget. Alice maybe."

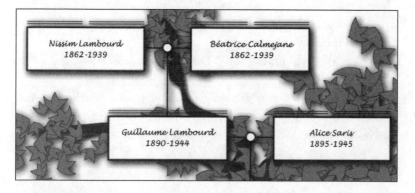

This isn't the most compelling story I've heard, Emma." Hugo shrugged. "I mean, lineage stuff? I was promised murder."

"Hush, it gets better. So, Guillaume and Alice's kids were Alexandre and Charlotte."

"Oh, yes, that's a great improvement. Do tell me about *their* kids, please."

"I will. But not yet. Because what's interesting about Alexandre was that he was a fighter pilot in the Second World War. Only he was killed, in 1943."

Guillaume Lambourd
1890-1944

Alice Saris
1895-1945

Alexandre Lambourd
1920-1943

Charlotte Lambourd
1924-

"How? France was out of the war at that point."

"He flew for the British. Meanwhile, his sister and parents were living at Château Lambourd, only the Germans had their eyes on the place."

"Of course, lovely house, great setting. Perfect place for some German efficiency to be installed."

"Not just that," Emma said. "The Lambourds were Jewish."

"Ah, right."

"Yes. And they saw the writing on the wall so they packed Charlotte off to Luxembourg under a false name, with falsified papers and quite a lot of their belongings. There, she married some banker."

"How old was she?"

"Seventeen or eighteen," Emma said. "While she was safely out of the country, sure enough the Germans took over the house and both her parents, who'd refused to leave, were sent to concentration camps."

"Did they survive?" Hugo asked.

"Sadly, no. But this is where it gets good."

"Finally."

She ignored the sarcasm. "Immediately after the war, Charlotte came back to Paris with her husband."

"Looking to reclaim the château, I presume."

"Right. Only, she couldn't prove who she was because her family had destroyed any record of her, to protect her in case the Germans caught her while fleeing. And of course the parents were dead so they couldn't speak up."

"She was stuck with her false name," Hugo said.

"Very much so. And while a few friends in Paris tried to help, the lack of paperwork did her in. And, of course, the new owner of the house was wealthy and influential enough to block her claim."

"So what happened?"

"I'm glad you asked." Emma gave him a wicked smile. "Her banker husband, the one from Luxembourg, was found dead in Parc Monceau."

"Murdered? You did promise me a murder."

"Unless he stabbed himself in the back and slashed his own throat . . ."

"Let me guess," Hugo said. "No one was ever caught."

"Correct. And within the year, our merry widow was married to the owner of Château Lambourd."

"Didn't waste any time, did she?"

"There wasn't much to waste," Emma said.

"Meaning?"

"He was rich man, at least twice her age," she said.

"Married him for his looks and vitality then."

"Well, he was vital enough," Emma said primly. "She was in her forties but they had four children. Although I think the last one was adopted."

"Impressive. Who owns the house now? One of them, I assume."

"Nope." Emma stood. "Charlotte is still alive. A widow once again, she owns it and it's her party the ambassador has been invited to."

"She's alive?" Hugo's eyes lit up. "How old is she?"

"Midnineties, I suppose. Still formidable, although she has a live-in nurse." Emma smiled. "You should go, maybe you could get her to confess to murdering her first husband."

"What about her second? Was that a suspicious death?"

"No idea. You can investigate that, too."

"Maybe I should." Hugo nodded slowly, deep in thought. "The black widow of Parc Monceau. That'd be quite something, wouldn't it?"

Four hours later, Hugo powered down his computer, stood up, and stretched out his lower back. He was up to date with returning emails and other pending tasks, and was ready for a glass of wine. He stepped out of the embassy to begin his walk home, and looked up at a blue sky he'd not seen all day. The usual July heat had been swept out of Paris by a cool front from the east, one that had sprinkled the city with raindrops for a couple of days before leaving behind a picture-perfect day. He strolled down Avenue Gabriel toward the expanse of parkland that would lead him toward the Louvre and, eventually, a nice glass of wine.

As he walked, his mind turned to the story Emma had told him. In truth, Hugo was not one for parties, especially formal ones, but he was a sucker for history, and a complete and total sucker for an historical murder mystery. He took out his phone and called the one person who might know more than Emma about the Lambourd story.

Her voice sounded strained when she answered. "Hugo, how're you?"

"Fine. You?"

"Busy wrapping up a story. My editor had a few changes she wanted so we've just finished fighting about that."

"Who won?"

"She did."

"Really? That surprises me."

"She's good at what she does and I trust her judgment," Claudia said matter-of-factly. "What's going on with you?"

"Wondered if you had time to share a carafe of cheap wine with me."

"You know perfectly well I don't drink cheap wine."

It was true. Born Claudia de Roussillon, she used the name

Claudia Roux for her newspaper and magazine bylines to avoid the appearance of cashing in on her blue blood and distinctive name. But despite her honest and humble intentions, she'd been unable to shake her upbringing—her first glass of port at the age of sixteen had been a 1963 Cockburns, her first glass of red wine a 1947 Pétrus, and her first (and only) car: a bullet-proof Mercedes with a driver. Cheap hotels, economy-class flights, and the thin house wine served by so many bars and cafés were not things she endured, Hugo well knew. Not out of snobbery, but habit and custom. "If I don't have to, why would I?" she'd once asked him, and he had no good answer.

Hugo named a café close to his apartment in Rue Jacob, in the Sixth Arrondissement of Paris, and she said she'd beat him there. He smiled at her competitive nature and hung up, but noticed he'd quickened his own stride subconsciously. He slowed, and reminded himself that this was his commute to and from work, a stroll through the ever-changing royal garden of the Tuileries.

On this evening, several families were taking advantage of the cooler weather to lay out blankets for picnics. One of those families, a husband and wife with two smartly dressed children, knelt on a dark red blanket in a circle, holding hands and their heads bent in prayer. Not far from them, an overweight father kicked a soccer ball with his toddler, who was dressed in the blue and white of the national team.

Hugo had just passed the Musée de l'Orangerie, and vowed to himself yet again to stop in one day and admire the Impressionist paintings it housed, when he heard two popping sounds ahead. *A little early for Bastille Day fireworks*, he thought.

Seconds later the rising swell of shouts and screams reached him, and when he heard three more *pops* he knew they weren't firecrackers. Instinctively he started running. As he did so he reached for the gun tucked under his arm, freeing it from the holster and holding it with both hands, barrel pointed to the sandy walkway. His eyes scanned ahead, past the people who were staring in disbelief, and past those who understood what they were seeing and were scattering in all directions.

And then Hugo spotted him. He was sixty yards ahead and to the left, a burly young man wearing a tattered jacket and with an army-green pack on his back. He had a pistol in each hand and stood looking down at one of them, shaking it as if it'd jammed. Hugo sped up, raising his own pistol, watching the man but also angling his run so that there was no one behind him.

Hugo was thirty yards away when the man threw the jammed gun to the ground in frustration and swung the pack off his back, kneeling in front of it.

At twenty yards, the young man looked up and saw Hugo.

CHAPTER THREE

T he man's faced registered no surprise, but he immediately started to raise his gun toward the running American.

"Drop it!" Hugo yelled in French. "Drop your weapon, *now!*"

The man either didn't hear or didn't care, and his gun was almost up when Hugo fired four shots in rapid succession. His first two rounds thudded into the dirt to the left of and behind the man, but the third hit the gun, ripping it from his hand and sending it spinning into the grass. The fourth shot slammed into the gunman's torso a split-second later, knocking him backward onto the ground. Hugo slowed to a walk and closed the rest of the distance between them, his gun pointed at the man who lay sprawled on his back, not moving. Hugo's heart pounded in his chest, and his ragged breathing made it hard to keep a precise aim.

Hugo was still working to catch his breath as he circled the still figure, surely just a teenager, looking for any signs of movement and any other weapon. His ears picked up the sounds of yelling and screaming all around him, and further away sirens, but his attention was locked onto the man on the ground. Hugo stepped closer and saw the entry wound, a circle of red slightly left of the center of his chest. Hugo quickly spotted the two guns and kicked them further away from the man, and then stooped to throw the backpack out of reach. The young man still hadn't moved, and from the placement of the hole in his chest was unlikely to, so Hugo holstered his gun and knelt beside him. He put his fingers to his neck, but felt nothing except his own hands shaking with adrenaline.

"Hey, are you hurt?" The shout had come from a man with a crew cut, a fit young man who moved like an athlete and was running fast toward Hugo while holding a phone to his ear.

"No, but this guy is," Hugo called back.

"I've called for an ambulance." The man reached Hugo and stood over him, wariness on his face. "I saw you shoot him, *monsieur*, please tell me where your weapon is."

"In my shoulder holster," Hugo said. "You're police?"

"*Militaire*," the man replied.

Hugo nodded and reached, slowly, for his embassy credentials, which the soldier scanned before handing back. "*Merci.*"

Hugo put them away quickly and swung one leg over the gunman, and clasped his hands, left over right. He pressed them against the man's chest and felt blood spill through his fingers, but nevertheless began compressions. The rising wail of sirens told him help was close, but not close enough.

"Do you know if anyone else was hurt?" Hugo asked the soldier who was on his cell phone. "Go look for victims, I heard four or five shots but don't know whether he hit anyone or not."

"*Bien*, I will." The soldier jogged off, and Hugo focused on the steady beat of the compressions. More than a few people held their phones up, capturing the scene with cameras and on video for posterity. Or, more likely, their social media accounts. The grassy area all around him was littered with abandoned blankets, folding chairs, and picnic items, but people were starting to edge toward him, the uncertainty in their eyes mixed with curiosity. Hugo tried to ignore them and focus on the job at hand, but his arms were beginning to tire and his breathing was labored.

After another minute, the soldier returned. "One is dead," he said. "Two other people are wounded, but they are alive and on their way to hospital."

"*Merci.* You mind taking over for a moment?"

"I don't know." The soldier frowned and made no move to relieve Hugo. "He killed someone and tried to kill more. He tried to kill you, *n'est-ce pas?*"

"Tried and failed."

"Then let him die. Or let God decide if he wants him to live." The soldier glanced up, as if inviting advice from the heavens.

"It'd help to know why he did this," Hugo said, his teeth gritted with the effort and with annoyance. "And for that we need him to live."

The soldier looked at him for a moment, and then shrugged. "*Merde.* I suppose so." He moved to Hugo's side and knelt, strong arms extending over the gunman. When Hugo took his hands away they were covered in blood, and he wiped them as best he could in the dry grass a few feet away.

He could see the police cars now, and two ambulances, cruising through the Tuileries toward them, slowing to make sure they didn't hit anyone. They had shut off their sirens but from both ends of the park an army of flashing blue, red, and white lights streamed toward them. The police vehicles nosed in closest, forming a circle around Hugo, the soldier, and the posse of onlookers, who were quickly ushered back behind the flashing lights. Two medics jogged past the advancing police officers to where the soldier was starting to puff and sweat over his task, and he gladly moved out of the way to let them take over. When he stood, blood dripped from his hands, and he held them up, the frown back on his face.

"If that bastard has any communicable diseases . . ." He shook his head and glared down at the gunman.

"Agreed," Hugo said, and turned his attention to the three uniformed officers who'd approached. They'd not drawn their guns, but they looked like they might, so Hugo tried to reassure them.

"*Messieurs*, my name is Hugo Marston. I am the regional security officer at the United States embassy."

The largest of the three moved closer. "You have identification?"

"In my inside pocket, yes. But . . ." Hugo held up his bloody hands. "You're welcome to reach inside."

The officer barked an instruction to his colleague, who ran to the trunk of one of the police cars. He returned a moment later with a plastic container of hand wipes. The *flic* opened the lid and held the container out to Hugo and the soldier.

"Take as many as you need. And you should go to the hospital, to make sure you didn't catch anything."

"We will," Hugo said. "And thank you."

The burly officer, clearly in charge, stepped forward. "I am Brigadier Raphael Caron, and I will be in charge here until I'm not. First of all, our information is that there was only one gunman, monsieur. I need to make sure that is the case."

Hugo nodded. "As far as I know, yes. I only saw him."

The *flic* looked at the soldier. "And you?"

"Same, just him."

Hugo finished wiping his hands as best he could, and then he reached for his credentials, passing them to the senior officer, who spotted the holstered gun, but didn't say anything. He looked over Hugo's badge and identification card, and handed them back.

"*Merci,*" Caron said. "And now I need your gun, please."

"My gun? I'm afraid that's not possible."

"There will be an investigation, monsieur. That will include a look at this man's life, but also an autopsy and ballistics. For that, we need your gun. It is standard procedure."

"I know it is," Hugo said politely. "However, this gun is the property of the United States government, and I have diplomatic status such that I am not required to hand it over."

Caron bristled. "I don't understand why your government wouldn't want to assist us in this investigation as fully as possible."

"You misunderstand," Hugo assured him. "I'd gladly let you have it, but since I don't own it, and since some lawyer or bureaucrat in Washington will have a fit if I hand it over, I just ask that you let me call my boss and get clearance."

"Who is your boss?"

"The US ambassador to France." Hugo gave Caron a friendly smile. "It's okay—I have him on speed dial."

Hugo called Ambassador J. Bradford Taylor and caught him enjoying an appetizer of olives and nuts, along with a tall Americano cocktail in the Hotel Crillon.

"Hugo, what's going on?"

"Hey, boss. You seen the news yet?"

"No. Why?"

"Are you drinking already?"

"Working session with some folks from the State Department, as it happens," Taylor said.

"Right. Working."

"Don't be impertinent," Taylor said. "What can I do for you?"

"About fifteen minutes ago, I shot a man in the Tuileries."

"Sounds painful." Taylor chuckled.

"I'm not kidding, boss."

There was a moment of silence. "Holy shit, Hugo. What the hell happened?"

"He had a gun and was letting rounds off, shot three people. He was about to shoot at me so I shot him first."

"Good God. That's insane—are you all right?"

"I'm fine. Looks like he won't make it, though."

"I don't give a damn about him."

"Yeah, well. The thing is, the cops here want to take my gun." Hugo looked over as the paramedics moved the gunman onto a gurney. Brigadier Caron was going through the man's jacket pockets, while beside him another officer held several large plastic evidence bags.

"It's US government property," Taylor said. "And you have diplomatic immunity, so . . ."

"Yeah, I know all that, boss, but they need it for the investigation. I shot the gunman with it. Of course they need it."

"Great." Taylor groaned. "That's going to mean paperwork for you, me, and them."

"I know it. I just wanted to get your blessing before I hand it over."

"Get a receipt, whatever you do."

"Will do." Hugo looked up as Brigadier Caron approached and held something out for him to look at. "I gotta run, boss. Some of the guy's blood got on me, so I'm going to get checked out at the hospital. And while I'm there, I'll keep an eye on him and give you an update on his condition."

"Sounds good. Make sure you get yourself taken care of. And I already told you, I don't give a damn about the gunman. I'll find out whether he's alive or dead from the news."

Hugo paused, his eyes locked onto one piece of evidence in particular. "Well, I can give you one pretty important update right now, I'm afraid."

"What're you talking about?"

"Here's the thing." Hugo watched as Caron dropped the blue, rectangular booklet into its own evidence bag. "The shooter appears to be one of us."

"Meaning?"

"He was carrying a US passport. Which, if I'm not mistaken, means you better hurry up and finish your important, high-level State Department cocktail, because as of right now you *do* care what happens to the shooter. Not to mention the obvious issue, on top of that."

"Shit, an American?" Hugo could hear the lightness leave the ambassador. "Go ahead, Hugo, mention the obvious issue."

"Okay. I think it's fair to say that you also now have an international incident on your hands."

"Just what I need. Look, I'll finish up here—go get yourself checked out at the hospital." The ambassador sighed. "A goddamn American, eh? Why can't they ever be Canadian?"

CHAPTER FOUR

Three hours later, Hugo walked out of the hospital to an awaiting black Cadillac. The driver, a young woman with big eyes and dreadlocks, smiled.

"Mr. Marston, glad to hear you're okay. I'm Cecilee Walker. I don't know if you remember me."

"Of course I do." Hugo nodded. "You drove me to the airport once, and on that ride I asked you to call me Hugo, not Mr. Marston."

"Yes, sir, that's right." Her smile widened. "I guess I'm the one who forgot."

"No problem." He climbed into the front passenger seat. "There was no need for a car. I could've taken a cab."

"Not really, Sir . . . I mean Hugo."

"What do you mean?"

Walker put the car into gear and eased away from the curb. "If you'd taken a cab, you would've gone home."

"Which is where you're taking me now. Right?"

"Not really, no."

Hugo turned to look at her. "Then where are we going?"

She was still smiling. "You don't like surprises, huh?"

"Not after a day like today, I most certainly do not."

"We're going back to the embassy."

"Why?"

She glanced at him, and then looked back at the road. "It hasn't occurred to you, has it?"

Hugo sat back and closed his eyes. "Any more guessing games and I'll fire you."

"No, you won't."

"Then I'll shoot you."

Walker laughed. "Hugo, think about what you just did."

"Got into a car?"

"You're a hero, Hugo. You stopped a mass shooting."

"If I stopped it, it wasn't a mass shooting."

"You prevented—" She sighed, the way a disappointed parent might. "Don't play word games with me. You're a hero."

"A very tired one, who would like nothing more than to go home right now."

"Weren't you just lying around in a bed at the hospital?"

"Getting poked with needles, thank you very much."

"Welcome." She shot him a worried look. "So is everything okay?"

"A few results to come back, but I don't have rabies, tetanus, or leprosy. At least I think that's what they said."

"A good start, then."

"As good as it gets. Now then, you were taking me home."

"Eventually, yes." This time the look she gave him was more sympathetic. "I'm afraid the ambassador wants to get to work on this shooter, figure out who is he is and why he wanted to gun people down in the Tuileries."

Hugo looked at her with suspicion. "But he knows I can't do that. I'm a witness and, technically I suppose, a potential suspect," he said. "Plus, the entire Paris police force will be doing that, *and* we have good people in the office who can help out. Like Mari—what's she doing right now?"

Mari Harada was Hugo's number two. Months after the death of Ryan Pierce, his long-time second-in-command, Hugo had called to see if she'd be interested in coming to Paris. It was a promotion for her within the State Department, so she said yes, and Hugo immediately requested her transfer from the Berlin office. They'd first met at a conference in Italy, where she'd impressed him with her lecture on the rise of nationalism in Western Europe. Afterward, he bought her coffee and found out she'd also worked for the FBI. She'd been a forensic anthropologist and their paths hadn't crossed, but it was a professional coincidence, and a bond between them. She'd had to leave the Bureau after contracting multiple sclerosis, and was now using an electric wheelchair and state-of-the-art voice-to-text software, so she didn't have to type.

Ambassador Taylor had been on Hugo to get someone in to ease the RSO's workload, and had assured Hugo he wasn't "replacing" Ryan at all—he was filling a position. And when Taylor saw her résumé he was all aboard. In the couple of months she'd been working at the embassy, Taylor had been more than impressed with her enthusiasm and intelligence, especially in matters technological, which had become her forte since she was less able to get to anthropological sites. Taylor had even pointed to her tastefully appointed office as an example to Hugo, and a counterpoint to his sparsely furnished one. She had decorated it with calligraphy from Bodhidharma and a pair of replica Jomon vases to reflect her father's Japanese heritage, and on the wall behind her desk she'd hung a print of the 1917 self-portrait by Christian Khrog, who was her favorite Norwegian painter and, like her mother, from Oslo.

As she steered the car onto Rue de Rivoli, Cecilee Walker threw Hugo another look. "Oh, Mari will be there, don't you worry."

"Right. And everyone knows she's ten times more competent than I am, so take me home and let her handle it."

"No can do."

"What if I give you a direct order?"

"Someone higher than you in the food chain already gave me one."

"I know, I know. But he's used to me disobeying his orders, so you wouldn't get in trouble for not doing his bidding."

Walker laughed quietly. "It's not his bidding that I'm doing."

"I don't understand." Hugo turned to look out of the window to his left, where the Tuileries lay in darkness. He'd seen on the news that police had closed it early, ushering an already nervous public out and leaving a dozen men and women to patrol inside, more to restore a sense of security than anything else. Hugo looked back at Walker. "If you're not doing his bidding, then . . ."

"Well, he wants you there, don't get me wrong."

"Walker, I'm warning you . . ."

"You're right—Mari can do all the background stuff with the Brigade Criminelle. That's not why he wants you at the embassy."

"Then why?"

"To meet someone."

"Is it Oprah? I've always wanted to meet Oprah."

"You probably can now, but no, it's not. I'm taking you to meet the president of France."

Hugo turned in his seat to stare at her. "You're kidding me."

"Nope." She gave him a wink. "I told you. You're a hero now. And presidents love to meet heroes, you know that." She pointed to the glove compartment. "I put a hairbrush in there for you."

"A hairbrush?"

"Yeah. Come on, Hugo, you know how it works. One president plus one hero equals . . ."

"Oh, good God. You're right." Hugo groaned again. "That equation equals cameras."

He looked out of the window at the traffic ahead of them, toward the embassy, which sat overlooking Place de la Concorde. He'd spent his career with the FBI avoiding the limelight. He always let others handle that side of things, but Cecilee Walker was right. This time, it was all on him. He reached for the glove compartment, and a hairbrush he most definitely needed to use.

CHAPTER FIVE

The Lambourd dining table was polished to perfection, and set with the precision of a Swiss watch. Just as it had been every year for a century. But now, the polisher-in-chief cowered in the hallway between the dining room and the kitchen, listening to the argument and knowing she shouldn't.

"You ought to let him rot in there!" It was the voice of Charlotte Lambourd, dry and brittle, and uncommonly angry. Tammy Fotinos was at once grateful for her gift for languages and slightly regretful. She'd needed to be fluent in French to get the job at the château, but might have been happier being oblivious to the mother-son argument.

"For goodness sake, Maman, it was a stupid mistake. You want him to miss the dinner, and the party, for a stupid mistake? What will people think if he's not here because he's in jail?"

"How many of those does he get, Marc?" The old lady snorted. "And I already know what people think."

"You don't know what it's like for him." Marc Lambourd's voice was sullen now. "It's been hard for him not knowing his mother, hard for me since."

"Stop making excuses, for God's sake," Charlotte snapped. "She died in childbirth, he was never attached to her emotionally, he didn't lose her in that way."

"But I did, and he's almost seventeen and lost out on knowing her at all. Just how long are we allowed to grieve for?" Marc was sarcastic now. "You let me know the timeline and I'll fill him in. Tell him to get over it."

"Telling him doesn't do a damn thing. You've done that his whole life. He's always been that way, and you've never done anything but *talk* to him. A few nights in jail will get his attention."

"Yeah, neglect and excessive punishment, back to the basics you know, eh, Maman?"

"Don't be a baby. My children turned out just fine."

"Oh, we did, did we?" Marc Lambourd laughed. "That's good to know."

"Well, if you didn't you've got no one to blame but yourselves." Tammy took a few steps back toward the kitchen when she heard the old lady shuffling her feet. "I'm going for a nap. Do what the hell you like, but get that boy under control. This is still my house, and I have certain expectations." Tammy imagined her waving a finger in her son's face. "For you and for that boy of yours, dead mother or not."

Tammy waited for them to leave the room, counting to sixty in her head to give them time. She loved this house, loved its location, its history, and the multitude of magnificent furnishings. She'd worked one summer in Disneyland, had a blast there, but this was like the real thing, being transported to somewhere even more magical. Even her role, effectively as a servant for this week, was part role-play, part real transformation. To take pride in polishing a table for other people, to take ownership in setting it absolutely perfectly, was something no modern American girl should aspire to. But royalty and history had always been like magnets to her, almost part of her soul, and to be this close to living history overcame any hesitation about playing a subservient role.

She moved forward toward the dining room, her mind back on the job at hand. She carried a notebook of precise instructions, what went where and when. For a hundred years the Lambourds had been served by the Grenelle family, but the old man had arthritis now and his wife and daughter had lost interest in playing at servant. Tammy had volunteered for it the previous year. She'd manned the reception desk for six months when the house was a museum, and so she was the first person the temp agency had approached, in case she wanted to

make some good money while the museum was closed to the public for
that Bastille week.

"You'll have exact instructions on what to do," they'd said. "No
cooking, just setting everything up and cleaning afterward. We'll pro-
vide a chef for the dinner, and waiters for the party. You just help make
sure everything runs smoothly."

She'd agreed immediately, needing the extra money and thrilled
to be getting an inside look at the Lambourd family. One of them was
even a real princess. It had been thrilling.

She stepped into the dining room, pausing when she saw Marc
Lambourd was still there, staring out of the window at the luxurious
gardens.

"Oh, sorry, Monsieur Lambourd, I didn't mean to . . ."

He looked over at her, his face expressionless. He was a handsome
man, with dark hair and darker eyebrows. But there was a tiredness
about him she'd not seen the previous year. Eventually, he spoke. "*Pas
de problème.* Tammy, nice to see you again."

"And you, monsieur."

"I'm glad we were able to get you to come back this year. I know
Fabien will be as pleased as I am." He laughed gently, and then his eyes
narrowed. "My son. I think he liked you. He was not . . . inappropriate,
I hope."

"*Non, monsieur. Pas du tout,*" she reassured him. *Not at all.* That
wasn't strictly true, but Marc himself had been a little forward and, in
her opinion, inappropriateness was in the eye of the beholder anyway.

"Did you overhear the discussion with my mother?"

"*Non.* I mean, a little, nothing . . . much. I hope everything is all
right."

The corner of his mouth turned up in the slightest of smiles. "With
my mother and me, or with my son?"

Tammy shrugged, at a loss for how to answer.

"He's in jail, Tammy. Arrested last night for a pushing match with
some hoodlum in Pigalle. My mother thinks he should remain there
for a night or two, to show him the error of his ways."

"Oh," was all she could think to say. And then: "I'm sorry."

"Set a place for him, if you please. I've already hired someone to get him out. If not for his sake, then to annoy my mother." That small smile again.

"Yes, sir, I will."

"Thank you."

"You're welcome," she said, but kept her thoughts to herself.

CHAPTER SIX

They waited for Hugo in Ambassador Taylor's office, a grand space housing his expansive desk, two leather sofas, four matching armchairs, and (for winter) a stone fireplace. Hugo had called it a rich man's study because it belonged in a château, and not in the outwardly impressive but inwardly rather drab US embassy.

Two of the president's security detail stood outside the office, and they scrutinized Hugo's ID before opening the door for him.

"Hugo, come in, come in." Taylor rose from one of the armchairs and, behind him, so did the president of France. In the far corner a photographer had set up a camera on a tripod, facing a bookcase and ready to go to work, but trying to look as inconspicuous as possible. The president, Marie Antoinette Bissett, moved toward him. She was a tall woman with striking blue eyes and a jaw that any Hollywood actor would die for. Her name, the Marie Antoinette part, had spawned a thousand cartoons and jokes about her losing her head, but Hugo had followed her rise through the ranks of French politics, and seen how every barb had missed its mark, or wound up pricking the thumb of the jokester who'd thrown it. She'd grown up poor in the suburbs of Paris, on the city's outer edges, and had little time for pomp and circumstance. And, in most cases, tradition be damned. She moved past the ambassador, not waiting for an introduction.

"Monsieur Hugo Marston." She extended a hand, and when he took it, her grip bordered on assault.

"Madame President." Hugo gave a small bow. "*Enchanté.*"

"We can talk in English," she said. "I need the practice. And I promise you, the pleasure is all mine. On behalf of myself as a Parisian, and on behalf of the wonderful people of this city and this nation, please accept my sincere thanks for your brave actions this evening."

"You are too kind. I did what anyone else would have done. I was just lucky to be in the right place at the right time."

"You'll forgive me, Mr. Marston." President Bissett gave a gentle laugh. "You shot the weapon from his hand before he could kill innocent people. You stopped a slaughter in one of the most popular and busy, not to mention peaceful, places in Paris."

"Like I said, you're very kind and I appreciate the—"

"Monsieur Marston. Whether you like it or not, you are a hero."

Ambassador Taylor chortled. "Trust me, he doesn't like it. Shall we get the pictures over with?"

"The sooner the better," Hugo said.

They moved to where the photographer stood, and let him arrange them as he saw fit—Hugo the hero between the president and the ambassador. He took a dozen quick shots and then checked the screen on his camera. "Very good, thank you."

They left him to pack up and show himself out, and Taylor led them back to the chairs.

"Please, Madame President, have a seat."

They took their places and President Bissett leaned forward to talk. "Once we know more about who this shooter is, perhaps why he did this, we will have a small ceremony. I would like to award you the Honor Medal for Courage and Devotion. It is more than deserved."

"Well," Hugo began, "I'm grateful, of course—"

"Hugo, you are *not* turning down a medal from the president of France." It was an order from the ambassador, not a question. "As President Bissett says, like it or not you saved lives this evening."

"I also took one," Hugo said grimly. "And being a realist, Madame President, do you think it wise to go slapping medals on Americans when it seems likely the bad guy was one of us?"

"Wait." President Bissett sat up, concern on her face. "What did you just say?"

Hugo glanced at the ambassador. "I assumed you'd told her, sorry."

"Told me what?" she pressed.

"This is why you're not a diplomat, Hugo," Taylor said grimly. "Madame President, we don't know who he is or where he's from. Hugo was shown on scene a passport that may or may not be a United States passport, and may or may not belong to the dead suspect."

President Bissett frowned. "That would complicate things."

"It would, but since we don't know anything definitive right now we're not advertising this," Taylor said. "For extremely obvious reasons."

"I understand," Bissett said. "But I expect to be the first to know when you do hear something definite."

"Of course," Taylor said. "But I'm sure you'll hear it from the French police long before we do."

"Speaking of that, who's working on this?" Hugo asked.

"Not you."

"Come on, boss, I was right there."

"And you know perfectly well that makes you a witness, which means you can't be an investigator."

Hugo knew Taylor was right, but he also knew it meant he'd be the last to hear anything.

President Bissett spoke up. "Even though it's obvious what happened, I'm told there does have to be a formal investigation into the shooting of that man. As well as looking into him and his motives, of course."

"That's pretty standard," Hugo said. "And you know I'll cooperate. Who's conducting it?"

"If I remember rightly, there's a division with the Brigade Criminelle called the Special Investigations Unit, which handles all officer-involved shootings."

"Great. They'll have my full cooperation. And they know where to find me, right behind my desk."

"Actually," Ambassador Taylor began. "You're going to need to take a few days off."

"Boss, I'm fine. I don't need days off, and I don't need to see a counselor, which I'm sure is the next suggestion."

"Days off isn't a suggestion, Hugo, it's a requirement. Every agency in the world puts their guys on administrative leave after a shooting. And since we'll be working with the locals on this, and here at the embassy, you can't be around."

"Great." Hugo sank back into his chair. "How long?"

"A few days. Hey, all the more reason to come with me to the Bastille Day party, at Château Lambourd."

"Emma was trying to sell that to me, but you know I'm not a party person, boss."

"I went to that two years ago," President Bissett said. "Trust me, you should go. The house is magnificent, the party exquisite, and the people thoroughly fascinating."

"How so?" Hugo asked.

"Let's just say that there are a lot of ghosts in that house."

"I don't believe in ghosts," Hugo said.

"All the more reason to go. That place is . . . like I said, fascinating. Great history."

"Of murder and mayhem," Hugo said.

"That's what makes it great." President Bissett stood, and the two men did the same. "I have a dinner to attend, and I will need to make a statement to the press." She put out her hand. "Thank you again, Monsieur Marston. You saved lives tonight. We will never know how many, but make no mistake, you saved innocent lives."

When she'd gone, Ambassador Taylor poured them each a whisky, and they settled back into the armchairs.

"You're okay, Hugo?"

"Fine. Really."

"You shot someone tonight, so you know I have to ask."

"Sadly, he's not the first. But yeah, I get it. Thanks for looking out for me."

"There's going to be a lot of news coverage, too. Here and at home. I'm surprised your phone's not blowing up."

"It probably is." Hugo grinned. "I dropped it off in my office before heading up here."

Taylor smiled. "Good idea. You talk to Claudia? Tom?"

"Just Claudia. Right before I left the hospital, just to let her know I was fine."

"Glad to hear it."

"You know, she agreed with you."

"That you need days off and counseling?"

"No. That I should go to that damn party tomorrow night."

CHAPTER SEVEN
THE KILLER

It's not that I particularly enjoy killing. What I enjoy, what I *need*, is the rush that goes along with it. When your soul is a little empty, when you don't feel the full range of normal human emotions, you have to latch onto the ones you *do* feel. But, like shoes or furniture, even the more extreme emotions get a little worn out, so to really feel their full power you have to turn up the volume. For example, where it used to be enough to flash strangers in a park, nowadays to feel that same surge of power and danger I have to sexually assault them. Not rape, I'm not an animal, just a grab or a grope to widen their eyes.

And don't get me wrong, I'm not some kind of serial killer with ten, twenty, fifty names on my headboard. I've only killed twice, and both times it was necessary. Not self-defense, exactly, but . . . necessary.

Tonight's dinner will, all by itself, be murder. A dwindling family getting together, maybe for the last time. One hopes. Our tensions and resentments tucked out of sight like the napkins that lie over our laps, our smiles as polished and precise as the silverware. By the time the cheese cart comes out I'll be asking for my steak knife back to sever a few heads, I'm pretty sure. So many grudges and resentments served up alongside the onion soup and lamb chops.

I'll watch the interactions with the eyes of an outsider and wonder if all families are like this, to some greater or lesser degree. The matriarch who brooks no impudence, is resistant to change, and hangs onto tradition like it were the strings of a parachute. Siblings maneuvering to curry favor with her, just in case a few more trinkets might be slid their way before she croaks. Old slights resurrected deliberately and with surgical precision, bringing back to life childhood paranoias and insecurities that follow each person like a ghost, invisible to most but inescapable to those they haunt.

It's so cloying, this house. Everyone who visits is enchanted with its history, the suggestion that its owner may have committed murder on these very grounds (but good God, no one dares say anything aloud), the beauty of the place, the art on its walls, the centuries-old furniture filling its rooms. Rumor has it a member of the English or French royal families has slept in every bed in the house. There are twelve beds in seven bedrooms, so either that's a handful of energetic blue-bloods, or those beds need changing out.

I wonder if my actions tonight will screw up the party. If I'm honest, and I rarely am, it's one of the reasons I'm doing this, to see if the old lady will continue to hang onto those parachute strings, whether she'll insist the party goes on as normal or be the first head of the Lambourd family in a hundred years to not hold the party of the year. I think I know the answer already, but I'm still looking forward to watching it all play out.

And lest anyone think I am committing murder lightly, I am not. There is method to my madness, which of course brings up the question of whether psychopathy is, in fact, madness. A larger question, and not one I intend to entertain right now.

After all, I have more planning to do.

CHAPTER EIGHT

Tammy Fotinos slipped out of her lover's room just after two o'clock in the morning. The dinner had gone well, at least as far as she could tell, even though some of the family members had drunk more than they'd eaten. Her lover was tipsy to be sure, but sober enough to slip her a note as she cleared the dessert plates, and definitely sober enough a short while later to strip her naked in under a minute. They'd barely said a word to each other—no time for small talk in those thirty minutes, just the taste of expensive port on their lips and the smell of leather-bound books and old but polished furniture in the bedroom.

She closed the door behind her and checked the long hallway to make sure no one would see her creep back downstairs to her room. She needed to make it halfway, to the staircase that led down to the second and then the ground floor, and her room in what used to be the servants' quarters.

It still is, silly, she thought.

It was dark, but not quite pitch-black thanks to the light spreading thinly from the sitting area that lay by the staircase, and she moved slowly toward it, aware of every creak of the floorboards beneath her bare feet.

She felt the way she did the last time this happened, exhilarated but also a little sullied. She really liked her lover and, in flashes, thought maybe she was liked in return, in the same way. But she also noticed moments of coldness, of remoteness, and couldn't decide if they were a defense mechanism or signs of true disinterest. Her fingers trailed against the wallpaper as she walked, her eyes on the area of light ahead, but her mind giving her flashes of an imagined future, one where she was a part of a family like this, where she lived in a house with such history as this. A silly dream, yes, but no one fantasized about reality because what would be the point of that?

The floor creaked beneath her feet and she paused, dreams dissolved by the surge of adrenaline that made her body quiver. If she were caught she'd be fired for sure, probably thrown out on the spot. She was a terrible liar, and if the old lady herself fixed those fierce blue eyes on her, no way she could come up with a story. She wasn't supposed to be on this floor at all, ever, let alone . . . consorting with family members.

And there was something about this family that scared her, even when she was following orders. Marc and his son Fabien were good examples. Both brooding but polite, charming but not warm. Fabien a chip off the old block with the gleam in his eye that said *rogue*. Édouard, who seemed to watch the world with a kind of timid disapproval, as if the people in it were too dirty and ignoble to warrant his good graces. Erika, the older sister, she was the one who gave Tammy her instructions when Marc wasn't around, the one who decided on the details Marc didn't care about, like which china to use and which napkins. But like the others, she was distant and acted almost as if she didn't want to be there. Last of all was Noelle, the one Tammy found the most interesting. She'd heard Noelle was adopted but couldn't imagine the old witch doing something like that, certainly not out of altruism. But it'd explain why of all the kids she was the most anxious, the one who alternated between trying to please and absenting herself from the family. Tammy had tried talking to her several times, frankly the only sibling she dared strike up a conversation with, but Noelle had never really responded. A polite reply, a distracted look, and then off about her business.

And all of them, Tammy thought, even Noelle, exuded a deep intensity that seemed to come from their shared family history, from the traumas and secrets of the past, and from the rivalries of the present.

She waited, holding her breath for a full minute before creeping forward. A sound from below, maybe a door but maybe nothing, pulled her toward the top of the stairs and she leaned over to stare into the darkness below. All quiet.

Her room seemed miles away in the dark, and she started down the staircase that would take her to the second floor, then the ground floor and safety. She grew more confident step-by-step, the worn carpeting rough but reassuring under her bare feet. She reached the wide second-floor landing and paused to listen again. All was quiet, and she was just about to start down the final staircase when the sound of someone breathing right behind her made her freeze with fear. A second later she flinched and her heart leapt wildly in her chest when she felt something drop over her head, past her face, and loop around her neck. It tightened.

A new necklace? was her last, and most ridiculous, thought, as the garrote tightened quickly, cutting into the delicate skin of her neck, squeezing so hard she couldn't even squeal a protest. She felt her body arch as the wire bit into her flesh and pulled her backward, and she stumbled back onto the landing, her fingers fluttering at the white-hot band encircling her throat, digging into the skin too deep for her fingertips to find purchase. Within seconds, the blood vessels in her neck conspired with the garrote to starve her of oxygen and fill her head like an overblown balloon, clouding her brain with pressure and pain until she fell first to her knees, and then into total darkness.

Hugo's phone rang at six the next morning, Saturday, and it took him a moment to read the name on the display. "Cecilee. What's up?"

She cleared her throat and said, "Sorry to wake you, sir. But I'm on my way to your apartment. There's been an incident."

"An incident?" A flash of terror as he pictured another mass shooting, a successful one this time.

"Yes, sir. An American girl was strangled last night." Walker paused, and then went on. "It was at Château Lambourd."

"Oh dear." Hugo swung his legs out of bed. "That's not good. At all."

"No, sir. That's why I'm on my way to get you."

"What ever happened to my mandatory days off?"

"That was before an American girl got herself strangled. And everyone else is working the Tuileries shooter."

"Ah, so I'm the last resort. I see how it is."

"You and me both. Anyway, the ambassador wants you there on site overseeing the investigation."

"The French police will love that," Hugo said. "Do you know who the lead detective is?"

"Yes, sir, and you're in luck. It's Camille Lerens."

"Thank God for small mercies." Hugo felt the relief wash through his body. Lerens had become a friend over the past few cases they'd been involved in, having never shown the suspicion of foreigners the way other investigators in the Brigade Criminelle did. Hugo knew why that was. She'd faced enough barriers in her own life. As a black woman born into a man's body, she'd once told him that a laser-like focus on the job was the key to winning people over, and she was most definitely good at her job, just as Hugo was good at his. What else mattered?

"I'll be at your place in three minutes," Walker was saying.

"Wait out front, I'll be out as quickly as possible. And Cecilee?"

"Yes, sir?"

"If I have to tell you one more time, it's Hugo, not sir."

"Yes, sir. Got it." She laughed and hung up before he could respond.

Hugo dressed as quickly as possible, pulling on his cowboy boots with one hand and brushing his teeth with the other. He clattered down the stairs to find Cecilee parked right outside his door on Rue Jacob.

"Morning," he said, sliding into the front passenger seat.

"Sorry about the early start," Walker said.

"Not your fault. So tell me about the dead girl. Why was an American at the château?"

Walker pulled away from the curb and accelerated down the street toward Rue de l'Université. "She was working there. In the old days, I suppose they'd refer to her as a servant."

"That so?"

"Yeah, hired to help out with the family dinner last night, and the party tonight."

"Right, the party. They going to cancel that, I assume?"

"No clue, si—, Hugo. Anyway, she's Tammy Fotinos, twenty-two years old, originally from California. Literature student in Paris to study or work on a novel or something. Worked at the château punching tickets for museum visitors, then hired by a temp agency to work the dinner and the party. You know, since she knows the place. Did so last year, too."

"Tell me about the crime scene."

"She was found at the top of the stairs, on the second floor. Three floors in the house, her room was on the lowest, so she was either coming up or going down."

"When was she found? And do we know roughly when the attack happened?"

Walker signaled left and they crossed the river at a speed that would get them pulled over, if any cops were awake and alert at that time on a Saturday. "She was found by one of the family members. Can't recall which one, but it was right after the attack."

"And she was strangled?"

"Technically, garroted."

"Good lord." Hugo looked out of the window as Paris flashed by, catching fleeting glimpses of the city's early birds, opening up their cafés and bakeries, the little *tabacs* that sold cigarettes and other essentials to those who'd run out overnight.

"Yeah. My thoughts exactly."

Hugo turned his attention to the route Walker was taking. "The house is on the east side of Parc Monceau," he said. "This way we'll end up on the west side."

"Yes, sir, I know."

Hugo raised a quizzical eyebrow, letting the "sir" go but unclear on why she was headed to the wrong side of the park. "Is there traffic blocking the other way?" he asked.

"No idea." She flashed him a smile. "We're not going to the house."

"You said the ambassador wanted me on scene."

"He also said you never take anything for granted, never make any assumptions."

"Cecilee, what the hell are you talking about?"

"He said I should give you a minute to think it through."

Hugo wasn't a fan of puzzles on an empty, and uncoffeed, stomach, but he was even less happy about the ambassador pulling a fast one on him. He turned his mind back to the phone call and all they'd discussed since. Then he smiled.

"I don't think I'll need the full minute," he said.

"No? You sure?"

"I'm pretty sure, yes."

"So, you know where we're going."

"I do."

"You have to tell me before we get there, or it doesn't count."

"I should remind you, young lady." Hugo gave her his sternest look. "That at this precise moment you work for me, and not the ambassador. This kind of treacherous undermining—"

"You have about thirty seconds, Hugo."

Hugo gave up the pretense at annoyance and sat back. "She's not dead."

"Who?"

"Tammy Fotinos. You never told me she was dead. Strangled, attacked, garroted, yes. But not dead. So, we're going to the hospital to try to talk to her. The Clinique du Parc Monceau, I assume?"

Walker just smiled, and then turned a hard left onto Boulevard de Courcelles. They raced in silence past the historic park on their left, toward a young lady who was either very lucky or very unlucky, but who, without doubt, would be scarred for life, if not physically then emotionally.

CHAPTER NINE

Hugo recognized the policeman standing guard outside Tammy Fotinos's door.

"Well, well, Paul Jameson, how are you?" Hugo said, shaking his hand. Hugo didn't know Jameson's full history—there were some shady parts in there about a woman and a job on nuclear submarines—but Hugo did know that his bald friend was the only Scotsman in the ranks of the Paris police. Always ready with a smile, and always crisply dressed, Jameson had quickly become Lieutenant Lerens's go-to man. Hugo introduced him to Cecilee Walker, and then nodded at the closed door.

"The local hero," Jameson said with a grin. "You did a great thing out there, my friend, saved a lot of lives."

"Well, thank you," Hugo said. "But you of all people would have done precisely the same thing had you been there."

"Ay, but I wasn't there and I didn't, so take some credit."

"I can try," Hugo said. "So how's our patient doing?"

"Not great," Jameson said. "But I'm told she'll live."

"Glad to hear that at least."

"So the boss just called, wanted me to fill you in on a bit of a twist."

"Lerens?" Hugo asked.

"Yeah. She said she called you but it went to voicemail."

"Must have missed it." Hugo pulled out his phone and saw the notification. "So, do tell."

"Turns out there were two crimes committed at the château last night."

"Is that so? Someone else get assaulted?"

"No. Four paintings were stolen from the main living room. No one noticed until now because of all the other excitement."

"That's . . . interesting."

"You think it's related? I mean, has to be, right?"

"I would certainly think so," Hugo said. "Way too much of a co-incidence."

"Right. The guy probably stumbled across her in the middle of the night and, afraid she'd seen him, tried to top her."

"Plausible," Hugo nodded. "You think I can talk to her?"

"A doctor came out of her room about five minutes ago, and she made sure to tell me not to bother the lass."

"Not surprising. She has a job to do and doctors can be as jurisdictional as cops."

"Ay, well, here she comes, so best of luck to you."

Hugo turned and found himself looking into the eyes of a woman wearing a white coat and a grim expression.

"*Bonjour, docteur, je suis—*"

The doctor raised a hand to cut him off. "We can speak English. That is one of the reasons I am her doctor. I married a Scotsman named Fergus."

"Ay, look at that, we're everywhere," Jameson joked, getting a smile out of Hugo and a frown from the doctor.

"Ami Roberston, how can I help you?"

"Thank you, Doctor Robertson. I am the regional security officer at the American embassy, and I am assisting the police with their investigation into the attack on Miss Fotinos." Hugo dug out his badge and showed it to the doctor. "I would very much like to speak to her, if at all possible."

"She is in poor condition right now—talking hurts her already-damaged throat. I would recommend that you come back tomorrow."

"I would love to do that, truly," Hugo said. "But time is of the essence here. There is a murderer out there, and I would like very much to find them before they decide to strangle someone else."

"Not a murderer, surely. After all, she is alive."

"That much may be true." Hugo nodded. "But in my experience, someone who is willing to strangle a young woman and leave her for dead is already a murderer in their heart of hearts. That a trail of bodies has yet to be laid down doesn't change who they are, or minimize our need to catch them."

"I see. Well, I will need to accompany you in there and would ask you keep your questions to a minimum. As you can imagine, talking is physically difficult for her. Reliving the experience may be a lot more problematic."

"Of course." Hugo moved aside and let the doctor open the door to the room. Hugo and Cecilee Walker followed.

"Tammy, these people are here from the embassy," Doctor Robertson said. "They want to ask you a few questions, but I have told them to be brief. And if it becomes too painful, please let me know. The most important thing is your quick recovery."

To you, maybe, Hugo thought. *I'm okay with slowing the recovery a tad to catch a potential killer.*

The doctor stepped aside and Hugo sat in the chair by the bed. He was pleased to note, out of the corner of his eye, Walker bringing out a tape recorder and setting it on the table close to them. Tammy Fotinos saw it, too.

"Much easier and more accurate than taking notes," Hugo said, reassuringly. "And I'll be as brief as possible. I can come back as many or few times as need be."

Tammy nodded, large brown eyes locked onto Hugo. "Okay," she said, and Hugo heard the rasp even in that one word.

"Tell me what happened," he said gently.

"It was late, and I was going to my room." She stopped and rubbed her throat, and then reached for the cup of water on the table. She took a sip and carried on. "I was on the second floor, about to go down to my room, when I thought I heard something downstairs. I looked over into the hallway but couldn't see anything. Then suddenly this . . . thing looped over my head and I was pulled backward."

Hugo nodded. "Do you know who did this?"

"No." Tears filled her eyes. "I couldn't breathe, and it hurt so much. After a few seconds I felt like my head was going to explode, I couldn't see or hear anything, and then . . . I guess I blacked out."

"You're doing great." Hugo handed her the cup of water and waited while she drank. "Is there anything at all you can tell me about the person. Height, a smell, anything they said . . ."

"He didn't say anything at all. And I didn't smell cologne or anything." She looked down. "I'm sorry, it all happened so fast. So fast."

"That's all right," Hugo said, "I totally understand. You just said 'he'—was there something that made you think it was a man?"

"I mean, no. Not really. I just assumed because he . . . they, seemed so strong. So fast."

"Can you think of anyone who might want to hurt you, Tammy?" Hugo asked. "Even if it seems like a stupid reason to you, it might not be to them."

Tammy shook her head and winced. "No. I really can't. I'm sorry." She put a hand to her mouth and coughed, a dry, hacking sound that got the doctor's attention.

"I think that's enough for today," Robertson said. "Tammy has swelling and tissue damage that will worsen if she talks, or coughs, too much. You can come back tomorrow."

"Of course." Hugo stood and picked up the recorder, but didn't turn it off. "Sorry, one last question. This was well after midnight. And you were found in your nightclothes, your robe. What were you doing up on that floor at that time?"

"That's another weird thing about all this." Fotinos shook her head slowly, and winced. "I've been wondering that myself, because I honestly can't remember."

They were in the car before either of them said anything, and it was Cecilee Walker who spoke first. "You know she was lying, right?"

"What about?"

"Not remembering."

"And what makes you say she was lying?" Hugo asked.

"Two things." Walker started the engine and steered them out of the parking lot, toward the château. "The way she looked down before answering, and how she clutched at the blanket as she said it."

"Very observant, I noticed that too."

"Plus, she remembers the attack but not why she was up there?"

"Doesn't make sense, I agree, but trauma does strange things to the memory. I'm not ready to call her a liar just yet. Was anything found on the landing near her?" Hugo asked. "Seems like that'd maybe help answer the question for us."

"I don't know, but we can ask Lerens."

"Who found her?"

"I'm not sure." Walker smiled. "Another question for Lerens."

Hugo glanced at her. "So why do you think she would lie about that?"

"Dude, come on, you know perfectly well."

Hugo gave her a quizzical look. "We've gone from 'sir' to 'dude' in record time."

"Sorry, sir. Hugo." Walker smiled, embarrassed.

"I was kidding, I don't mind a little enthusiasm so please don't worry about it. What's your theory?"

"Simple. She was . . . visiting someone and didn't want us to know."

"Maybe."

"One of the Lambourd kids. I mean, they're grown up but . . . Well, not old lady Charlotte, is what I mean."

Hugo chuckled. "You're probably right about that. How old is she?"

"Ninety-something. I'd guess her days of sneaking around are over, especially after midnight." Walker drummed her fingers on the steering wheel. "But that leaves us with the five family members as five possible lovers."

"Six, if you count Charlotte Lambourd's live-in nurse," Hugo said. "Let's head to the Lambourd house and pick one."

Walker didn't need telling twice, and quickly had them in the light weekend traffic. Within minutes they were crunching to a stop in front of the Lambourd house.

Hugo got out of the car and looked around. The house loomed in front of them, not the largest mansion he'd seen, but considering it was in the middle of Paris, impressive enough. Three stories high, the house was a shallow U shape, and each wing was connected to a one-level stone building. Less ornate, they looked like they would have held horses, and perhaps later motorcars. The house itself reminded him a little of the Petit Trianon at Versailles, a château on the grounds of the Palace of Versailles that had been built in the 1760s by Louis XV—square and sturdy, but with beautiful clean lines and many tall windows to let in the light. A stone balcony sat over the large double doors of the entranceway, where a uniformed policeman was watching them.

"Need me to come in?" Walker asked.

"No, head back to the embassy if you don't mind, see if they need anything there. I'll call if that changes."

"Sounds good."

Hugo approached the house as Walker turned the car around and drove slowly away. At the front doorway he asked for Lieutenant Lerens. The *flic* looked at Hugo's credentials and spoke into a shoulder mic, waited a few seconds, and then stepped aside.

"You'll find everyone in the main living area, second floor," he said. "And Monsieur Marston, thank you for what you did in the Tuileries yesterday." He put out a hand.

"You're very welcome," Hugo replied, shaking it.

The ground floor's staircase led them up to a large landing, and straight ahead of them the open doors to the main living area. Hugo stopped looking for Lerens and gave himself a moment to enjoy the ornate beauty of the eighteenth-century French furniture and art that adorned the landing and the living room. Books were his thing—his collection of rare and first editions was small and steadily growing—but a man able to admire the beauty of a well-preserved endpaper, a man capable of enjoying the look and feel of a cloth spine with gilt lettering was perfectly adept at appreciating the still-colorful weave of a two-hundred-year-old carpet or the exuberant decoration of a rococo *chaise longue*.

"Hugo, come in, you have some catching up to do." Lieutenant Camille Lerens waved him toward her in the living room where she stood with a uniformed officer. Hugo moved slowly forward, still taking in the grand portraits on the walls and the beautifully maintained antique pieces of furniture.

"Am I allowed to sit on any of it?" he asked, as he shook Lerens's outstretched hand.

"I've been told to shoot anyone who tries. How are you, Hugo?"

"Fine, considering."

"Considering you're a national treasure now? I should be hugging and kissing you, not shaking your hand."

Hugo shot her a stern look. He knew she was joking. Almost as well as anyone she'd know how little he was enjoying the spotlight. "The case, Camille. Tell me what we know, and let's not talk about the other business."

"Very well. First, meet Jean Oiseau." She gestured to the uniformed officer.

"*Enchanté,*" Hugo said, as they shook hands.

The *flic* gave a small bow and said, "Monsieur, let me say thank you for what you did yesterday. I know you will say anyone would have done the same, but I suspect I would have missed. So thank you."

"You are welcome. I barely had time to think." Hugo smiled. "If I had, I might have missed, too."

"I doubt it," Lerens said, and turned to Oiseau. "Would you please relieve Jameson at the hospital, have him come here?"

"Of course, lieutenant. Right away."

Hugo expected a snap of heels, but Oiseau gave them both a nod and strode from the room, his back straight and his cap tucked under one arm.

"Good policeman," Lerens said. "He doesn't quite know what to make of me yet, and he needs to relax a little. Otherwise, smart and efficient, I like him."

"He'll get the hang of it. Of you."

"Or else, right?" Lerens chuckled. "Did you manage to talk to the American girl?"

"I did." Hugo gave her a summary, including his theory that Fotinos had paid a nocturnal visit to one of the Lambourds, and watched the frown on Lerens's face deepen.

"*Merde*, I was hoping she'd seen her attacker. Or could tell us *something* about him. Or her."

"Me too. Anyone here see or hear anything?"

"No one has offered any information, no. This is one of those families . . . I don't know if they love or hate each other, but each one seems to be more tight-lipped than the last. And they want us out of here by lunchtime, to set up for this famous party they're having."

Hugo raised an eyebrow. "Going ahead with that, then?"

"So they say. People have come in from all over France, and beyond, I was told. A murder might have been different, but not . . ."

"Not a mere garroting. Of course. Makes perfect sense."

"Hugo, I've not had a lot of dealings with people like this. French nobility, whatever you want to call them. But I know enough about them to say they think differently from normal people. There's a degree of . . . I don't know, hardness of heart, I guess. Or maybe it's just that their priorities are different. I don't know, exactly, but keep an open mind and don't judge them by normal standards."

"Don't worry about that. I don't think I know what normal standards are anymore."

"*Bien*, me neither, despite a lifetime of people trying to tell me what normal is and isn't." They both smiled, knowing exactly what she meant. "Anyway, I've had initial words with everyone, but wanted to wait until you were here until I got into too much detail."

"Thanks, I appreciate that," Hugo said. "Who found her?"

"The nurse, Karine Berger, at around three in the morning."

"That's odd. I glanced at the chart at the end of her bed, and it says she was admitted around six am."

"Yes," Lerens said. "She refused an ambulance and instead they got her into her bed and called a doctor. Before he arrived, though, her throat began to swell and she had trouble breathing, so they called for an ambulance."

"That explains it. So what's the deal with the stolen paintings?"

"I don't know yet. Charlotte Lambourd noticed they were missing and told one of my men, who passed it onto me right away. He took a note of what they were and where they were hanging, but nothing other than that. I figured the family could tell us more."

"I certainly hope so. Where are they all?"

"Either sulking in their chambers, or downstairs in the impressive kitchen. They let me have this room for interviews."

"I see." Hugo looked around the room. "Trying to intimidate?"

"That was my thought."

"Charming," he said. "So, where do you want to start?"

"Well, if you're right about Miss Tammy having an illicit dalliance, I suggest we focus on finding out who that might be with."

CHAPTER TEN

Lieutenant Lerens went to the ground floor to find their first interview subject, and Hugo took the opportunity to step out onto the broad landing to see the scene of the crime. There was nothing to look at, really, just an open landing with a few pieces of plush furniture and planter pots to make the area seem warm and comfortable. Nowhere looked less like a crime scene, he thought, but nevertheless took a couple of photos with his phone, and then made his way back into the large living room. He took a moment to evaluate the space. As well as the old art and antique furniture, there was a smattering of family photos in heavy silver frames, and Hugo studied several of them, trying to figure out where they might have been taken. None at the château, he concluded.

A few minutes later, the matriarch of the family came in first with Camille Lerens. She'd insisted on it when she intercepted Lieutenant Lerens the moment she entered the large kitchen. "You will speak with me first," the old woman had said, brooking no disagreement. Now, she settled onto the sofa, sitting in the middle to force her interviewers to bring chairs over to sit opposite her.

Lerens introduced Hugo, and the widow nodded but did not offer a hand to shake. For Hugo's part, he couldn't help but glance at the tiny hands and fingers knobbly with arthritis, and wonder if they'd once held the knife that cut the throat of her husband.

Lerens placed a digital recorder on a small Guéridon table to her left and to Madame Lambourd's right. The old lady glanced at it but made no comment.

"Thank you for speaking with us," Lerens began. "And I'm sorry your family has had to suffer this trauma in your home."

"In a way, I'm quite pleased," Charlotte Lambourd said. "By that I mean it could have been so much worse."

Lerens nodded. "Yes, I suppose that's true."

"I want you to ask your questions and get out of here. I don't mean to be rude, Lieutenant, but my family gets together once a year, and only once a year." She straightened her back. "And at my age, every get-together has the potential of being the last. As I'm sure you know, we have an event this evening. We would like to put this nasty business behind us and focus on celebrating France this evening."

Interesting, Hugo thought. *Not only does she want us out of here as soon as possible and with minimum fuss, but no apparent concern for the condition of Tammy Fotinos.*

As if reading his mind, Lieutenant Lerens pushed back against her apparent callousness. "Madame Lambourd, a young woman, working for you no less, was almost murdered in your home last night. In a horrific way, if that matters. I need to be clear with you that finding out who did this is infinitely more important to me, and to my colleague Monsieur Marston here, than a party."

To Hugo's surprise, Madame Lambourd relented, giving them a soft smile. "Of course, I understand completely. And please, forgive me if I sound uncaring or unsympathetic. For one thing, I didn't know the girl, though I'm told she worked for us a year ago. My memory, you know. But, much more important than that, you have to remember the . . . tragedies, yes, that's the word. The tragedies I have seen in and around this house. The loss of family members, my two husbands, and of course the house itself. For the young lady last night, I am sure it was the most traumatic experience of her life. For me, it is not even close to being that. So you see, for me, it's not a matter of being indifferent or uncaring, nor of pitting her attack against what you see as a mere party. The Bastille Party is a Paris tradition, it is history. Like this house itself, and these are the things that help us live through the tragedies of life, make sense of them, perhaps. The large tragedies, and the lesser ones."

"Indeed," Lerens said. "I just have a few questions, then we'll let you get back to it."

"Thank you." Madame Lambourd shifted forward on the sofa, as if prepared to answer one quick question before she left.

"Did you see or hear anything last night after midnight?"

"I did not."

"Do you know of anyone who might have wanted to hurt Mademoiselle Fotinos?"

"I do not."

"Do you . . . and please excuse me for asking this so directly, but do you know whether Mademoiselle Fotinos was having a relationship with anyone?"

"Anyone in my family, you mean." Her spine stiffened again.

"Yes, I suppose so."

"Well, my eldest, Marc, used to play the field but is now very much in love with his fiancée, so not him. My other son, Édouard, despises Americans, so I highly doubt it was him. And my grandson Fabien is barely old enough to tie his shoelaces, and he's certainly not capable of doing anything discreetly, so not him either. He's a wild boy, that one, but he is still a boy so I insist an adult is present if and when you speak to him. Anyway, as far as someone having relations with the young lady, that would be a resounding no."

"Well," Lerens began, carefully. "That's only half the family."

Madame Lambourd looked directly at Lerens, then Hugo, and then back at the lieutenant. Then she sighed heavily. "Good heavens, people. I understand that that sort of thing takes place, I'm not a fool. But I can assure you that neither of my daughters is that way inclined, and even were they, that sort of thing doesn't take place here."

"It would explain why Mademoiselle Fotinos was up and about around midnight," Hugo offered. He liked that Madame Lambourd was a little off-balance at the idea something so improper as homosexual behavior might occur under her roof.

"Yes, as an American I'm sure you think that sort of unnatural behavior is perfectly acceptable. However, as libertine as we French can be, love and . . . yes, lust too . . . are displayed and acted upon the way God intended, between a woman and a man. At least in this residence."

"I see," Lerens said. "Can you tell me about the paintings that were taken?"

"The two over the fireplace were family portraits. The other two . . ." She furrowed her brow in thought. "I'm so sorry, in all the excitement I can't seem to recall."

"That's fine," Lerens reassured her. "We'll ask the other family members."

"Yes, I suppose you will." She stood. "Now, if that's all, I have things to do."

Hugo and Lerens stood out of politeness, and watched as she walked slowly from the room, leaving them alone.

"She was lovely," Hugo said. "But 'as God intended'?"

"Absolutely delightful." Lerens raised a scornful eyebrow. "Do you have any idea how much I wanted to tell her I was born into a man's body?"

Hugo smiled. "I'm guessing quite a lot."

"More than that. Desperately."

"Well, if that should ever come to pass, please make sure I'm there. I would love to see that old shell rattled good and hard."

"With pleasure. I mean, she can stab her husband and move into this place like a murderous cuckoo taking over the family nest. But God forbid two women want to make love."

"Yeah." Hugo thought for a moment. "You believe that? That she killed him?"

"I have no idea. But having just spent time with her, I'd hardly rule it out."

CHAPTER ELEVEN

As they waited for the second member of the family to enter the drawing room, Camille Lerens checked her watch. "If they really want us out of here, do you think we should split up and do one-on-one interviews?"

Hugo thought for a moment. "How many are there?"

Lerens flipped through her note pad. "There's still Charlotte's kids—Marc Lambourd, Erika Sipiora, Édouard Lambourd, and Noelle Manis. Oh, and Marc's son Fabien."

"Don't forget our jolly widow's nurse."

"Karine Berger, yes. So that's six altogether."

"No one we can rule out immediately?"

"Not that I know of."

Hugo looked at his own watch. "Then maybe we should get to it. Is there somewhere else we can use?"

"I was told I could use the parlor, through there." Lerens indicated high and ornate double doors to their left.

"Remind me of the difference between a drawing room and a parlor," Hugo said, only half-joking.

"Easy. One is here, the other is over there." Lerens smiled and got up, making her way to the doors. "Just make sure everything is recorded. Your French is good enough, yes?"

"I guess we'll see."

"That's not reassuring, Hugo."

"If I screw up a question or answer, we can always come back. It's not like they're homeless vagrants that will be moving on to somewhere we can't find them."

"That's for sure." Lerens looked around at the splendor of the large room. "Paul's downstairs. I'll radio him and have him bring up two people at once."

Hugo was pleased that Jameson brought him Erika Sipiora, the one he knew least about and the only one with an official royal title. He rose when she entered the room.

"Princess Erika, my name is—"

"Please, please." The woman waved a hand to shush him. She was almost six feet tall and strongly built, with auburn hair that was pulled back into a practical pony tail. Judging by the cut of her matching tweed jacket and skirt, she had an eye for the finer things in life, but the smile she shone on Hugo was of humility. "None of that princess stuff, I beg of you. I didn't marry my late husband for his title, or to get mine. I had no choice in that matter. Because he made me a princess, he was the only one who was allowed to call me one." She reached Hugo and thrust out a hand. "Hugo Marston, I presume."

"Yes, that's right."

"Oh, don't look so surprised. As of yesterday evening, you're a national treasure. They're preparing a spot for you in the Louvre as we speak, I believe."

"Thank you. I just did what any law enforcement officer would have done, nothing special about it."

"Nonsense. I hear you shot the gun right out of his hand."

"By chance, I assure you." Hugo looked around the room, and changed the subject. "This is a beautiful house."

"Isn't it?" Sipiora agreed. "Dripping with history, too."

"Absolutely. And maybe we can start there."

"Meaning?"

"The four paintings that were taken. Your mother said two were family portraits."

"Yes, Nissim and Béatrice. My great-grandparents."

"Taken from this very room."

"Yes." She walked to the fireplace and gestured to a blank area of wall. "Right here."

"And the other two?"

"Also from in here." She pointed to either side of the French doors that led onto a long balcony, overlooking the back gardens and, beyond them, Parc Monceau.

"What were they?"

"It's funny, when someone told me they'd been stolen I actually had a hard time remembering. Picturing them. You can look at something every day and not really see it." She laughed and shook her head sadly. "Makes me think that those paintings watch us more than we see them. Anyway, one was by Piero Sansalvadore, of a square in Florence, and the other was a country scene of some sort."

"Valuable?"

"The ones of my grandparents aren't, no. Just sentimental value. The other two, I have no idea. They're old but that's about all I can tell you." She walked back over to the sofa that Hugo had been sitting on. "Shall we?"

"Yes, of course." Hugo shifted down to one end, as it didn't look like Sipiora was about to find anywhere else to sit. Once settled, he put his recorder on the table in front of them.

"Your French is very good, but my English is better," she said, matter-of-factly.

"I think since this is a French investigation we should probably stick to—"

"Nonsense. English it is, and if they don't like it, well, too bad." Her smile matched her words: short, sharp, and unmoving.

"Okay, fine by me," Hugo said. "Do you mind telling me a little about yourself and your place in the family?"

"My place in the family . . . I think that's a novel, not a police statement, but I know what you're asking so will do my best. I am the firstborn of Charlotte and Alfred Lambourd . . . Ah, your face, Mr. Marston. You don't play poker, do you?"

"A little Texas Hold'em, from time to time, why?"

"Then I suspect you lose. Your face will give you away every time."

"It's just that someone said your brother Marc was the firstborn, nothing major."

Sipiora clapped her hands together, and laughed. "Nothing major? Oh, dear, Mr. Marston, you don't know much about French nobility, do you?"

"Enlighten me."

"Well, that's another tangent but suffice it to say, and so we're being completely accurate, that Marc and I are both firstborn."

"Ah, twins."

"You *are* a good detective, well done." She gave him a wink. "Yes, that's correct. He preceded me by one whole minute, but we're both the firstborn."

"Got it. And you now live in Luxembourg?"

"I do. Most of the time. My late husband was from there, so I have the house, but it's quite large and I rather rattle about in it, so I tend to travel a lot. I can afford to, and have no real ties binding me there, so why not?"

"And when did you get to Paris?"

"Yesterday. By train. I don't fly anymore if I don't have to. None of us do."

"None of you?"

"The family. It sounds silly but you might call it the Lambourd phobia. Ever since our uncle died in a plane crash, we don't fly." She laughed. "That was in the war in 1943, so I know how silly it seems. I sometimes wonder if it's more of a control thing coming from my mother than a result of that plane crash. Anyway, I'm rambling, sorry."

"That's quite all right," Hugo said. "Every family has its foibles. So do you have anyone left in Luxembourg?"

"As I said, no ties binding me there." She looked down, and clasped her hands on her lap. "I did have a daughter, but unfortunately she passed away when she was three. Kidney disease."

"I'm sorry to hear that. And your husband?"

She looked up and smiled. "He was a little older than three when he died. He lasted until he was ninety."

"Oh, so quite a lot older than you."

"I'm not sure if you're trying to flatter me, or judge me, Mr. Marston."

Hugo held up an apologetic hand. "I'm sorry, that terrible poker face sometimes extends to my words. I'm sorry if I offended you."

"You didn't. But at the risk of offending you, I would like to get to the point of this. Lunch plans, you know, and I have a dress to pick up for tonight's event. Will you be attending?"

"Possibly, I think so. Ambassador's orders."

"Oh, it'll be fun, I promise. When the house is filled with people drinking champagne, you can almost feel its past looking down on you, admiring the incredible guests and their ridiculously expensive finery. This place was made to be shown off, and not just as some musty old museum."

"Then I shall try to adjust my attitude," Hugo said gamely. "So, getting to the point, how well do you know Tammy Fotinos?"

"Poor girl. Barely at all. She worked for us last year, did a fine job but, and I know how bad this sounds, but part of doing a good job as a servant means not making your presence known. She did what she was supposed to, and did it well. I'm sure that's why we hired her back this year." She smiled conspiratorially. "You've met my mother. You can imagine she's not easy to please, so when someone meets her standards, well, she hangs onto them."

"Makes good sense," Hugo said. "So as far as you know, no one had anything against her, any reason to hurt her?"

"Good heavens, no. Certainly not within the family. We may be an odd group, Mr. Marston, but in my experience we tend to reserve our antipathy for each other, not outsiders."

"Was anyone having a . . . dalliance with her?"

"Dalliance?" Sipiora snorted with laughter. "I didn't know people still used that word. But no, not that I'm aware of." She frowned in thought. "That said, my nephew Fabien was paying her a lot of attention with his eyes last night. And he's at that age where anything in a skirt . . . well, you know."

"It's been a few years, but yes," Hugo said. "So you don't know of anything definitely happening between them?"

"Why don't you ask him? Or her, for that matter?"

"We will. And, for the record, you didn't see or hear anything last night at the time she was attacked?"

"I don't know what time that was. But no, I'm sure I didn't. I was in bed by eleven, asleep soon after. I didn't see or hear anything unusual at all."

"Well, thank you for your time. If there's anything you can think of that might be helpful, please let us know."

They both stood, and Sipiora said, "You're welcome. And if you have more questions yourself, maybe you can ask them with a glass of champagne in your hand this evening." She put out her hand, and her grip again was firm, dry, and fleeting, as if they'd finished a drab business meeting. "Oh, my little brother, Édouard, is nervous about talking to your colleague—mind if he comes to see you?"

"Not at all," Hugo said. "Please send him my way."

CHAPTER TWELVE

Édouard Lambourd looked like he was scared of Hugo, too. Dressed in a light gray suit, with waistcoat even, he all but tiptoed into the drawing room of his own house. He swept back floppy, sandy hair from a high forehead and didn't offer to shake hands.

"My sister says to do this in English. Do you mind if I sit here?" He gestured to the chair opposite the sofa Hugo had been sitting on.

"Not at all. And why did she tell you that, do you know?"

"Because . . ." He dropped his gaze to the floor. "I probably shouldn't . . . Please, forget I said that."

Hugo thought for a moment, and then smiled. "So that if we use your statement against you later, you can claim you didn't understand the question properly?"

"I didn't . . . that's not exactly what . . . I meant. No."

"Monsieur Lambourd," Hugo said, switching to French, "we can conduct this interview in French or English, whichever you choose. But whichever it is, I will ask that, should you not understand me or have even the slightest bit of doubt about what I'm asking, you speak up. Otherwise I will assume you do understand. Are we clear on that?"

"Yes, yes. Of course."

"Would you like to do this in French or English?"

"I don't suppose you speak German?" Lambourd said, with a weak smile.

"Not enough, no."

"Well, me neither. Be a nice short interview, wouldn't it?" Lambourd sighed. "English, I suppose."

Hugo leaned forward. "Is there some reason you're so nervous to talk to me and my colleague, Monsieur Lambourd?"

"Well, I mean, your colleague, yes. For obvious reasons."

"They're not obvious to me. Can you explain?"

"I'm just not comfortable with that sort of thing. Nothing wrong with it, I'm sure, it's just not something I'm used to."

"What *sort of thing*?" Hugo pressed, enjoying Lambourd's discomfort.

"Well, I mean, what would I call her?"

"I'd suggest Lieutenant Lerens."

"Yes, of course, but I mean . . ." Lambourd looked around helplessly. "I suppose I don't really know what I mean."

Hugo sighed, hoping that Lambourd would notice the heavy dose of disapproval it contained. "Perhaps we should get to the point. How well did you know Tammy Fotinos?"

"Not at all. Pretty girl, but I only saw her a few times. Here at the house."

"She slept here, did she not?"

"Yes. In the serv . . . downstairs. Ground floor."

"Servants' quarters, I'm well aware. When did you get into town?"

"Yesterday. I took the train in from Nice—that's where I live."

"A long ride?"

"No one in our family flies, unless we have to."

"Your sister mentioned that, the family phobia," Hugo said.

"Quite ridiculous, I expect, especially as it stems from my uncle being shot down in the Second World War more than seventy years ago."

"I prefer trains myself. What do you do in Nice?"

"I'm an art dealer. And an art consultant."

"What's an art consultant?"

"When people buy art I go into their home and recommend where they hang it. Or maybe how they frame it, if that's not already done."

"You tell people where to hang paintings? In their own homes." For a slight man, Édouard had surprisingly large hands, Hugo noticed.

"Yes. Believe me, it's a valuable service and a lot of people have more money than sense, art sense that is, and so need the help. And are very grateful for it."

"Can I assume you're familiar with the paintings that were stolen last night?"

"You can." Lambourd nodded. "And you're probably wondering if they're valuable, if they were worth stealing."

"I am," Hugo said.

"The pair of my grandparents is not at all valuable." He pointed to the left side of the large French doors. "The Sansalvadore, possibly worth a couple of thousand euros. But probably not."

"And the fourth?"

"That was by Charles-Émile Jacques. A French painter who was part of the Barbizon School, lived and worked in the mid-1800s. It was called *Sheep and Shepherd*, or something equally unimaginative." He sat looking at Hugo for a moment. "As for whether it was worth anything . . ." He thought for a moment. "Maybe ten thousand euros? Something like that, I would guess."

"Thank you, that's good to know." Hugo looked around. "Do you have other paintings or pieces of art that are more valuable than that?"

Lambourd smiled. "God, yes. A lot. I'll tell you this—whoever stole those pieces was either very unlucky or very stupid."

"Or they didn't finish."

"Maybe, but I don't know why they'd even start with those pieces."

"If you're right about their value, me neither," Hugo agreed. "So, if you don't mind, what time did you go to bed last night?"

"Oh, I would say around ten. I watched television in my room for an hour or so, and was asleep by midnight."

"Is that your normal routine?"

Lambourd hesitated. "Nothing's normal when I come here."

"Meaning?"

"My family is an odd collection of people. I'm sure we'd have nothing to do with each other if it weren't for the blood ties."

Hugo nodded his understanding. "Which of them are you closest to?"

"My mother, probably." That weak smile again. "But I wouldn't use the word 'close.'"

"What about Erika?"

"You know, I'm actually curious what you thought of her."

"Why?"

"She's very good at . . . putting on a front. She's an extrovert. Like Marc—he is too. They are both charming and funny and convincing."

"That's an odd word choice. Convincing?"

"*Convaincants.* I said it right, yes?"

"Yes, that's the word. But tell me what you meant by it."

Lambourd shrugged. "Just that. When they say something, people believe it. They have . . . confidence."

"And you don't?"

"Perhaps not."

"I see. Well, tell me this. Is there anyone in the family, or in the house, who might have a reason to harm Tammy?"

"Not that I know of. I assume she was having an affair with someone, and either that person did it or someone who was jealous."

"Who might she be having an affair with?"

"You should ask her."

"I'm asking you."

"I don't know."

"Was it with you?"

Lambourd snorted. "No. Not possible."

"You're not married, so why not?"

"You think married people can't have lovers? This is France—we invented affairs."

"You know what I mean," Hugo said sternly.

"I am not interested in . . ." He waved a hand in front of him.

"In women?"

"In sex. In relationships. I am asexual, I suppose one would say. I have interests but none of them involve being with other people. Of either gender."

"Is it possible your brother was seeing her?"

"He is engaged." Lambourd laughed gently. "He may have sown his wild oats in the past, but those days are gone. And while discretion was never important to him, I would be very surprised."

"His son?"

"Fabien is Marc all over again, two peas in a pod I think the expression goes. But I wouldn't know about anything between him and the American girl."

"Marc and Fabien are close?"

"Very. If Fabien is a little wild from time to time, it is Marc's fault. He dotes on the boy and, in my opinion, hasn't gotten serious with a woman in years not because they're not good enough for him, but because they're not good enough for Fabien."

"So Marc thinks very highly of his fiancée."

"We all do. Fabien included, from what I can tell." He looked at his watch. "Now, if we're about done . . ."

"May I speak frankly, Monsieur Lambourd?"

"I suppose so."

"I'm not understanding something about this family, this household, and I was hoping you could explain it to me." Hugo cleared his throat, more for dramatic effect than anything. "You see, a young woman was almost murdered here last night. Garrotted. A horrific crime. And it just seems to me that no one here really gives a damn. No one wants to help, everyone has plans for lunch or afternoon tea or whatever other thing, and the only thing that really seems to matter is that you all clam up and say as little as possible until you can successfully stage your annual party." Hugo sat back and spread his hands wide. "Did I get any of that wrong?"

Édouard Lambourd sat staring at Hugo for a moment, but when he spoke his voice carried more anger and, perhaps, strength than Hugo had expected.

"You come in here, a foreigner, and you start picking at a noble French family, start poking around our home on the day of the most important event, historical event, any of us have ever known. You try to get us to tell tales on each other, to drive us apart, and for what? Because some silly girl got herself into a bad situation?"

"Oh, so you think it's her fault someone garroted her?"

"And how do you know that someone didn't come in from the outside? We don't have alarms or cameras in here. The locks are as old as the rest of the house, which means an imbecile could pick them, I'm sure. There are no guards, no dogs, so I'm wondering why you're so intent on blaming someone in the family."

"I'm not intent on—"

"Maybe it's for the headlines, is that it? It certainly seems like you enjoy being in the newspapers, maybe this little heroic act of yours has given you the taste for it."

"That's ridiculous, I'm just—"

"From where I sit, it's no more ridiculous than accusing one of my family of attempting murder. Not by a long shot. No one here is capable of anything like that, so I suggest you look elsewhere, Mr. Marston. You and your complicated friend from the Brigade Criminelle." Lambourd stood up and swept past Hugo, leaving the drawing room door to close behind him of its own accord.

When Hugo looked up he saw Camille Lerens standing in the door to the smaller parlor. "What was that about?" she asked.

"Someone was a little huffy that I was asking too many questions about the family. Sensitive fellow, our Édouard Lambourd, and quite a temper."

"Good to know," Lerens said. "I finished with Marc and have been waiting for Noelle. He checked on her and apparently she gets migraines, had one this morning, so is moving a little slowly. On her way now, though."

A knock on the door was followed by its opening, and Noelle Manis poked her head around to look at them.

"*Bonjour.*" She stepped into the room and closed the door behind her. "I'm sorry to keep you waiting. I wasn't feeling well." She was tall and slender, with lush brown hair and a face that might have been pale from her migraine, or her natural complexion. She was a few years shy of fifty years old, Hugo figured, but could pass for being in her midthirties. She crossed the room and offered them her hand, and a firm grip.

They arranged themselves and Manis sat primly, her hands on her lap, waiting for the questions. Lieutenant Lerens clicked on her digital recorder and began.

"Can you tell me where your bedroom is located?" she asked.

"Of course. If you go up to the third floor, it's the one furthest to the left, at the end of the hallway."

"And what time did you go to bed last night?" Lerens asked.

"I think around eleven. I usually stay up a little, though, and watch something on my tablet." She gave a sad smile. "The only one without a television in my room, which is what you get for being the youngest."

"Did you see or hear anything out of the ordinary last night?"

"Nothing at all. That poor girl, someone told me she's going to be all right, but how awful for her."

"She's going to be fine, physically," Lerens said.

"I can't imagine who'd want to hurt her—it makes no sense at all. No one in the family, for sure."

"Do you know if she was having any kind of sexual relationship with anyone here?"

"In the family?" Manis opened her eyes wide. "Good heavens, no. Do you think that's what was going on?"

"We don't know," Lerens assured her. "It's just something that we have to explore."

"No, I really don't think so."

"I hear Marc used to be quite the man around town," Hugo interjected.

"Well, yes. In years gone by, that's true, I suppose. But not since he got engaged to Catherine."

"I see." Something about her tone, the way she said the name, told Hugo that Noelle Manis wasn't a fan. He decided to press that button. "You don't approve?"

"Well, it's not my place to approve or otherwise." She shrugged. "I did think the engagement came very quickly after their meeting. And the one time she spent time with us, at Erika's in Luxembourg, she didn't seem to fit in very well. Or even be a good fit for Marc."

"How do you mean?" Hugo asked.

"She was very clingy. Beautiful—I can see why Marc fell for her and wants her on his arm. But she's younger and . . . well, clingy." Manis looked at Hugo and then Lerens. "Marc and I have discussed this. I'm not telling you anything I've not said to him."

"How did that conversation go?" Hugo asked.

"Fine, really." Manis shrugged. "Marc and I have always been close. By that I mean closer than with the others, you'd hardly call this a warm and cuddly family. I don't recall much parental affection. The most physical contact I had with my mother growing up was over her lap when she'd decided I'd disappointed her." She smiled, as if trying to make light of what she was saying. "And then the contact was with the hard side of her hairbrush."

"Was she harsh with the others?"

"Yes, I think so. I mean, I think we'd all agree that Marc has always been the favorite, her favorite. But she was still hard on him, Édouard too. Belt for the boys, brush for the girls seemed to be the rule. Everyone felt like they got it more, including me. I think her patience had worn out by the time I came along, but the others will probably see it differently. My point is just that in a family where appearances and status mean more than love, Marc was the one who was kindest to me."

"The oldest looking after the youngest?" Hugo suggested.

"Something like that." She laughed gently. "Ironic, too. Erika was supposed to be born first, but Mother had some complication and they took out Marc first. He loves telling that story. I'm surprised he didn't tell you. He can be a little . . . status conscious, I suppose."

"Which makes me wonder why he's not firmer with Fabien," Hugo said. A shift in Manis's eyes and a tightening of her jaw made him think he'd hit a nerve.

"He . . . makes exceptions for Fabien," she said.

"Exceptions?" Hugo pushed.

"Has a blind spot. To reality sometimes."

"What do you mean?"

"As I've said, Marc and I are close, but one area . . . the first area of disagreement has been over Fabien."

"Anything in particular?" Hugo asked.

"Yes, actually. But I don't mean to sound rude when I say that's family business. I can't see how it'd be relevant and so I prefer not to talk about it."

"I think maybe we should decide if it's relevant," Hugo said, keeping his tone soft.

"Nevertheless, it's a family issue and that's all I have to say on the matter." It was the first note of steel in her voice, and Hugo let it go. For now.

"On another note," Lerens said, "a moment ago you used the phrase, *By the time I came along*." Lerens hesitated. "I'm sorry to ask, and it probably doesn't matter in the slightest, but someone mentioned you were adopted. Is that right?"

"So I'm told," Manis said. "When I was a baby, I don't remember a thing about it, of course. And, as you would imagine with this family, no one ever really talked about it. I don't even remember being told—it was just something I always knew." She cocked her head. "What other family secrets can I spill?"

"I am curious," Hugo began. "Why didn't Marc's fiancée come for the weekend?"

"You'd have to ask him." Her eyes were wary. "I really don't know the exact reason."

"He told me she had other plans," Lerens said. "But I'm not sure I believe him entirely. After all, this is the party of the year, and if she likes being seen on his arm, that'd be—"

"I think I said, *he* likes her being seen on his arm," Manis corrected. "Look, there's tension between me and her, and between her and the family. What she doesn't understand, and will need to if she wants to marry into the Lambourd clan, is that there's always going to be tension. You just have to learn to live with it."

"You speak from experience," Hugo said. "You're married?"

"Was. For ten years. Then he decided he liked men better than women." Again the sad smile. "What could I say about that, other than goodbye?"

"Not much, I suppose. I'm sorry," Hugo said. He turned to Lerens. "Anything else?"

"Not that I can think of." Lerens stood and put out her hand. "Thank you for your time and candor. Can you ask either Fabien or Karine Berger to come in?"

"Of course." Manis shook hands with them both and then let herself out of the living room.

"Quite the family," Lerens said.

"You're not kidding."

"Dysfunction aside, not one of them saw anything, heard anything, or can think of anyone who'd hurt Tammy Fotinos."

"Correct. You'd think with all these creaky old doors and floor boards, someone would have heard something."

"Yeah, like a young woman being almost strangled to death." Hugo shook his head in frustration. "Maybe young Fabien will confess to everything and make our lives easier."

"I don't think so," Lerens said, as they watched the door open and Noelle Manis come back in.

"So there's a bit of a problem with you talking to Karine and Fabien," Manis said.

Her tone caught their attention. "What's wrong?" Lerens asked.

"I'm very sorry, but Mother has forbidden Karine to speak with you."

"On what basis?" Lerens asked.

"That she didn't do anything wrong and is already traumatized by what happened."

"Please tell your mother we will absolutely need to speak with Karine at some point. We can have a counselor present, and your mother can even be there. But we will need to talk to her." Lerens sighed in frustration. "And what about Fabien—what's the problem with him?"

"He's not here."

"What do you mean?" Hugo asked, not liking her tone. "He went out?"

"It's just . . . no one knows where he is," Manis said. "He seems to have disappeared."

CHAPTER THIRTEEN

"What does that mean, *disappeared*?" Hugo asked.

"No one has seen him at all this morning," Jameson said. The Scot had returned from the hospital and been keeping the family company downstairs.

"And no one thought to mention it until now?" Hugo asked.

"Ay. I get the feeling this family won't be helping any more than they absolutely have to. And that includes offering information without being asked."

"Do they seem worried?" Hugo asked.

"I just finished talking to his father, for heaven's sake," Lerens said, exasperated. "How did he not mention it?"

Jameson shrugged. "You want me to get him back up here?"

"Yes, please." When he'd gone, Lerens said, "Just what we need, a runaway teenager."

"He'll turn up. Probably not a fan of authority and, as you say, he's a teenager."

"Yeah, hopefully." Lerens sighed. "So, what do you make of things so far?"

"Well, it seems like whoever stole the paintings didn't know what he was doing. Not if he wanted to make any money off them, anyway."

"Is there any other reason to steal art?"

"To enjoy it," Hugo offered. "But two of the paintings were of family members, and a stranger isn't going to get much pleasure from those."

"The paintings themselves were on the smaller side compared to the others in here, so in one way it makes sense he'd take those. And, I suppose, he attacked Tammy Fotinos on his way out."

"That seems odd to me," Hugo said.

"Why?"

"Well, she told us she was on her way to bed when she was attacked from behind."

"Right. He saw her coming down the stairs, waited until her back was turned, and attacked."

"But why? I mean, she'd not seen him and was on her way to bed. If he'd waited thirty seconds she'd have been out of the way and he could've slipped out then, or stolen more stuff."

"Maybe he panicked?"

"And just happened to have a garrote with him?" Hugo gave her a dry smile. "Is that something French burglars typically carry?"

"So you think the theft of the paintings is a distraction."

"Maybe, yes."

They turned as the double doors opened and Jameson led Marc Lambourd into the room. He was a tall man, dark-haired and handsome, wearing moleskin trousers, a pink button-down shirt, and a blue sports jacket.

"Monsieur Lambourd," Lerens said. "I wanted you to meet Hugo Marston—he's helping me with this investigation."

Lambourd and Hugo shook hands. "Pleasure to meet you," Hugo said. Lambourd just nodded.

They took their seats, and Hugo let Lerens do the talking. She said, "Someone mentioned that Fabien hasn't been seen this morning."

"So I'm told."

"You yourself haven't seen or spoken to him at all today?"

"He's a teenager. I go days without seeing or speaking to him."

"Today isn't your normal day, though," Lerens pointed out. "And didn't you just bail him out of jail?"

"Not bail, they're dropping all charges. I expect that's why he's avoiding me—he knows I'm tired of cleaning up his messes."

"I see," he said "Kids aren't as attuned to circumstances as we'd like them to be."

Hugo spoke up. "Plus, it's my understanding that you and Fabien have an unusually close bond."

Lambourd shrugged. "I don't know what you mean by that. If it's unusual for a father and son to love each other, then maybe so."

Hugo smiled. "I think maybe it's more that father and son like each other."

"Ah, perhaps," Lambourd conceded. "At the very least, we are very alike, and I am very lucky that I have his friendship."

"I assume you've tried calling him?" Lerens asked.

"Of course. About thirty minutes ago, I called as soon as I was told he'd not been seen, but it went to voicemail. And he's not read the texts I sent him."

"Do you have a tracking app?" she asked.

"No. I give the boy his independence as much as possible."

"If you could write his number down, I can have someone ping his phone, find out where he is."

"Is that really necessary?"

"Monsieur Lambourd." Lerens held his gaze for a moment. "A woman was almost murdered here last night. Your son should be here, and he's not. Are you not concerned?"

"I am not concerned that he's involved, if that's what you're suggesting. Nor am I concerned that he's in danger. He is an expert in martial arts and is a sensible boy."

"Martial arts aren't much use against a gun," Hugo said. "Or even the element of surprise."

"This is not America," Lambourd snapped. "Not everyone has a gun on their hip."

"Monsieur Lambourd, please," Lerens said. "I need his phone number. If we locate him and he's fine, then we can clear him, leave him alone, and start worrying about other things."

Lambourd dictated the number and Lerens typed it into her phone, dialed the prefecture, and spent a few moments talking to someone back at the Brigade Criminelle, passing on Fabien's phone number. "They'll get a warrant and have it tracked. Shouldn't take an hour."

"Fine. Please let me know what you find out." Lambourd stood. "Is that all you need from me?"

"Actually, there is one thing." Hugo remained seated. "Would you mind having a word with your mother on our behalf?"

"What about?"

"She doesn't want us to talk to Karine Berger."

"Why not?"

"That's not clear to us," Hugo said. "And, as you might imagine, not wanting us to talk to her makes us want to talk to her even more."

"Probably because you'd be wasting your time."

"Meaning?"

"My mother is a very loyal person. And Karine . . . has her issues." He pursed his lips, as if wondering how much to say. He continued. "Look, Karine is perfect for my mother. She does as she's told, doesn't talk a lot, and doesn't require . . . a lot of time for herself. My mother's needs are great and she's a demanding person. Karine isn't the sort of person likely to get a good job anywhere else, so while she works a lot and spends her life with my mother, she is paid well. And my mother will protect her."

"Why does she need protecting?"

"She's . . . we call her a nurse but she's not trained or anything. She's more of a companion and she's . . . a very simple person. She could be bullied into saying something that she shouldn't. Or something that wasn't true."

"That's not how we operate," Lerens said.

"Maybe not. But my mother doesn't know that. And wouldn't believe it if you told her."

"What exactly does she do for your mother?" Hugo asked. He wanted to change the subject, make both Lerens and Lambourd less defensive.

"Whatever *Maman* needs. From trips to the store to trips to Bordeaux and beyond. She takes care of her when she's sick, and generally makes sure my mother is comfortable. I've seen Karine carry her from the car to her bed several times. She's as loyal to my mother as my mother is to her."

"I wasn't clear about something," Hugo said. "Were you implying that Karine has some kind of learning disability or mental impairment?"

"I have no idea. I barely know the woman."

CHAPTER FOURTEEN

When they were alone in the room, Hugo and Camille Lerens sat in silence for a moment. A heavy wooden clock on the mantle above the fireplace *tick-tocked* in a hollow, almost baritone voice, and Hugo thought about the people who'd passed through and lingered in this room before him. Like many Americans, he was a sucker for history, *real* history. Stories of kings and queens, art that was hundreds of years old, homes that had survived wars and, or so it seemed to Hugo, held onto family secrets of people like the Lambourds.

Hugo wandered to the windows overlooking the garden, and beyond it the park, where Charlotte Lambourd's first husband had been found murdered. Had she done it to get the house back? But who would kill their husband and marry a man and bear three children for him just for a house? The truth was, he'd seen people kill for less. Far less—a handful of coins, or just an insult.

"You're looking pensive," Lerens said.

"Just thinking about this house. All that it's seen over the years."

"You think houses see things?" Lerens was amused.

"You know what I mean."

"No, tell me."

"I think people project their emotions onto things, invest their lives and even their souls into places just like this."

"That's a . . . very un-Hugo-like sentiment."

"Let me ask you this, then. If you were blindfolded and led into a building, do you think you could tell whether it was newly built, or old like this?"

"Could I tell the difference?"

"Right. Do you think you could?"

Lerens thought for a moment. "I would have to say yes."

"Right. Because there's something intangible, unexplainable, about old houses like this."

"They smell of dust and polish. What happened to Mr. Logical? You'll be turning to religion next."

"No, that's not fair," Hugo said, laughing gently. "I've always told you that I believe in a person's ability to sense when something's not right. Either in the moment or more generally."

"Yes, you have said that."

"Call it instinct, a sixth sense. I've trusted mine plenty of times, and been thankful for doing so."

"Especially when dealing with Tom."

"Most definitely. But my point is . . . well, I'm not sure what my point is."

"Something about houses retaining the history of the people who've lived in them?" Lerens offered.

"Yes. Something like that." He gazed out of the window at the beautifully manicured gardens. "And died in them, too." He came out of his reverie when his phone buzzed in his pocket. He answered it when he saw who was calling. "Mr. Ambassador, how can I help?"

"I'd like a sit rep, please."

"Yes, sir, I'm doing just fine. And you?"

"Hugo. Don't be difficult."

Hugo chuckled. "So, as well as the attack on Tammy Fotinos, who is going to be fine by the way, someone stole four paintings from the house last night."

"What? Why?"

"We're working on it. Not priceless works of art, by any means."

"Well, that puts a wrinkle in the picture. Pardon the pun."

"Pardoned, boss," Hugo said. "Camille thinks maybe Tammy encountered the burglar in the middle of the night and he attacked her to keep her quiet while he got away."

"But judging from your tone of voice, you don't."

"Not yet, no."

"Why?" Taylor asked.

"The use of the garrote. The fact that she didn't see him, which we know because she told us. He could've waited for her to go downstairs to bed—he didn't need to strangle her."

"Any chance the Fotinos girl is hiding something?"

"Oh, I think she is." A cold hand clutched at Hugo's stomach. "At first I thought it was a secret meeting with someone in the family. Now I'm wondering."

"Like, she might have been in on the burglary, and her accomplice decided not to share the spoils?"

"That's not impossible."

"You better go talk to her again."

"I'll wait until tomorrow. She has a very protective doctor by her bedside, and she's not going anywhere."

"That's fine." Ambassador Taylor cleared his throat. "So, I've arranged a couple of interviews for you."

"We're hiring?"

"No, Hugo, don't play dumb."

"Boss, I don't have time for that."

"You'll have to make time. Believe it or not, some cases in France get solved without your involvement."

"Not this one." He glanced at Camille Lerens and winked. "Lieutenant Lerens just told me I'm invaluable and she can't do without me for even a moment."

Taylor sighed dramatically. "You're a terrible liar, Hugo. Maybe I should talk to her myself?"

"She just went to the restroom, sorry boss."

"You saved lives. You may be a reluctant hero, but a hero you are. And heroes give interviews."

"Can I just give one to Claudia?'

"One what?" Taylor snickered. "Sorry, that was the thirteen-year-old who lives inside me. And no, you can't. We can't be playing favorites among the media, not on a story this large."

"Fine. They want us out of the house this afternoon anyway, so I can do it then. At the embassy?"

"Yes, I told them they could set up in my office. Other than a bland conference room, it's the only place big enough. Three o'clock."

"What can you tell me about the shooting investigation? I've not had a chance to check the news."

"Well." Hugo heard the hesitation in the ambassador's voice. "I probably shouldn't tell you too much. Not before your interview."

"Worried I'll spill the beans?"

"You're not supposed to know the beans, Hugo. In theory you're a suspect in the shooting death of a man."

"You know, that's really weird because I thought I was a hero."

"Funny."

"Should a suspect in a shooting case really be giving an interview?"

"When he's also a hero, yes."

"Well played, sir."

"Three sharp, Hugo. Brush your hair and wear a tie."

"I'm not wearing a tie, boss. The hair I can do, but no tie." He hung up before Taylor could say anything else.

"You're giving a television interview?" Lerens asked.

"Apparently."

"So what happened exactly? We've not had a chance to talk, and all I know is what I've seen online or on television."

"We haven't. It all happened so fast, to be honest. I was heading out for a glass of wine, then suddenly heard gunshots and saw the guy, right there. I just . . . did what I was trained to do, I guess."

"And you feel all right about it?"

Hugo smiled. "You sound like Ambassador Taylor. Thank you for your concern, but yes, I do feel fine with it."

"I've never shot anyone," Lerens said. "I hate to think how I'd feel after."

"You can't know until it happens. Obviously, I hate it, but after a lot of years in law enforcement I have these pretty secure compartments in my head. Shooting someone who is trying to kill innocent

civilians, well, that fits into one of the safest and least leaky compartments."

"Someone told me you shot the gun out of his hand."

Hugo rolled his eyes. "Good God, not you too."

"Is it true, cowboy?" Lerens asked, a twinkle in her eye.

"I'm not a cowboy, and yes, while it's technically true it wasn't my
intention. I shot center-mass where he happened to be holding the gun,
and the first bullet happened to strike it and knock it out of his hand.
Pure luck."

"No one will want to believe that."

"Well, it's true."

"A handsome cowboy striding through town with boots on his
feet and a six-shooter on his hip, a glint in his eye and a pretty lady
waiting for him. He spots a bad guy, a ruthless killer, and takes him
out with two shots, pinging the gun out of his hand for good measure."

"Enjoying yourself, Camille?" She was toying with him now, and
Hugo pretended to be irritated.

"Very much. Shame you weren't wearing your hat."

"It's a fedora, not a cowboy hat. Plus, I took four shots and missed
with two of them."

Lerens waived a dismissive hand. "Irrelevant parts of a legend always fall away, leaving just the good bits behind. No one needs to know
about those missed shots." She held up a finger to silence Hugo as her
phone chirped. "Lerens here." A pause. "That was quick." Another
pause. "Thank you. Can you send that to my phone, in a text? Thanks
again." She hung up and turned to Hugo. "Well, well."

"Some news?"

"Time to saddle up, cowboy. They located Fabien's phone. Let's go
find its owner."

CHAPTER FIFTEEN

I t took less than ten minutes to drive from Château Lambourd to the abandoned Renault Mégane, which sat on the grassy verge beside Avenue de l'Hippodrome, one of the few east-west roads that took traffic through the Bois de Boulogne. Sitting on the western edge of the city, the park occupied about two thousand acres and had been everything from a hunting ground for robbers to the hunting grounds of kings. Hugo hadn't been there more than a few times, and wondered if it still was as it had been when he first came to Paris: scenic and serene during the day, but as the sun slipped from the sky and the day-trippers left, they were replaced by those looking to sell, and buy, sex and drugs, and by even more nefarious characters looking to help themselves to both at no expense. Lieutenant Lerens stopped her car behind the marked police unit that was keeping an eye on things until they got there.

They got out of the car and, from where Hugo stood, and in the middle of the day, it seemed like a peaceful place, and it felt good to be away from the roar of the traffic that endlessly looped through the city's roads, pleasant even to be away from the beautiful but always-crowded streets of the Latin Quarter, where he lived, just a stone's throw from the River Seine. He looked around and took in a lungful of fresh air, and then joined Lerens, who stood looking into the broken-out rear passenger window of the abandoned Renault. It looked like it had been there weeks, not hours, dusty and dirty, the wheels caked in mud and one headlight broken.

"Anyone in it?" Lerens asked the uniformed *flic*, who stood to attention as she approached him.

"*Non, personne,*" he said. *No, no one.*

"Did you run the plate?"

"Yes, I was first on scene and figured you'd want to know whose it is."

"Excellent," Lerens said. "I most certainly do."

"It belongs," the officer began, and dug a notebook out of his breast pocket, "to an Alain Juin, lives in Montmartre. He reported it stolen five days ago."

"Did you search it?"

"*Non*, Lieutenant. I just looked inside." He gestured to the grimy windows. "Had to use a flashlight, but saw the phone they'd pinged. It's right there on the back seat."

"Well, the crime scene people are on the way. They'll photograph it as is, then get to work processing it for prints, DNA, all that stuff." Lerens started to turn away, and then turned back, a little hesitant. "You didn't see any blood in there, did you?"

"No. And I thought about popping the trunk to make sure there's . . . well, you know."

"No one inside?"

"Right. But they told me not to, so I just tapped on it to make sure no one was alive in there. No response, obviously."

Lerens nodded. "If someone's in there, the emergency has passed. So let's hope not." She stepped away from the car further into the verge, lowering her voice so only Hugo could hear. "What do you make of all this?"

"It's odd. Very odd. Did Fabien have a car at his disposal?"

"I checked, and yes, he did. There are two at the château that the family members can use. But the thing is, they also come with drivers. Which suggests that, if he's the one who stole this car, he didn't want people to know he was going somewhere . . ."

"Or who he was going with," Hugo added.

"Then why not just rent a car?" Lerens asked. "Or use a ride-share company?"

"Because both of those leave a trail."

"I'm not sure stealing a car is any less risky."

Hugo gave a wry smile. "Only if you get caught."

"And why leave his cell phone behind?"

"One of two possibilities," Hugo said. "At least the way I see it. Either someone else stole the car and is the reason his cell phone is sitting on the back seat."

"You're suggesting foul play."

"Or he did steal the car and is trying to make it look like he didn't."

"Leaving the phone for us to track and find."

"Right."

"Care to make a bet on which one of those it is?" Lerens asked.

"Not much of a gambling man, I'm afraid. Mostly because I hate losing."

Lerens laughed. "Good, because I'd have no idea which side to take."

Hugo looked at his watch. "If the crime scene people are on the way, there's not much for me to do, so if you don't mind I'll head back to the embassy and prepare for my interview."

"Prepare?" Lerens raised a manicured eyebrow. "What if there's a body in the trunk?"

"There's not."

"You sure about that?"

"Someone dumped the phone in an already dumped car." Hugo gestured to the trunk. "I don't smell anything and I'm pretty sure this vehicle's been here a while."

"It does look that way." Lerens was quiet for a moment. "So this television thing, you answering questions or giving a speech?"

"The former, I think. But you can bet my boss will have certain things he wants me to say, and a fair few things he doesn't."

Lerens pointed at the three police cars headed their way along Avenue de l'Hippodrome. "One of those should be Paul Jameson—you can irritate him by making him take you. And if he argues, tell him it was my idea."

"He won't argue," Hugo said. "He's one of the good ones."

Ambassador Taylor's office had been transformed from a place of quiet reflection, and occasional negotiation, to something more resembling a movie set. Three large cameras, several banks of lights, audio booms, and some equipment Hugo couldn't identify sat around two of the ambassador's armchairs. *The scene of the interrogation*, Hugo thought.

He lurked beside his boss's desk, watching as Taylor spoke to the overly made-up male reporter. Eventually, Taylor walked over to Hugo, who grimaced and said, "Remind me why I agreed to this."

"You didn't," Taylor said. "Under orders."

"Then you can't blame me if I screw it up."

"Can and will."

"Anything specific you do or don't want me to say? I have no idea what they know or what they're going to ask me."

"I was just told the passport was fake, but don't mention that."

"So he's not an American?"

"That we won't know until we identify him," Taylor said. "But that passport information is for your ears only."

"Got it. Any other information you want to hand me that I have to keep to myself?"

Taylor shrugged. "The interview is going to be in French, so just listen carefully and use your discretion."

Hugo gave Taylor a look. "Real helpful, thank you."

"It's not live—it's for broadcast tonight, so if you say anything really dumb maybe we can beg them to delete it."

"Again, thanks for the guidance."

The news reporter approached, his hand extended. "Monsieur Marston, I am Pascal Gross, delighted to meet you."

"Likewise," Hugo said, shaking his hand.

"So, the way this will work is that you'll give one interview to me, and I'll share it with the other channels. Kind of like a pool reporter.

The ambassador didn't want you to give a dozen interviews to a bunch of different people."

"He's thoughtful that way," Hugo said.

"Shall we get started?" Gross smiled, and Hugo was reminded of an alligator, except this one had perfect teeth.

"I suppose so."

Gross led Hugo to the chairs, and as soon as they sat down a woman appeared in front of Hugo and clipped a tiny microphone to his shirt. "Can you say your name and count to five, please?"

"Sure." Hugo did as he was told, and the woman apparently received a thumbs-up from one of the technicians.

"You want some powder? You're a little shiny in a few places."

"Not unless I have to."

She looked at Gross, who nodded, and then left and returned moments later with a powder puff, dabbing at Hugo until she was satisfied.

"Just so you know, there are three cameras. One on my face, one on yours, and one capturing us both." Pascal Gross picked up a notepad from the floor beside his chair, and smiled at Hugo. "All three are rolling, so are you ready?"

"I think so."

"Great." Gross straightened himself in the chair and looked over Hugo's shoulder, presumably into a camera. "My name is Pascal Gross, and I am here at the United States embassy in Paris, with Hugo Marston, the man who stopped the Tuileries shooter yesterday. Monsieur Marston, thank you for giving us this interview."

"You're welcome."

"And I should thank you, too, for stopping the gunman from gunning down more people than he did."

"Again, most welcome."

"Tell us what happened in your own words, if you don't mind reliving it."

"Sure. It was like any other evening, really, I was going to meet a friend for a drink—"

"That would be Mademoiselle Roux?"

You've done some homework. Or spying. "Yes."

"If you don't mind me interrupting, Mademoiselle Roux is quite a well-known journalist. I think people might be interested in how long you've been together."

"We're just friends."

"*Vraiment?*" Pascal Gross flashed his most ingratiating grin. "Then I've been misled. Please, carry on."

Hugo nodded "Well, I was just walking through the gardens when I heard a popping sound ahead of me."

"Did you recognize the noise?"

"Initially, no. But then I heard more and quickly realized what it was, so I ran in that direction. I saw him seconds later. He had two guns, one in each hand. I think one must have jammed or something because he knelt down to do something with it. Anyway, I pulled my gun at some point and kept running toward him."

"Why didn't you shoot from where you were?"

"There were too many people out there. I wanted to get as close as I could to improve my chance of hitting him, and only him."

"Did you say or shout anything to him?"

"Not at first. I wanted to get as close as possible before he saw me. After that . . . I don't recall, to be honest. I may have told him to drop his weapon. Weapons. But I don't really remember."

"What happened next?"

"I do remember the moment he looked up and saw me. I could almost see his eyes focus in on me. He started to raise his gun toward me, so I fired. Four times in all, I believe."

"You shot the gun out of his hand, did you know that?"

Hugo smiled. "I missed with the first two shots, and the third happened to hit his gun, yes."

"Knocked it out of his hand."

"Yes. Yes, that . . . happened."

"And the final shot killed him."

"I suppose. I know they were giving him CPR. I didn't hear what happened after he was put into the ambulance."

"You shot him through the heart. Knocked the gun out of his hand and then shot him through the heart."

"People keep forgetting the first two shots," Hugo said.

"You're from Texas, yes?"

"Correct. Austin, to be exact."

"And everyone carries a gun in Texas, isn't that right?"

"Well, not really." Hugo laughed softly. "I know some people, maybe a lot of people, think that's true, but no. It's not nearly as common as you think."

"But everyone is allowed to carry one, *n'est-ce pas*?"

"I mean, most people would be allowed to, yes."

"Do you always carry your gun in Paris?"

Something in Gross's voice caught Hugo's attention, told him to tread carefully. He glanced toward where the ambassador had been standing, but the lights made it impossible to see if he was still there.

"I carry it for my job. And our embassy sought permission from local authorities to allow me to carry it when I'm outside of the emb—"

"But when you are off-duty? You have somewhere at work you could leave it, do you not?"

"Well, yes, of course."

"Then why do you not do that?"

"I don't know. Habit mainly. And I'm thinking it's lucky I *was* carrying it last night."

"I think most people in this city would be quite unhappy to know there is a gun-carrying American walking their streets."

"I don't know about that," Hugo said, trying not to sound testy. "But after last night—"

"Ah, last night." Gross held up an admonishing finger. *Here we go, the performance for the cameras*, Hugo thought. "Last night, there were two gun-toting Americans in Paris. And they had a shoot-out in one of the most beautiful, most historic places in our city."

"A shoot-out? That's not what happened."

"Do you see yourself as a hero, Monsieur Marston?"

Hugo fought the urge to look for his boss again, or to get up and walk away, but he was new to this and had no clue how him abandoning the interview would look. *Stay calm and polite*, Hugo told himself.

"No, I was lucky that I was in the right place at the right time, and my training kicked in. So no, I don't consider myself a hero, not at all."

"What can you tell us about the man you shot?"

"Nothing, I'm afraid. The Paris police are conducting the investigation and because I was involved, I'm not a party to anything they've found."

"He was an American, you're not denying that."

"I don't know whether he was or not."

Pascal Gross cocked his head, suspicion in his eyes. "Is the investigation trying to bury the fact that the gunman was an American? Is that why they had you do the interview, so you can deny all knowledge?"

"I thought you'd asked to interview me, that was my understand—"

"Are you aware of the reports that the gunman was seen two days earlier loitering outside this very embassy?"

"So you know who he is?"

"No, but my information is solid."

"I know nothing about that. And if it's that solid, you need to share it with the authorities."

"Wouldn't that seem odd, an American comes to the embassy, your place of work, and then two days later you just happen to interrupt his attempt to kill people in the Tuileries?"

"What are you suggesting?" Hugo bristled. "I don't know who that man was. I'd never seen him before in my life, and if he came to the embassy at some point—"

"What I'm suggesting, Monsieur Marston, is—"

And then, with a loud click and the gentle whine of electronic equipment shutting down, the ambassador's study went dark.

CHAPTER SIXTEEN

"A false-flag operation," Ambassador Taylor said. He was sitting in Hugo's office with his feet on the desk. Hugo sat slumped in a chair opposite him. "That's what he was suggesting."

"That's ridiculous."

"I know. But that's what some of those idiotic so-called journalists are peddling."

Hugo shook his head in disgust. "Anyone pushing that isn't a journalist, they're a conspiracy theorist."

"For the few remaining newspapers and all the online news sources it's about getting attention these days, getting people to click the link," Taylor said. "Getting the story right, the truth, that's merely a potential by-product of asking outrageous questions."

"So who vetted this guy? Who the hell authorized him to do the interview? Couldn't you find a real reporter?"

"It was his turn on the pool rotation, and believe it or not he used to be a real journalist. He told a couple of . . . exaggerations while out in the field and fell down in the pecking order of respected reporters. I gather he clawed his way back on to television but, apparently, he's got a chip on his shoulder."

"And now I have a target on my back. From hero to murderer in short shrift."

"You're still a hero in my book, big guy," Ambassador Taylor said with a smile.

"And that's what matters," Hugo said. "But this pisses me off. Why the hell would we run a false-flag op?"

"We wouldn't. It's ridiculous."

"But what's their stupid theory?" Hugo asked.

"I don't know. Maybe to improve US-Franco relations. We make you a hero and if everyone loves you, everyone loves America and Americans again." He gave a wry smile. "It's been a while."

"Right, we shoot innocent people in the Tuileries and sacrifice some schmuck so that people will like Americans again. That makes no damned sense."

"Hey, I'm not the one—"

"And the dead guy, was he in on the scheme according to the conspiracy nut jobs?"

"I imagine it depends on which message board you go to."

"Are people actually buying into this crap? I mean, seriously."

"Of course. Some people will always buy into a good conspiracy, especially if the big bad United States government is behind it. If people can believe a school full of dead children was faked, then you know they can believe we staged this."

Hugo thought for a moment. "So who was the gunman? We have to know that by now, surely."

"Hugo, you know I can't tell you anyth—"

Hugo leaned forward. "They're now saying I killed a man, a fellow American, to make myself a hero. I think we're past the niceties of keeping me in the dark."

"Okay, fine." Ambassador Taylor sighed. "The truth is, we don't know yet."

"What? How is that possible?"

Ambassador Taylor shrugged. "We don't know who he is."

"Was the passport real?"

"Yes and no. It's a real passport but looks like it was obtained by using fraudulent documents. The name on the passport isn't someone we can identify."

"No prints or DNA on file?"

"Prints, no, and the DNA isn't back yet. The lab is backlogged but they're expediting it." Taylor grimaced. "Never heard that before, eh?"

"What does *expediting* mean, exactly?"

"A week at best, I'm told."

"What if his DNA isn't on file?" Hugo asked.

"We'll figure out who he is, Hugo. You know we will."

"Step it up a little, eh?"

"Trust me—I have the secretary of state crawling up my ass on this one. I'm going as fast as I can."

"Anything else of note?" Hugo asked.

"You could say that." The ambassador held Hugo's eye. "He was carrying a badge."

"What kind of badge?"

"It said CIA, had a little wallet with it and an ID card."

"Fake?"

"Very," Taylor said. "Not made of plastic, but almost. It wouldn't fool anyone who took so much as a second glance at it. Very odd."

"It is." Hugo nodded. "So who is working this?"

"Your buddy Marchand."

Hugo had helped Adrien Marchand solve a murder that had taken place at the Dali museum in Montmartre. After initially, and wrongly, suspecting one person Hugo had pointed him in the right direction . . . led him, others might say. But despite their initial personality clashes, Hugo thought Marchand was an intelligent and hardworking detective, open to looking at new evidence and changing his mind when that evidence warranted it. Plus, Hugo suspected Marchand had a point to prove to Hugo, which would work to Hugo's advantage and, hopefully, ferret out the truth about the shooter's identity.

"Okay, well, if you don't mind slipping me a little reassuring information from time to time, I'd appreciate it. Leave a note under my pillow if you need to, I don't much care."

"Full-time ambassador, part-time tooth fairy. I can do that."

"So, in the meantime I lay low and avoid the press, is that the plan?"

"Half of it." A smile spread over the ambassador's face.

"I don't like that look, boss. Not one bit."

"Avoid the press, for sure."

"Great, I'll go home and have Claudia bring me food and wine. Lots of wine."

"Nope. Media will be camped outside your building, for sure. You can't be enjoying fine wine and beautiful women at a time like this. Not there, anyway."

"What do you mean, *not there*?"

"Hugo, this is the perfect time for you to go to the Lambourd's party."

"That's tonight."

"Precisely. No media allowed."

"I'll go, but I'm not staying late. I'm exhausted and, in case you'd forgotten, in the middle of an investigation there. I can't exactly party and powwow with my suspects."

"It'll be fun, and with the champagne flowing, loosening tongues, what better way to catch a few people off-balance?"

"I prefer to record my interviews in a controlled environment, not squeeze information from drunk people over canapés."

"So wear a wire."

"I'm serious," Hugo insisted.

"Jeez, Hugo, lighten up. You're not interviewing suspects, you're looking for clues. And hell, maybe you'll have some fun while you're at it." Ambassador Taylor swung his legs off the desk and stood up. "Well, if I need to order you to go I will, for diplomatic purposes. Just seems like a smart detect—"

"Fine, I said I'd go." Hugo held his hands up in surrender. "As long as Claudia comes with me."

Taylor walked to the doorway. "Use that famous Marston charm—how could she resist? Come to think of it, I'm sure she's invited in her own right."

"You did say no media was allowed there," Hugo reminded him. "So maybe not."

"She'll be invited as Claudia de Roussillon, French nobility, not Claudia Roux, pain-in-the-butt journalist. Ask her." Taylor winked at Hugo, and then left the room, closing the door quietly behind him.

Hugo dialed Claudia. "Hey, it's me," he said when she answered.

"Busy man, nice to hear your voice." Hers sounded bright, and instantly Hugo was glad he'd called.

"What are you doing this evening?" he asked.

"Trying to find a reason not to go to a party. You want to give me one?"

"The Lambourd party, by any chance?"

"Yes," she said. "How did you know?"

"I'm an outstanding detective. I'm also a wonderful party companion."

"Oh, I'd love to take you, Hugo, but you have to be invited."

"Which I am."

"Well, great. But you'd rather do that than have a quiet dinner?"

"No, but Ambassador Taylor isn't giving me that option."

"Ah, I see." Claudia sighed. "Fine, I'll go with you, but if you ignore me for work, there will be trouble."

Hugo chuckled. "You are very sexy when you get strict with me."

"I'm not joking, Hugo, there will be no investigating on our date. Or else."

CHAPTER SEVENTEEN

THE KILLER

There's a slow rise of excitement at the house. There always is the afternoon before the party, but it's more evident this time, even more so than previous years. Strangers in the black and white uniform of servants carry folding tables and chairs outside to the garden, while more of them bring boxes of food, plates, and cookware into the house. They remind me of ants, trooping in and out with their heads down, not stopping to look around or talk to anyone.

I have mixed feelings about having strangers in my house. Our house, I'm sorry. My house in the future, is the plan. One of the plans. Anyway, I don't like the feeling of not knowing who all these ants are, not being able to control them, know what they're doing every moment. But it occurs to me that the more people, known and unknown, who come through this house tonight, the harder it will be for the police to point fingers at any one suspect. Maybe I should be worried about all the extra pairs of eyes that will be on the property today and tonight, but I'm not. In my experience, people are blind. They see things, yes, but it's a mix of what they want to see and what they expect to see, which means they miss a lot. And that's good for me.

And so my own excitement is mounting, too, only for different reasons. Obviously.

But I'm also a little annoyed.

I was sloppy with the American girl, and am lucky she didn't see me. Well, doesn't remember seeing me, because she actually did. I looked into her eyes as they went blank, a moment I've recently discovered. I've never believed in God or the existence of a soul, mostly because I'm damned sure I, myself, don't have one. But about a year ago I came close to changing my mind when I slid a scalpel between the ribs of a drunk man on a Metro platform. I almost missed the moment because his fetid alcohol breath gasped out at me, making me pull away and close my eyes in disgust. But I opened them again just as he sagged back against the tile wall, and caught him staring at me with surprise on his face. He probably didn't feel any pain—the drunken slob was too liquored up to feel a shark bite his leg off—but he knew what was happening to him and his eyes were wide with the shock of it.

It took three seconds, maybe four, but the life went out of those eyes just like that. It was quite remarkable, and if you think about it, there's no reason that one's eyes should change that way. But they did. The soul leaving the body? I still don't believe that, but I don't need to for it to be an interesting, and enjoyable, phenomenon.

But that's no excuse for being careless.

My plan is progressing well, and the disappearing act has got everyone worked up, including those investigators. Although the two lead cops are pretty cool characters. The woman, someone told me she used to be a man, is actually quite attractive. Has a confidence about her, like she doesn't care if you know her past, or what you think about her. I like confident women.

I'm not happy about the American, though, especially the way he watches people, like he can see into their minds. And he uses that technique where he stays quiet and makes the other person fill the space by talking. Clever, unless you're expecting it.

I'm a little surprised they're going ahead with the party. I can see ignoring the fact that some drifter of an American girl got hurt—after all, she'll be fine. But add to that a member of the family disappearing? Well, that's the matriarch for you. She's like a grizzled actress who insists on taking the stage no matter what, looking past the real world and its tragedies, and just repeating over and over, *The show must go on!* until it does.

Which is perfect for me, because I like a good show, and I'm orchestrating a four-act play. The first two are complete, the third comes tonight, and, unless those cops are a lot smarter than I think, the final act will go unnoticed by everyone but me.

It will be a sight, unseen.

CHAPTER EIGHTEEN

Hugo was finally allowed to go home, escorted into his building by two gendarmes, who pushed through the half-dozen reporters camped out on Rue Jacob wanting a quote or two from the sharp-shooting American. Safely inside, the *flics* waited in the lobby under the watchful eye of Dimitrios, the concierge, as Hugo climbed the stairs to his apartment, grateful for a few moments of peace and quiet before he had to change for the party.

Those hopes were dashed the minute he walked in the door.

"Tom, I thought you were in England."

"Delightful to see you, too," Tom said. He was stretched out on the couch, shoes still on, with a book on his lap. Hugo saw it was one of his, *The Unrepentant*, by Ed Aymar. A pair of glasses perched on the end of his nose, and he looked over them at Hugo. "You gonna shoot me right between the eyes, Wyatt Earp?"

"I would love to. And if you don't get your feet off my couch I will." He sank into a chair opposite his friend. "Reading glasses?"

"Technically it's a disability, so you can't make fun of me."

"They come with hearing aids, some kind of package deal?"

"Funny. Didn't you hear what I just said?"

"Yes, my hearing is like my eyesight: just fine. Yours on the other hand . . ."

"Fuck off, Hugo." Tom swung his legs off the sofa and put the book on the coffee table between them. "They're from a high-end store in London. Cost a fortune so I know they look good."

Hugo smiled. They'd come a long way together, he and Tom.

Roommates at Quantico, they helped each other through training, and over their years with the FBI they'd shared the same postings several times. Hugo had gone on to train and work in the Behavioral Analysis Unit, whereas Tom had honed different skills, ones that eventually got noticed by the CIA. They lured him away and even Hugo didn't know the full extent of everywhere he'd been and everything he'd done. Didn't know the half of it, most likely.

And now here was Tom, the secret agent extraordinaire, the man who'd killed for his country and turned himself into a functional alcoholic in an attempt to drown his demons, here he was pushing his glasses up to the bridge of his nose like a disappointed driving instructor.

"They look great, Tom. How was England?"

"Surprisingly sunny. For the three days I was there."

"You've been gone two weeks."

Tom grinned enigmatically. "Business trip."

Officially retired, the CIA made use of Tom's experience on a part-time basis, paying him handsomely and letting him travel in comfort, as long as he wasn't too specific with those around him about where he was going, or why. Hugo had long ago given up asking.

"As long as you got your fill of fish and chips while you were there."

"And these glasses." He took them off and looked at Hugo. "So what the hell happened out there? And why did you give an interview to that hack? Kind of dinged your hero status there."

"None of it was my choice, I promise you that."

"You really shoot the gun out of his hand?"

Hugo groaned. "Good lord."

"Well?"

"The third shot happened to hit the gun, which he was holding center-mass."

Tom nodded approvingly. "Nice. I have no idea why you're fighting this, Hugo."

"Fighting what?"

"The hero narrative. Man, play it right and you could retire and write your memoirs."

"I'll have plenty of time for that," Hugo said. "I like my job. Plus, I couldn't afford this place without it, and then where would you live?"

"Ever the altruist, thank you. You working on something? Need help?"

"You hear about the American girl strangled at Château Lambourd?"

"Who strangled where?"

"It's the home of a noble French family. The girl was a servant, basically. Someone garroted her in the middle of the night, but didn't kill her."

"Was it Colonel Mustard in the library?"

"Funny. It was on the landing by the stairs, and if I knew who did it, I'd have said."

"Got the great Hugo Marston stumped, has it?" Tom sounded a little too pleased. "Sounds like you do need my help."

"Actually, I do. But not on that case."

"On what, then?"

"The shooting. Ambassador Taylor has me in the dark, since I'm a *subject of interest* or some damn thing."

Tom nodded, serious now. "Well, they have to investigate, make sure it was a good shooting."

"Yeah, I know that. But it's frustrating not knowing what's going on, and in the meantime I'm being hounded by the media and some of them, as you saw, want to turn me into the bad guy."

"What do you want me to do?"

"The dead guy was carrying a fake CIA badge."

Tom snorted. "Because agents carry badges to identify themselves in case they get caught?"

"Exactly. Anyway, seems like that'd give you reason to ask a few questions, no? Kind of a jurisdictional entranceway."

"It might," Tom said. "Anything specific you want to know?"

"Yes. I want to know everything you can find out about the shooter. And as soon as you can."

"You know me, Hugo. An absolute whirlwind of energy and

activity." Tom stood. "So I'm gonna take a nap before dinner, then
have a good long sleep tonight. I'll get to work first thing on Monday."

"Sooner."

"Fine." Tom let out an exaggerated sigh. "I'll make a few calls tomorrow."

"Discreet ones, please."

"You wanna do this yourself?"

"Fine, fine, I'm sorry," Hugo said. "You do your thing, I'll do
mine."

"Which is?"

Hugo looked at his watch. "I'm sorry to say, my thing tonight is
attending a black-tie event."

Tom started for the bedroom. "Well, you have fun with that.
Don't get back too late, and no girls in the apartment."

Hugo smiled. *It's my apartment, Tom.*

Claudia and her driver, Jean, picked Hugo up from outside his building, after he all but sprinted past the remaining three reporters, who
weren't expecting him at that moment and didn't have time to get pictures or ask questions.

Hugo waved cheerily at them out of the back window, and settled
in next to Claudia.

"You smell good," he said, nuzzling her. She did, a sexy mix of
jasmine, vanilla, and something he couldn't identify. She laughed and
playfully pushed him away, and then drew him back in close again, saying she didn't mean it. Hugo was glad—it'd been too long since he'd
seen her, in fact long enough that her hair had grown past her shoulders, further softening her already beautiful features.

When they got to Château Lambourd and climbed out of the
car, Hugo noted that she looked even better than she smelled. She
wore an off-the-shoulder light blue dress that hugged her figure down
to the knee-length ruffled hem. A pair of silver heels made her taller

than usual, and Hugo used her extra height to his advantage, planting kisses on her welcoming lips several times before they headed to the entrance.

The château was resplendent, too. Candles lined the path to the main doors, and two liveried footmen stood to attention either side of the open doorway. A string quartet was set up in the courtyard to welcome guests, and Hugo recognized Vivaldi's spring *concerti*. There was no one checking invitations—Claudia said they were doing that remotely from one of the former stables, using hidden cameras and facial recognition software. She didn't know how she knew that, so Hugo wasn't convinced, but crashing this party required a black tie or evening gown, so even the uninvited would have looked good.

Inside, in the large and open reception area, white-jacketed waiters proffered silver trays carrying champagne and hors d'oeuvres, while newly arrived guests laughed and chatted in small groups and the sweet sounds of the violins drifted in and around them like a gentle breeze.

"Quite the party," Claudia said. "I'm surprised I've never been here before."

"Me too. How is that possible?"

"My father used to come, but they don't allow children to this party, and as an adult I've always had other things to do. Travel, mostly."

"I think you'll be impressed with the place. Off this foyer, all downstairs, is the functional stuff, huge kitchen area, wine cellar, servant quarters."

"Where that girl was staying when she was attacked?"

"Yes, but she was attacked at the top of those stairs, the second floor." Hugo glanced in that direction to show Claudia.

"What was she doing up there?"

"She says she doesn't remember, but I think that wasn't true."

"Then what?"

"I suspect she'd paid someone a visit, but doesn't want to either get them in trouble with us, or get herself in trouble with the family."

"A midnight tryst, how exciting," Claudia said with a wink. "Who do you suspect?"

"I thought I wasn't allowed to investigate tonight?"

"You're not. We're just talking." She swiped two champagne flutes from a passing waiter and handed one to Hugo. "*Santé.*"

"*Santé* to you, too." They clinked glasses.

"Well?"

"I have no idea who she was seeing, if anyone."

"You asked her?"

"Gosh, no, didn't think of that," Hugo said sarcastically, earning himself a punch in the arm. "Let's go up to the second floor and see the main living rooms."

Claudia looped her arm through Hugo's, and they walked up the stairs toward two more footmen, erect and unmoving.

"I wonder if they're there to stop drunk people falling down the steps," Claudia whispered.

"Let's get drunk and find out," Hugo whispered back. At the top of the staircase another open space held giant vases brimming with flowers. Sweet-scented lilies, bloodred roses, and cascades of wildflowers that filled the area with color and the soft smell of spring. Hugo cursed silently as his phone buzzed with a new text, and he took a discreet look at the screen.

Call me. It was from Tom.

Hugo hesitated, and Claudia noticed.

"What was my rule?" she said sternly.

"It's Tom. Probably unhappy about the empty fridge. Or something else domestic like that."

She raised an eyebrow. "Really?"

"Yeah, probably not. You going to be mad if I call him back?"

"Yes."

"He'll hound me until I do, if I know Tom." At that moment another text came in: *Now!* and Hugo showed it to her. "See?"

Claudia crossed her arms and pretended to be angry. "Well, make it snappy. And don't be surprised if you come back and find me chatting with some other handsome hunk. Or hunkette."

Hugo kissed her lips again and started for the staircase that led to the top floor, but one of the two footmen standing in front of the bottom step put out a hand to stop him.

"Oh, so you're not just ornamental," Hugo said in English. He switched to French when the man gave him a quizzical look. "I need to make a call, in private." He dug out his credentials and showed them. The footmen glanced at each other, and one of them nodded. "*Merci bien*," Hugo said and trotted up to the third floor.

The thick rugs and even thicker wood floors muted most of the hubbub below, and Hugo sank into a plush velvet armchair away from the top of the staircase to call Tom.

"This better be good, my friend, you made Claudia mad at me for calling you."

"Well, now you can have makeup sex. So you're welcome."

"It's not that kind of party. You have something for me?"

"Yeah, couple of things."

"That was quick," Hugo said.

"Nap didn't work out so I made a phone call or two. Five actually. Anyway, first of all the dude you shot isn't necessarily American."

"I know. At least, I know the passport was a forgery."

"You knew that already?"

"Yes. I didn't mention it?"

"No, you fucking didn't."

"Sorry," Hugo said. "Did you ID him then?"

"Not yet, no one has. But I did ID the gun."

"And what does that tell us?"

"Not good things, Hugo. Not good at all."

"Stop playing cute, Tom, Claudia is waiting for me. Impatiently."

"Okay, well, here goes nothing. Like I said, the dude may or may not be American," Tom said slowly. "But the gun definitely is."

"I thought someone said it was a Glock. That's Austrian—"

"No, you idiot. I don't mean where it was made, I mean where it came from."

"And that is?"

"US soil, I'm afraid. To be more precise, our fucking embassy. Hugo, it's one of yours."

CHAPTER NINETEEN

Hugo felt the blood drain from his face. "Tell me exactly what you mean by that," he said. "And how you know."

"A few weeks ago you replaced your section's .40 calibers with nine millimeters, right?"

"Yes."

"The ones you were replacing were supposed to be shipped back to the States."

"That's right. You're saying they weren't?"

"Most of them were, but two of them missed their flight. Actually, one was scheduled for destruction because it'd malfunctioned."

Hugo pictured the scene in the Tuileries. "The one that jammed, that he put down."

"I only got info on one of them, but that's a pretty safe bet."

"How the hell could that happen?" Hugo asked, more of himself than Tom.

"No idea, I'm still looking into it."

Hugo's mind was racing. "With all the paperwork that went into that swap, surely this means we can figure out who stole them."

"Your bailiwick, not mine, but it seems like it'd narrow the field."

"But how the hell did they end up in the hands of someone who, apparently, doesn't exist?"

"No idea."

"How did you find this out, Tom?"

"You know I can't tell you that. For your sake."

"Then just tell me if your source was someone at the embassy."

"No. Police contact."

"How would they know it was an embassy gun?"

"Paperwork, actually. All foreign weapons, including ours, have to be registered with the French police. They like to know what's coming in and going out."

"Which means the whole world will know pretty soon."

"Yep," Tom said. "I imagine so. On that note, you want me to go out and talk to those reporters, say some nice things about you?"

"No, I most certainly do not."

"Well, tough shit. Dimitrios just texted that my pizza is down there. Seems like a shame to waste a trip down those stairs."

"Tom, don't you da—" But he was speaking to a void. Tom had hung up.

Hugo took a deep breath and slowly stood. *An embassy gun. From my own security section! How is that possible?* He didn't know the answer to that question, but he certainly knew how it'd play out in some parts of the media. The ones alleging a false-flag operation would go gleefully bananas, and even those who didn't normally buy into conspiracy theories might have second thoughts. And Hugo couldn't blame them. An embassy gun used to shoot French citizens by a man carrying an American passport, then an embassy employee coming to the rescue? Pretty far-fetched coincidences.

Suddenly Hugo didn't feel like being at a party, didn't want to smile and meet new people, make small talk. He thought he heard voices at the foot of the staircase and moved away, wanting some more time to think. He studied a painting ten yards along the hallway, depicting a pheasant hunt and snowy trees. Seconds later his attention was drawn to the sound of voices again, this time coming from behind a closed door to his right. They were muffled, yet urgent, and as they were speaking French Hugo struggled to identify them.

"—you call those people friends?" a woman was saying.

"I've never met them, but I trust him."

The woman laughed. "And that's the problem, right there. You can't see what everyone else can."

"Everyone made up their minds years ago. He's a child, for God's sake, he's maturing."

"Is that what you call it? He's a menace, and he's either gotten himself into trouble or his friends have put him in it. Neck deep."

"He'll be fine. He'll be back here before the end of tonight—he loves this party."

The woman sounded more resigned now. "If I loved him like you did, I'd be more worried. Not just about tonight, but the direction he's headed in, generally."

Given the context, Hugo was certain the man was Marc Lambourd. The woman had to be one of his sisters, but he couldn't tell which one.

"Thanks for the advice. Although your total lack of interest in the family makes it somewhat ironic."

There was a pause, then. "And what does *that* mean?"

"It means the only thing you like about this family is its home. This place."

"We all do. That's a ridiculous thing to say."

The man said something in a low voice that Hugo didn't catch, and the female replied, "I contribute to this family as much as anyone."

"Oh, so then what did you do to help for the party?"

"I wasn't asked to do anything. Maman always arranges everything."

"As far as you know. For God's sake, she had to take a break because you had a damned computer delivered and she didn't want it littering the hallway until you deigned to move it. She had to climb two flights of stairs to have the delivery person put it outside your bedroom door."

"She didn't have to do that."

"You know she hates having tradesmen unattended in the house."

"Well, I've said for years she should put in an elevator. Or one of those chairs that slides up the bannister. Anyway, it was a printer, not a computer."

"That's not the point. The point is that you're busy taking care of you, while everyone else is focusing on . . . the family, the party."

"Except Fabien, who's chasing tail and stealing cars. Apparently."

As fascinating as family dynamics were, especially those of a family like the Lambourds, Hugo felt that he'd eavesdropped enough, and walked quietly to the top of the stairs. He still had that sinking feeling in his stomach from finding out where the gunman's weapon had originated, but he dragged his mind back to the present, and was curious to see who Marc had been talking to. When he reached the reception area on the second floor, he stopped. Over several gray heads, he could see Claudia in the main living room talking to an older couple.

He texted her: *Look to your left, and join me. Bring champers.*

A moment later, she looked over at him and winked, and then turned back to her companions with a smile. Hugo watched as she disengaged from them, swiped two fresh glasses of champagne, and headed toward him.

"You on a stakeout?" she asked.

"Something like that." He nodded toward the staircase. "Just overheard a family squabble up there, and now I'm curious to see who'll come down those stairs."

"You couldn't tell who it was?"

"Marc Lambourd was one."

Claudia nudged him gently. "And here comes the other."

Hugo looked over and watched as Marc Lambourd descended the stairs still deep in conversation with his sister, Erika Sipiora, who looked very different from when she'd met with Hugo previously. The austere look was gone—now her lush auburn hair flowed down and onto her bare shoulders, and the split in the side of her silk green dress made it all the way to her right hip. Hugo felt a hand on his backside, and then a sharp pinch.

"You're staring, my lover," she said playfully.

"I bet you are, too." Hugo looked back at Claudia to confirm his suspicion and, once he had he reached behind her and returned the pinch.

"Ouch! You monster." She laughed and leaned into him. "Do that again and we'll have to find a vacant room."

Hugo stood by the large window overlooking the back garden of the house, watching as a team of men set up the annual fireworks display. Claudia, who'd excused herself to find a ladies' room, had mentioned that once it was all set up, partygoers would drift out of the château and mingle on the expansive lawn until fireworks time. His phone rang, but he didn't recognize the number. He normally wouldn't answer without knowing who was calling, but this would give him cover not to talk to anyone.

"Hugo Marston," he said.

"Ah, Monsieur Marston." Hugo didn't recognize the voice, but it was a Frenchman calling. "My name is Paul Ancette and I am the outreach coordinator for LLLF."

"That's a lot of Ls. What does that stand for?"

"*La Libéralisation des Lois sur Fusils.*"

"The liberalization of gun laws? You're like the French NRA?"

"*Exactement, oui.*" The man went on. "Traditionally we're more oriented toward protecting the rights of farmers and hunters to own guns, but we're always in favor of pushing gun ownership legislation. Anyway, we have our annual conference in just one month. We'd like you to be a guest speaker, talk about your heroic acts to stop a madman."

"I see. The thing is, we don't know if he was a madman, and since there's an investigation into him and me, I should decline."

"Oh. Well. What a shame." The man sounded crushed.

"By the way, how did you get my number?" Hugo asked.

"I didn't—the embassy forwarded the call to you. What about after it's all over, the investigation, do you think—"

"Well, thank you for thinking of me," Hugo said cheerily, before hanging up. He pocketed his phone and turned to look out of the window again, when a voice spoke up behind him.

"The great American hero, *n'est-ce pas?*"

Hugo turned and found Marc Lambourd standing in front of him. "Monsieur Lambourd, nice to see you again."

They shook hands, Lambourd's eyes never leaving Hugo's face, as if he was waiting for a reaction.

"And you. Enjoying yourself? To be frank, I'm a little surprised you were invited. My mother doesn't hold much fondness for policemen."

"Too many speeding tickets?" *Or something more sinister, perhaps?* Hugo smiled. "Anyway, I'm not really a policeman."

"Then you can drink as much champagne as you like."

"Not too much." Hugo reached out and swiped a cracker piled high with caviar. "But the *hors d'oeuvres* are delicious."

"I'm glad you're enjoying them."

"You're not?"

"I am a big believer that you are what you eat. Just like the fuel you put in your car can make it run or foul it up, so the food we put in our bodies dictates how we function. How we live. So, I only drink the best wine, and rarely, and eat organic food and no red meat."

"Impressive."

"Well, I say that." Lambourd smiled self-deprecatingly. "The truth is, I indulge once every couple of months, have something I'd normally consider unhealthy. But I truly believe I can do that only because I eat well the rest of the time."

"I wish I were that disciplined."

"It takes practice, believe me. So, speaking of impressive, I just found out you had an audience with our esteemed president after your heroic act." The sarcasm was invisible, but Hugo was pretty sure it was there.

"I did, yes."

"Did she know at the time an American was the shooter?"

"We still don't know that." *The gun, on the other hand . . .*

"Is that so? My sources mislead me then."

"As you can imagine, they're not telling me much about that investigation." Hugo shifted, wanting to change the subject. "Have you heard anything from your son?"

A flicker of worry passed over Lambourd's face, but it was gone in an instant. "Not yet. As you're one of the investigating officers, I was hoping you may have an update."

"No, sir, I'm afraid not. I promise the moment I do, I'll let you know."

"I'm sure he's just gotten into some scrape with his friends." The veneer cracked a little, and the look of worry returned. "Everyone thinks I'm too soft on him, and maybe I am. He's my only child, my son. And despite all of this"—he waved at the splendor around them—"he's not had an easy life. Maybe *because* of all this."

"I'm in no place to judge or advise," Hugo said. "I don't have kids, so I wouldn't know what I was talking about."

"All I can tell you is, most parents would do pretty much anything for their child."

"Most?"

"You've met my mother, have you not?" Lambourd didn't smile because, Hugo assumed, he wasn't trying to be funny. "When Fabien was born, I vowed to do a better job than my mother did with us. To her, love was communicated by faint praise on a good day, a leather belt on a bad day, and complete indifference most other days. Maybe I've gone too much in the opposite direction, but if you ask me, too much love beats not enough."

"I'd agree with that," Hugo said.

"Here comes someone who doesn't always." Lambourd's grim look dissipated as a beautiful woman in a white dress approached. "Monsieur Marston, I believe you know my sister Noelle."

"*Enchantée*, monsieur," she said, shaking Hugo's hand. As before, her grip was surprisingly strong. "What important world affairs are you gentlemen discussing?"

"Your nephew, actually." Lambourd opened his mouth to say something else, and then his eyes looked past Manis. "Will you excuse me? My mother needs me for something. Even at my age, and she at hers, I daren't keep her waiting."

"Truer words were never spoken," Noelle Manis said. She watched him leave and then turned to Hugo. "If I'd known how dysfunctional this family was, I would never have . . . been born, I guess."

"Aren't most families screwed up in their own way?"

"Nothing like this, I promise you."

"How so?" Hugo knew he shouldn't be asking work questions, which this was, but Claudia had obviously gotten buttonholed by someone, and Manis might give him good insight, maybe even information, about the family.

"Take Marc. I'm sure he told you of his promise to raise Fabien differently from the way he was raised."

"He did. And it sounded very sensible, if you ask me."

"Maybe."

Hugo wondered if a glass or two of champagne might help Noelle tell whatever story she'd kept to herself when they first met, but she didn't seem even a little tipsy. He tried anyway.

"Unless his leniency causes problems within the family," Hugo said. "Which I gather it has."

"Yes, and what's frustrating is how self-righteous Marc is about it." *Nice deflection*, Hugo thought. *Intentional?* "About other things, too."

"Other things?"

"I'm sure he gave you his *you are what you eat* speech." Manis rolled her eyes. "Never mind the fish and chips he eats on his frequent trips to England."

"No one's perfect," Hugo said.

"So true. And when it comes to raising Fabien, you're right, his theory is sound, but if Marc didn't turn a blind eye to the boy's every misadventure, I might agree. That kid could punch the pope in the nose and Marc would make excuses for him."

"Can you give me any real-life examples?" Hugo asked.

"I know you want me to tell you what I wouldn't before," Manis said. "But you're out of luck."

"Fair enough." Hugo raised both hands in surrender. "One thing, though, for being so doting, Marc doesn't seem that worried about the car we found, or about Fabien's absence."

"No one is. Because he does this kind of thing all the time." She sighed. "It's like he's testing Marc to see how far he can go and, as far as I can see, it's as far as he wants."

"Being a parent isn't easy. Isn't he doing the best he can?"

Manis shook her head. "You asked, so let me tell you a story. And it's one example, one incident. One of the worst, but certainly not the only one."

"Please, go ahead."

"A few years ago, three maybe, Fabien was at a party. It was at the house of one of his friends from school, the parents were away or out, and about twenty of them got together and had a party." She took a sip of champagne. "Normal teenage behavior, right?"

"I'd say so, yes."

"Except that one of the girls claimed the next day that Fabien had raped her friend. Drugged her and raped her while she was unconscious. This family closed ranks before the kids' hangovers had worn off. The girl making the claim was ostracized, and the girl who was allegedly raped denied it. Said she'd been awake all night, and Fabien hadn't gone near her. Nothing would make her say otherwise, even though most people believed it had happened."

"What did Marc say?"

"Oh, he was furious, with the parents for leaving the kids unattended, with the friend for making up such a destructive lie, and even with the girl at the center of all this. With everyone except Fabien, who was the only victim in Marc's eyes."

"Maybe he really didn't do anything?"

"That's the thing about this family, the truth is always hiding. The truth you see is what they want you to see—they create reality to suit themselves."

"You said 'they,' but you're part of the family."

"I can't argue with that." She laughed gently.

"That reminds me, I'm curious about something if you don't mind me asking."

"Anything—I love to dish on the family."

"Your mother married twice, but is still a Lambourd, and your brothers have the Lambourd name. Did you use that name growing up?"

"Yes, I am divorced and am currently receiving immense pressure to take back my maiden name."

"From your mother?"

"Yes. She is a force, monsieur, please don't ever underestimate her. What she wants, she usually gets and that included this house and the Lambourd name. The story is, she only agreed to marry Alfred Fontaine if he took the family name, the real one. Sounds very modern, I know, but it has more to do with him being rich and desperate for prestige."

"And your mother reclaiming the Lambourd name."

"Oh, that was primary. She gave in a little, allowing her kids to use Fontaine as a middle name, but Lambourd had to be the surname."

"You all have the Fontaine middle name?"

"All except me."

"Seriously?" Hugo asked, surprised.

"Well, I added it myself when I was old enough to do so, but yes."

"Why was that?"

"Figure it out." She flashed an enigmatic smile. "Anyway, I'm doing a terrible job of explaining the family dynamic, and I'm making Marc out as a monster. He's not. He's loving and kind, and a good man. He just has one blind spot. Like you said, he's so blind to reality when it comes to his son, he's not even worried that he's missing."

"Are you?"

"I'm trying not to be. I'm also trying not to hope something bad happens to him."

Hugo cocked his head in surprise. "That's an odd thing to admit. You want something bad to—"

"Sorry, what I mean is . . ." She cast about for the right words. "If nothing bad ever happens to him, he'll never change. And eventually he'll trust the wrong people, insult the wrong people, and then something will happen that won't be fixable."

"He needs a shock to the system, you're saying."

"Yes, that, instead of being rescued every time. Exactly. Maybe this will be it, but who knows?"

"Well, the police are looking everywhere for him, I know that much." Hugo spotted Claudia—she was throwing looks his way, her path having been blocked by a rotund older man with a red face and a tendency, or so it seemed, to lean in close when he talked to beautiful women. "Speaking of rescuing, if you'll excuse me, my date is in need of just that."

Noelle Manis looked behind her. "Blue dress?"

"Yes."

"She's very pretty." Manis leaned in and put a hand on Hugo's arm. "Let's see if she's jealous."

"Trust me, she's not," Hugo said with a smile.

"Nonsense. All women are, to some degree." Manis removed her hand and looked back at Claudia. "I'll let you go save her because that man is Roger Gallant, who most certainly does not live up to his name. Plus, he's drunk already so you better get over there before he falls on top of her, which may be his plan all along."

CHAPTER TWENTY

Monsieur Roger Gallant, as it turned out, did not have a red face from drink, as Noelle Manis had suggested, but from outrage. And that outrage only grew when he first recognized Hugo from the Tuileries news coverage, and then realized that Hugo was attempting to prize the beautiful Claudia Roux from his clutches.

"Do you know who I am?" Gallant said testily, when Hugo put a hand on Claudia's elbow and asked to have a quiet word.

"I believe Roger Gallant is your name."

"Yes, of course, but do you know who I am?"

"No, *monsieur*, I have no idea, I'm sorry."

"I am the head of one of the largest news organizations in Europe, that's who I am."

"Congratulations," Hugo said, starting to steer himself and Claudia away.

"And I'll have you know, my organization doesn't much care for what you did."

Hugo stopped. "What I did?"

"What right do you have to walk the streets of Paris carrying a gun?"

"It's perfectly legal, I assure you. My embassy—"

"I'm not interested in whether it's legal. It's immoral. Laws can change, but morality stays the same. You carrying a gun is wrong, and I won't stand for it."

Hugo felt the heat rising under his collar. "Well, to be frank, I don't think there's much you can do about it."

"There are a lot of people who do my bidding—politicians and government leaders."

Hugo took a small step back, having discovered that it wasn't just beautiful women Gallant leaned into when he spoke to them. "I'm shocked they allow you . . . you . . . cowboys to roam the boulevards of our beautiful city armed to the teeth, like it was Texas in the 1800s."

"Texas nowadays, too, as it happens." Hugo smiled cheerily, deciding to needle the man if he couldn't escape him. "And I don't think I was armed to the teeth."

"And," Claudia chipped in, "there are a lot of people who are very glad that he was there, and carrying a gun."

"Exactly!" Gallant exclaimed.

Hugo and Claudia exchanged confused glances. "Exactly what?" Hugo asked.

"How *fortunate* that you were there. How *lucky* that you happened to show up right when another armed American was about to murder people."

"Ah, I see," Hugo said. "First of all, no one knows if he was an Amer—"

"Don't interrupt me, young man." Gallant waved a finger. "I don't know that I believe that conspiracy stuff, but I can certainly understand why people do. No, that's not my concern. What I don't want to have happen is for the small group of pro-gun people here in France to think they have a reason to be right."

"I don't really think—"

"I imagine you're now their hero," Gallant interrupted, disgust in his voice. "But my point is, you've already poisoned our system for too long—this would be the last straw."

"Poisoned what system?" Claudia asked.

"Americans. With your crass films, with your rap music, your revolting fast food, and your bland, foul, chain coffee shops. France has been forever altered, diluted, by your country. Like pouring water into a glass of fine wine. Everywhere I look, something American looks back at me. Clothing, those stupid peaked hats, even. And now you want to bring guns to our country?"

"I have no plans to do any such th—"

"I told you not to interrupt me. I'm just getting started with you."

Gallant looked startled as a hand grasped his upper arm, and Ambassador J. Bradford Taylor spoke in his most authoritarian voice. "No, Roger, you are not. You are finished with Monsieur Marston and his lovely companion, because I need them much more than you do."

"Well, I . . . just . . ." Gallant blustered, but he fell silent as Taylor led Hugo and Claudia away to safety.

"Your phone is turned off," Taylor said to Hugo when they were in the clear. His mood seemed to have soured considerably.

"No, I don't think . . ." Hugo turned to Claudia, who was smiling her most innocent smile. "Did you pickpocket me?"

"I have no idea what you're talking about," she said mildly. "And I'm shocked and horrified at such an accusation."

Hugo took out his phone and discovered that it had, in fact, been powered down. "Probably wiped your fingerprints off, didn't you?" he said to Claudia.

"Lieutenant Lerens has been trying to reach you," Taylor said. "She called my cell when you didn't answer her calls or texts, asked me to let you know."

"Thanks a lot, Mr. Ambassador," Claudia said sarcastically. "I'm already fighting a losing battle for his attention, and you're not helping. I know, I know, important investigation, lives at stake, I know all that."

"This is something he needs to know about." Taylor turned to Claudia and forced a smile. "Make it up to you with a fresh glass of champagne?"

She smiled and took his arm. "And something to eat, please."

Hugo watched them wander off and powered on his phone. The noise level had risen in the drawing room, throughout the house it seemed, and he headed downstairs to see if he could slip into the garden. He managed to tail an electrician outside, angling away from where the final touches were being applied to the fireworks display.

"Camille, sorry about that."

"Claudia turned your phone off?"

"Yes, actually, how did you know?"

"It's not the first time she's done it to keep your attention," Lerens said, laughing. "She's very ingenious."

"And very light-fingered," Hugo added. "What's going on?"

"Well, as much as I hate to interrupt your party it occurred to me that while you're there you might be able to get a few answers."

"I've been poking around as best I can, but I don't think it'd go down well if I start grilling people over the champagne and caviar."

"I wasn't talking about people in general."

"Someone in particular?"

"Yes. Marc Lambourd."

"Already had the pleasure of a chat with him. Anything in particular?"

"Yes. Turns out he has some nasty gambling debts, from a series of trips to Monaco."

"How bad are they?"

"Bad enough for him to be selling his house."

"Maybe he's just downsizing," Hugo suggested.

"Ever known anyone to get married and immediately downsize?"

"Fair point. Are you thinking maybe the people he owes money to might have Fabien?"

"He gets his kid back when he pays up?" Lerens was quiet for a moment. "Not the most original business strategy, but it can be effective."

"And would explain why he doesn't seem unduly worried about the boy's disappearance. He knows once he pays, Fabien will be let go unharmed."

"But what does that have to do with the attempted murder of Tammy Fotinos?" Hugo asked.

"No idea. Maybe nothing. But when you have two mysteries, it doesn't hurt to solve one of them."

"I don't know—it just feels like they're connected. The attack and Fabien's sudden and unexplained absence."

"Can you talk to Lambourd, maybe get him drunk and admit that's what's going on?" There was levity in her voice, but Hugo suspected she was only half-kidding.

"Do you know who he owes money to?"

"Not names, no. We're still working on that." She cleared her throat. "And Hugo, there's one more thing I need to tell you."

I know, but I have to pretend I don't. "What is it?"

"The gun that asshole used. It was stolen from your embassy less than a week before the shooting."

"My embassy?"

"Yes."

"How do you know?"

"We log the serial numbers of every weapon that comes into the country. As best we can, anyway. All official weapons, and that includes those used by foreign embassy staff."

"That's not good," Hugo said. "At all."

"The ambassador said much the same thing."

"I bet," Hugo said. "I hope you broke the news gently."

"Of course."

"Should you even be telling me this?"

"I'm not passing on information, Hugo. I'm giving you a warning."

Hugo didn't like her tone. "What do you mean?"

"You'll be getting a call from Adrien Marchand tomorrow, asking you to come in for your official interview."

"I've been expecting that. I don't know why it's taken this long."

"For officer-involved shootings the new protocol is to give the subject officer two nights of sleep before their interview," Lerens said. "Something about how memory works. But that's not my point."

"Then what *is* your point, Camille?"

"That he's now got some coincidences he wants explained, some very odd coincidences. And they all revolve around you."

CHAPTER TWENTY-ONE

Hugo texted Claudia for her to join him in the garden, and then took in the activity around him. Closer to where the lawn backed up to Parc Monceau a dozen men worked under portable lights, wires streaming down from panels, stretching across the perfect grass to the launch pad for the fireworks.

Hugo walked in the opposite direction. It was now close to ten, and the low light from the disappearing sun allowed him to see not much more than ten feet in front of him. The smell was what he noticed the most, of freshly cut grass and flowers, of soil that had been watered that afternoon. He looked up and was pleased that any clouds from earlier had disappeared, which would help the show come off better.

He wandered slowly through a rose garden, stopping in the middle of it to see whether Claudia had responded to his message. She'd not even read it. He started slowly toward the back door, intending to find her, when the figure of Édouard Lambourd stepped across the threshold onto the patio. The light caught his face for a second and Hugo thought he looked worried, an impression that remained when he saw how the man was hurrying across the lawn to the fireworks team. *A problem?* Hugo wondered. He decided to follow, head that way just in case—the artsy Édouard didn't seem like the go-to problem solver for matters technical.

Hugo was thirty yards away from the fireworks setup, and he could see the men had stepped away from their equipment. They stood in a semicircle by the hedge, with Édouard Lambourd in the midst of them. Hugo quickened his step.

One of the workers spotted Hugo and put out a hand to tell him to stop, but the embassy credentials impressed the man enough to let Hugo pass by. He stopped by a kneeling Édouard Lambourd, who had peeled back a piece of clear plastic and was using a flashlight to study an object that had been hidden in the hedge.

"What is it?" Hugo asked, and waited for the surprise to leave Lambourd's face and recognition to set in.

"It's one of the paintings. One of the stolen paintings."

"Are you sure?" Hugo asked.

"Absolutely. It's the one of our grandmother."

"That's great news," Hugo said. "But I need for you to leave it right where it is. That's evidence in an attempted murder case."

"It's a family heirloom, monsieur," Lambourd snapped.

"It will be, but right now it's evidence." Hugo was not about to be bullied. "Please leave it where it is."

His phone was in his hand, and he moved away so he could speak privately to Lieutenant Lerens. He told her what they'd found, and asked her to send a crime scene unit to the house.

"Of course, Hugo, but the Lambourds are not going to be happy about having our people there in their crime scene overalls."

"I don't think the Lambourds are ever happy about anything," Hugo said, checking to make sure Édouard Lambourd couldn't hear. "So just add this to the list."

He hung up and walked back to the group.

Édouard spoke up. "Don't tell me you're canceling the fireworks. Not for just a painting."

"No, sir, that's not my plan. Some folks from the Paris police will be here soon, though. They'll photograph the scene, the painting, exactly where it is. Then they'll take it to their lab for processing."

"Wait, what does *processing* mean?" Lambourd asked.

"They'll look for fingerprints and DNA."

"I don't want the painting leaving this property!"

"I understand that, but there's a process."

"A process that will damage the painting, most likely."

"They're careful, Monsieur Lambourd. This isn't their first time with a piece of evidence that's valuable. Or delicate." Hugo felt his patience ebbing. "I'll have them out of here as soon as possible. It's two hours until the fireworks, and I'm sure they'll be gone long before then."

"They better be." Lambourd eyed him for a second. "I need to tell my mother."

"That's fine," Hugo said. "If possible, it'd be good to just let family members know for now."

Lambourd grunted what may or may not have been agreement, then turned on his heel and marched back toward the house. Hugo addressed the men.

"Who found this?" he asked in French.

There was a moment of silence, then a man with a beard and tattooed arms raised a hand, and Hugo was pleased to see he was wearing gloves.

"I did."

"Well done," Hugo said. "Did you know what it was?"

"I thought it was trash when I first saw it. Thought it'd maybe blown from the park and got caught in the hedge."

"Then you took a closer look?"

"*Oui*. Used a flashlight. I knew about the theft—it was in the newspapers and online news. I wasn't sure that's what it was. It was wrapped up. But it looked like it could be, so I called my *patron* to come look."

"Excellent. Did you touch it at all?"

"*Non, monsieur.*"

"Not even the plastic wrapping?" The man shook his head, so Hugo turned to the rest of the men, some of whom had slunk to the back of the group, almost into the gathering darkness, as if afraid of what had been found. "Did anyone touch it?" A murmur of *no*. "Good," Hugo said, "I will need to take all your names and contact information. I apologize for the intrusion but this is an important matter. I'm sure you understand." Another soft chorus, this time of agreement. Hugo turned to the man who'd been identified as the boss of the crew. "Would you please do me a favor?"

The man nodded, eager to help. "*Mais oui*, of course."

"Thank you. Just stay right here and make sure no one moves or even touches anything, just until the police arrive."

"*Oui, monsieur.*"

Hugo glanced toward the house and saw Claudia on the patio, waiting for him. He walked over and she slipped her arms around his waist.

"Something happen?"

"The firework guys found one of the stolen paintings."

"Oh, wow, where?"

"Tucked in to the hedge where they were working."

"Which one? And was it damaged?"

"One of their grandparents, Édouard said. And too soon to tell. I'm more worried about contamination than damage, since the painting's not worth anything."

Claudia grimaced. The memory of contaminated DNA was too fresh in her mind, an unfortunate fluke that had landed her in jail facing a murder charge until Hugo figured out how her DNA had been found at a crime scene, one she'd never visited.

"So how do you think it got there?" she asked.

"It's possible the thief left it there right after stealing it the other night. Maybe stashed it to come back and get it later."

"Then why didn't he?"

Hugo shrugged. "Maybe he found out it wasn't worth anything. It has sentimental value to the family, but that's about it. Maybe he figured it wasn't worth the risk to try to sell it, especially since the paintings were all over the news."

"So he ditched all four there and when he came back, retrieved only the other three?"

"Possibly. Or he brought it back and left it there."

"That strikes me as risky behavior," Claudia said. "He could be spotted from either the park or the house."

Hugo smiled. "You making mental notes for your story?"

"Yep." She gave him a squeeze. "Only once you've solved, it though. It's not much of a news story until then."

"Then I better go wait for the crime scene team and get them back here as soon as possible. You mind hanging out here, to keep an eye on the guy keeping an eye on my crime scene?"

"Happy to. Just hurry back."

Hugo kissed her, tasting the sweet champagne on her lips, and then walked into the house. He crossed the main hallway to the front doors, but was stopped in his tracks by an angry voice coming down from the second floor.

"Young man! Come here at once!"

Hugo turned to see the face of Charlotte Lambourd peering down at him, and seeing the fury in those eyes he couldn't help but wonder again what had happened to her previous two husbands. He resolved to remain several feet away from her at all times, and *never* go into a room alone with her. Especially one that contained knives.

"Madame Lambourd, how can I help you?" he asked, and when she just stared back at him he started up the stairs with a sense of doom enveloping him like a shroud.

CHAPTER TWENTY-TWO

When Hugo reached her, she seemed impossibly calm given the rage that was clearly emanating from her small body.

"What have you done?" she demanded in barely accented English.

"I've . . . not done anything."

"I'm told the police are coming to my house. In the middle of my party. I would say that's something."

"Technically they will just be in the garden, and I will do everything to make sure they are both discreet and fast."

"People are already talking about it. I would suggest that discreet is no longer possible."

"Well, then," Hugo said, "we'll concentrate on the fast part of that equation."

"You do understand that you were invited as a respected member of the embassy staff, not as an investigator acting without directions or permission." It wasn't a question—it was a statement of fact.

"I wasn't the one who found the missing painting."

"And there's some reason you can't just rehang it and not disrupt the party?"

"Yes, as I explained to your son it's an item of evidence for now." He was pretty sure she knew this already and was just torturing him. "If we want to find out who attacked Tammy Fotinos and stole the other three pictures, this one might help us do that."

"Someone told me you're sticking to your theory. That the girl was sleeping with someone in my family."

"It's a possibility."

"In which case, that would be a further disruption, meaning I have no real desire to know who did that to her. She's fine now, isn't she?"

This lady definitely could kill and not lose sleep over it. "She will be fine, physically. Emotionally, who knows?"

"Emotionally," Charlotte Lambourd repeated, as if Hugo were trying to be funny. "Please. If she was sneaking around my house seducing members of my family, well, she may not have deserved what happened, but I can hardly be expected to be concerned with her emotional state. In my opinion, she put herself in harm's way."

Hugo bit his lip, desperately searching for words that weren't rude, or just plain angry.

"Adult women don't deserve to be punished for having sex," was the best he could do.

"If they do it illicitly in my house, with a member of my family, I disagree." She twisted her mouth in distaste. "Nevertheless, I strongly disapprove of you summoning the police without informing me first."

Over her shoulder, Ambassador Taylor was approaching, a look of worry on his face.

"Is everything all right?" he asked, looking back and forth between Hugo and Madame Lambourd.

"No," she said. "Ambassador, this man has invited the police into my home on the most important night of the year—it's unforgivable."

"It's not unforgiveable, it's necessary," Hugo snapped. "And this might be the most important night of the year to you, but—"

"Hugo, what's going on?" Taylor seemed genuinely perplexed by what was happening, and Hugo's uncharacteristic loss of temper.

"One of the stolen paintings has been found, in the garden by the park. A crime scene unit is on the way to take custody of it and process it."

"And none of this can wait until tomorrow," Madame Lambourd said testily.

"Right, we should just leave the—"

"Hugo, if I may respond, please?" Taylor interrupted.

"Have at it, boss." Hugo took a deep breath, exasperated but recognizing he wasn't exactly helping matters.

"Thank you." Ambassador Taylor turned to Charlotte Lambourd. "Unfortunately, these things can't wait. But if you like, I can oversee the collection process and make sure no one comes into the house . . . Hugo, there's no need for that, is there, someone inside?"

Hugo raised an eyebrow. "God forbid a mere police—"

"Right, thank you, so there you go. I can make sure all the activity is outside and minimally disruptive."

"Your man here has already offered to do that," Charlotte Lambourd said. "And I think I'd like to take him up on it." She turned her steely gaze on Hugo. "Once that task is complete, you may escort them off the property and enjoy the fireworks from the park like everyone else in Paris."

Without looking back at the ambassador, she turned and walked through the large doors across the open reception area and into the busy living room.

"You know," Ambassador Taylor began, "they say she might have killed both of her husbands."

"I've heard. And I'm sure they're both more than grateful."

"Quite possibly." Taylor turned serious. "So, Camille told you about the guns being stolen from the embassy. This is really, really bad, Hugo."

"I know, boss. I almost don't believe it."

"She didn't seem to have any doubt. Good of her to let us know, off the record."

"For sure." Hugo thought for a moment. "I assume you'll have Mari look into this?"

"It's the only thing she'll be doing, until she finds out what happened."

"Good. I know how bad this looks, but she's good, she'll figure it out."

"She better." Taylor took a long draught of champagne, emptying his glass. "Well, I guess you're dismissed for the evening. Do you want to tell Claudia or should I?"

"I'll do it," Hugo said. "You mind chaperoning her if she wants to stay?"

"That's been my cunning plan all along." He stepped back. "Here she is. Good luck."

Claudia drifted up to them and Taylor backed further away. "You were supposed to be right back," she said. "What's going on?"

"So . . . it's not my fault, but I've been asked to leave the party."

"What?"

"The old lady doesn't like that the police have to collect evidence."

"Hugo, you're not making sense. Are you seriously being asked to leave?"

"Yes, I'm sorry. She's upset because she doesn't want the police here tonight. I don't understand people sometimes. I mean what the hell does she expect when a piece of evidence is found?"

"Well, it's not a piece of evidence to her, is it?"

"Maybe not, but I don't have any discretion here—why can't she see that?"

"Hugo, sometimes your job . . . it's intrusive. You can't help that fact, or the timing, I know, but not everyone sees the crushing importance of dusting a worthless painting for prints and scraping it for DNA."

"Swabbing, not scraping," he said sulkily.

"You know what I mean. She lives for this party, and God knows it may even be her last one."

"This damned party. Someone was almost kill—"

"I know, Hugo, I know." She put a calming hand on his arm. "I'm just saying, not everyone is as personally invested in solving every crime as you are."

Hugo looked at her for a moment. "Does that include you?"

"What do you mean?"

"My investigations, do you find them intrusive?"

"Hugo, you saved my life in the last one. Well, saved me from prison, but it may have come to the same thing."

"Don't be evasive—I really want to know."

She pursed her lips in thought. "Well, sometimes, I suppose so. But you're my . . . whatever you are, so I understand that. I know what I signed up for, and I have no complaints." She smiled. "Except for tonight, getting thrown out of the fanciest party of the year, that kind of sucks."

Hugo smiled. "Well, it's me getting thrown out. You're welcome to stay—the ambassador said he'd take care of you."

Claudia rolled her eyes. "Because I couldn't possibly make it through a party alive on my own."

"Right, yes, sorry." Hugo all but blushed. "I'll go back to my apartment in the 1950s and keep quiet."

"As you should."

At the sound of voices below, they both looked down the staircase, across the entrance hall to where two of the footmen were blocking the path of the crime scene team.

"That's your cue?" Claudia asked.

"It is."

"Then go." She reached up and kissed him. "I love what you do for a living, and how good you are. The old witch may be angry, but I'm not. Call me later."

CHAPTER TWENTY-THREE
THE KILLER

So far, so good.

Part of the pleasure of all this is doing it right under everyone's noses. But it turns out that the Lambourds are all so self-involved that they can't see much beyond the end of that particular facial feature.

Getting the paintings where I needed them to be was the trickiest part. Well, not being seen doing it was, technically, the hard part. But that's the glory of the Bastille Day party *chez nous*—those who aren't wrapped up in their own petty dramas (my family) are so busy getting everything prepared that they pay little attention to anything or anyone else.

And the party went off without a hitch, as far as my planning was concerned. It's quite amazing how a place as quiet and staid as the château every other day of the year can come so alive for just one evening. Every room in the house flourished and took on a personality to entertain our guests. Even the large landing outside the main living room smelled like heaven, with explosions of color and scent welcoming people at the top of the staircase. Funny how we take something so beautiful and kill it, just to give ourselves a few hours of pleasure. They don't look already dead but they are, all of these flowers, their heads cut off somewhere along their long necks. That's not what we see, though, is it? We don't see that they're already dead—we just see their beauty.

Well, I do.

Flowers aside, the living room and parlor, normally staid repositories for furniture, antiques, and questionable family art, positively

147

brimmed with people, and along with the flowers you could smell the champagne in the air. I made the rounds, of course, charming those I could and ignoring those I couldn't. Which meant steering clear of my family for the most part, but they're doing the same thing.

The one downside was that people kept asking about Fabien, so I had to make something up about him being detained by business and likely to arrive any minute. I told my siblings to say the same thing, and that did the trick. Anyone who knows Fabien can understand how he'd screw up being at his own family's most important night of the year. He's a grown man, as good as, though, and someone who likes to find his own path. Yes, sometimes at the expense of others, but aren't we all selfish that way? *Another Fabien escapade*, that's all any of us needed to say.

I did have to keep an eye on that American, though. I've said it before and I'll say it again, there's something about him. He's different from other cops. Not that I've had a lot of experience with them, but you can just see how he looks at people. It's like he looks *into* them. Someone told me he used to be in the FBI, like one of those profilers you see on television. It makes perfect sense, too. I can absolutely believe he was.

Which means I will need to be careful around him. He will have dealt with a lot of people with my particular emotional disability. If I trip up around most people, my family or even the regular cops, they'll either miss it or I'll be able to cover it up. I'm not so sure about him, though, and I certainly don't want to underestimate him that way.

I suppose, if it comes to it, I can always kill him.

CHAPTER TWENTY-FOUR

"How's the Lambourd investigation going?" Lieutenant-Intern Adrien Marchand placed a plastic coffee cup in front of Hugo, and then took his seat across the small table between them. Hugo had been in a hundred interview rooms in his career, maybe a thousand, but this was the first time he hadn't gotten to choose which side of the table to sit behind.

"Slowly but surely," Hugo said. "I need to go interview the victim again when I'm done here."

"I gather they retrieved some of the stolen property."

"Two paintings, yes." Lerens had called him late the previous night, to let him know *both* of the family portraits were in the wrapped package. Two valueless paintings abandoned by a money-seeking thief? Or something different? Lerens had asked Hugo that question, but he wasn't ready to answer it, so didn't.

"That's good news. Any prints or anything?"

"They're working on that right now," Hugo said. "You'll forgive me if I answer my phone during this . . . interview."

"Actually, I'd rather you didn't." Marchand gave him a friendly smile, which may or may not have been genuine. "I like to treat all my sus—, I mean subjects, the same."

"Slip of the tongue there? Have you decided the outcome of this already?"

"Not at all. And after our last investigation, I'm sure you can understand why I'm being even more careful with this one."

"Makes sense." *Our last investigation* was when Marchand had

149

arrested Claudia on suspicion of murder. Ignoring Hugo's protestations of her innocence, but finally listening when Hugo used science to undermine the only, but compelling, piece of evidence Marchand had against her. Marchand had seemed grateful for the proof of innocence, wanting to catch the right person, not just close the case. But now Hugo wondered if the young lieutenant had received any blowback for arresting the wrong person, especially someone as well connected as Claudia.

"So, shall we start?" Marchand said.

"Yes, sure."

"As you know, this is being recorded by the two cameras in those corners, audio and video. For the record, you told me before you are willing to give a voluntary statement and have no wish for a lawyer to be present."

"Correct, and I do not."

"The door is shut for privacy and no other reason. You're free to leave at any time, and if you want to take a break just let me know. Also, because we're doing this in French, if you have any doubt at all about what I'm asking, I can repeat it or we can find a translator."

"Thank you, I'm fine with all of that."

"*Bien*. So, why don't you take it from the beginning, tell me what happened?"

Hugo did so, starting from the moment he left the embassy to when he stepped away from the gunman's lifeless body, leaving the paramedics to do their thing.

"Before the shooting, anything unusual at all happen?"

"No, not that I can recall."

"And you didn't recognize the man you shot?"

"No."

Marchand opened a folder that was in front of him and slid a photo over to Hugo. It was the young man he'd shot, the picture taken by the coroner most likely. *How old are you?* Hugo wondered. Here, pale and his eyes half-open, he looked even younger than when Hugo had seen him in the flesh.

"Have you seen this man before?" Marchand asked.

"Man? You mean kid."

"Yeah, he's young for sure. That's why we've not released this picture. So, have you ever seen him before?"

"No, I haven't." Hugo pushed the photo back to Marchand. "Do you know who he is yet?"

"You know I can't answer that."

"Yeah, you can. I think I have a right to know who I killed, don't you?"

Marchand pondered that for a moment. "I suppose you do. Thing is, we're not certain."

"Either you know or you don't," Hugo said.

"We don't. Yet." Marchand looked down at his notepad, and then up at Hugo. "Did you know he was using a gun from your embassy?"

Hugo feigned surprise. "Really? How did that happen?"

"I was hoping you could tell me."

"I'm afraid not. But a lot of people will be very unhappy about that, myself included."

"A lot of people are *already* very unhappy. People a lot more powerful than you or me, which means I need to figure out how that happened, and as quickly as possible."

"If I can help, just let me know."

Marchand nodded. "Are you involved in the process of decommissioning firearms?"

"Only the decision-making process."

"So it was your idea to change weapons? Put those out of service?"

"Yes."

"Why?"

"All of the people who are armed prefer the nine mill. Most of them own one. It made sense to me to have people carry what they prefer."

"I see. And the timing of the switch?"

"What about it?"

"Why then?"

"Budget reasons. It's been in the works for months but . . . government, you know how it can be."

"I most certainly do. So the timing was just a coincidence."

"I guess. Or maybe if he'd gotten his hands on those guns three months ago, or in six months' time, he'd have gone shooting in the Tuileries then."

"Quite possibly. Is that your usual route home, by the way?"

"Yes, it is."

"And you always carry a loaded firearm when you're not at work."

"Not always. I would say not even usually. If I'm on my way there or on my way home, though, I do, yes."

"I'm sure you know this, but a lot of people are less than thrilled that a man carrying an American passport shot at people in the Tuileries, and that an American carrying a gun shot him."

"Would they have preferred it if I hadn't?"

"It's not the shooting part that bothers people—it's the carrying of a loaded gun."

"Pretty hard to shoot someone without one."

"Yes, exactly. The general perspective is that neither of you should have been armed, that both of you were, and that whether he turns out to be an American or not, he was carrying a gun that you people provided."

"Yes, I'm aware of the ludicrous rumors and conspiracy theories. I have to assume you're just going to be dealing with facts, though, right?"

"Doing my best, Monsieur Marston, but you're not really giving many I didn't already know."

"I think that's how being innocent works." Hugo resisted the urge to make a crack about Marchand arresting innocent people. As he'd learned the previous night, antagonizing his host was counterproductive.

"Four shots, right?"

"Yes. Two missed, two hit."

"We recovered all four shell casings and two of the projectiles from the body. The two misses . . . we never found those."

"In the dirt," Hugo said. "He was kneeling and I was shooting from a standing position, so the bullets would have angled down into the ground. Come to think of it, I could swear I saw one of them kick up dirt."

"Quite possibly. We looked but didn't find them. Why four?"

"Because the first two missed."

"Of course. And you only needed two more to finish the job?"

"I don't like the way you phrased that." Hugo wondered if it was intentional, but he wanted to register his disapproval just in case. "I shot and the threat was obviously over after the fourth shot. As you know that's what we're trained to do, shoot until the threat is nullified. Then stop."

"Same for us, yes, of course."

"Glad to hear it," Hugo said. "The two people he wounded, I was told at the time they weren't badly hurt. Is that right?"

"Yes. One person is still in the hospital but will make a full recovery."

"Did either of them know the shooter? What about the person he killed? A woman, I heard."

Marchand smiled. "There you go again, with the questions."

"Put me in an interview room, I can't help myself."

"Well, I think that's all I have," Marchand said. "Do you have any more questions for me?"

"When will I know the results of your investigation?"

"You'll be one of the first, I promise."

"When you slap handcuffs on me?"

"No, no. I'd let you turn yourself in discreetly, don't worry." He saw Hugo's face and held up a hand in apology. "My attempt at humor, I'm sorry. I'll let you know as soon as I can, I promise."

Marchand stood and let Hugo out of the room ahead of him, and they walked together to the public area of the police station.

"Let me know if I can help in any way," Hugo said.

"I will, and thank you for coming in. Oh, on the gun issue. Please let us look into that. If you start asking questions or poking around, it will look . . ."

"Like I'm tampering with your investigation. I know."

"Thank you." They shook hands.

Hugo walked toward the entrance, out into the warm July air. He took out his phone to call Claudia. She'd been a little too tipsy to talk for long the previous evening, but just before he hit her number, Lieutenant Lerens's name popped onto the screen. He answered.

"You all done with Marchand?" she asked.

"Yep, just finished."

"How was it?"

"He didn't arrest me, so there's that."

Lerens laughed. "I'm glad about that."

"You have news?"

"As a matter of fact, I do." She paused for effect. "We got a print hit off the plastic wrapping."

"Great, who is it?"

"Are you still near the building?"

"Yes, want me to come back in?"

"No. I want some coffee. Pick somewhere close by and we can talk there."

CHAPTER TWENTY-FIVE

"Who the hell is that?" Hugo asked. He was staring at the front of a manila file, reading and rereading the name *Auguste Pierre Rabin*.

"He's a reformed criminal," Lerens said. "Or so it seemed."

Hugo waited until the waiter had dropped off their coffees before opening the folder. "Check fraud, car theft, car theft, car— . . . wow, he likes cars. Six of those."

"He does. But the last one was seven years ago, nothing since."

"What's he been doing? And where?"

"No idea what, but the last address we had puts him here in Paris three months ago. I guess he's been behaving himself, did for a while anyway."

Hugo furrowed his brow and dropped a sugar cube into his coffee. "Seems odd, no?" he said finally.

"What does?"

"He has a history of petty crime, all of it nonviolent from what I can see. Then he does absolutely nothing for seven years, and returns as a wannabe murderer and art thief?"

"That's why he chose paintings with no real value."

"Maybe," Hugo conceded.

"Or maybe he's been escalating and we just haven't caught him until now."

"I doubt it." Hugo tapped the file. "This guy is no genius. He was caught, what, a dozen times in three years for various dumb stuff?"

"Something like that."

"And then somehow stays off our radar for almost a decade while committing increasingly violent crimes?"

"When you put it like that . . ." Lerens nodded in agreement. "But it's definitely his print."

"Then let's go talk to him." Hugo stared at the photo and frowned. "Maybe he has one of those faces, but I feel like I know him."

"He looks like the henchman in every police show ever made."

"Yeah." Hugo put the picture back in the folder and closed it. "I also want to talk to Tammy again. Hopefully her voice is better. And her willingness to cooperate."

"Let's do that first," Lerens suggested. "Maybe she'll recognize our friend Auguste Rabin."

Lerens drove them to the hospital, and they both spent the trip in silence. Hugo tried to focus on why someone like Rabin would go dormant and then escalate, but he was also feeling the pressure of the Tuileries shooting. He was used to the stress that comes with hunting dangerous criminals, but not at all used to being so prominently in the public eye, especially while so many made him out to be the villain of the piece.

Two uniformed nurses stood at their station, and watched them approach. The older one examined their credentials before telling them that Tammy Fotinos had been moved to a new room.

"Was there a problem?" Hugo asked.

The nurse frowned as she looked down at some paperwork. "Someone called . . . A lieutenant named Lerens requested she be moved every two days for her safety. Do you know who that is? If so, take it up with him."

"I do, thank you," Hugo said with a smile. "Good thinking by that lieutenant."

The nurse grunted in reply and pointed down the hallway. "Second door on the right. The one with the policeman standing outside it."

They started in that direction, and as they walked Hugo said to Lerens, "I thought you decided she didn't need a cop at her door."

"I did. Until Fabien went missing. Until we're sure he wasn't the one who put her here in the first place, I'm taking all necessary precautions."

"I'm very impressed. And in agreement."

"Two good ideas in two days," Lerens said. "Glad I can make you proud."

The *flic* standing guard nodded his recognition of Lieutenant Lerens, and took a cursory glance at Hugo's credentials before stepping aside. Hugo tapped on the door and opened it without waiting for an answer.

Fotinos was sitting up in bed, poking at her cell phone. She looked startled at their sudden entry and looked nervously between them. "Hi," she said. "I . . . I wasn't expecting you."

"Expecting someone else?" Hugo asked lightly.

"No. Who would that be?"

"Whoever you're texting maybe."

"That's my mother. Back home. Letting her know I'm fine." She cleared her throat gently and stroked it, as if by habit now.

"Is she coming over?"

"She can't afford to," Fotinos said, her eyes dropping. "So I just told her I was in an accident and am fine. There's nothing she can do anyway."

Hugo nodded and waited as Lerens clicked on her recorder and set it on the tray table that hovered over the foot of the bed. "So," he said. "We have a few more questions."

"Like what?" Fotinos said, her voice scratchy and dry.

Camille Lerens placed a photo in front of her, and asked: "Do you know this man?"

Fotinos studied it for a moment, then shook her head *no*. "Who is he?"

"Auguste Pierre Rabin. Does the name mean anything to you?"

"No, I don't think so."

"Thank you," Hugo said, and handed the picture back to Lerens. "Now, about what happened the other night."

"I don't remember any more than I told you," Fotinos said.

"Okay, that's fine. But it's what you didn't tell us that I want cleared up."

"Like what?

"You get one chance to lie to me, Tammy. And you get one chance to correct it, no questions asked, no consequences."

"I didn't lie—"

"Just wait," Hugo interrupted. "You need to know that Fabien Lambourd has disappeared."

Her eyes widened. "Disappeared?"

"Yes. And he's my best bet for being the person you were visiting that night, am I right about that?"

Fotinos held his gaze for an admirably long time, then dropped her head and gently nodded. "I couldn't tell you before," she said.

"Why not?"

"He didn't want people to know."

"And?" Hugo pressed.

"Sometimes we did stuff that's . . . different." Fotinos shot a glance at Hugo and then looked down. "You know. They call it breath play."

"You mean, sexually?" Hugo asked. "Like choking?"

"Technically, it's strangling as you cut off the blood flow, not the air," Lerens said. "So, you thought maybe he did this, and it went wrong?"

"I mean, it doesn't seem likely. But who in the world would actually want to hurt me?"

"Someone stole paintings that night," Hugo said. "Whoever it was maybe thought you'd seen them."

"Oh. I didn't know about that. Why?"

"A good question, but one we can't answer at the moment."

"But you are looking for Fabien, right?"

"Yes, of course," Lerens said. "You have no idea where he might be? Has he been here?"

"Here?" Fotinos laughed. "I don't know him that well, but I'm pretty sure he's not the type to bring flowers to someone in the hospital."

"Do you know if he was into anything?" Lerens asked.

"What do you mean?"

"His phone was found in a stolen car. So, I mean, do you know of any mischief he was planning?"

"No, it's not like we were friends or talked very much. It was just a fun thing."

"And did anyone else know about it?" Hugo asked.

"No, that's why I was sneaking about like that—he made me promise to keep it a secret, that no one find out. He would've gotten in trouble with his family, and I would've been fired, so we made sure no one else knew."

"You have your phone," Hugo said. "Here's my card. If you think of anything else, please don't hesitate to call. Day or night."

Fotinos took the card and nodded. "I do have one question."

Hugo paused. "What is it?"

"You said someone stole some paintings that night. They might have done this to . . . you know, shut me up, I guess."

"It's possible."

"But why would a burglar be carrying a weapon like that?"

"I don't know," Hugo said. "I've been wondering the same thing myself."

CHAPTER TWENTY-SIX

uguste Rabin was less welcoming. No one answered the door of his small duplex in a working-class suburb of the city, on its southeastern edge. Lerens rang the bell a third time, and Hugo wandered around the side of the building. He tried to peek through a window, but the dirty glass made it impossible to see inside, so he kept walking. Through the slats of an old wooden fence he saw a man working in the back garden. Hugo went back for Lerens, and together they let themselves through the unlocked gate. The man was on his knees with a trowel in his hand, and he turned at the sound of the gate opening.

"*Bonjour*," Lieutenant Lerens said. She and Hugo had their credentials in their hands as they approached, but the man barely glanced at them. Which told Hugo plenty. "Auguste Rabin?"

"*Oui.*"

Lerens introduced herself and Hugo, but Rabin stayed where he was.

"Do you mind if we ask you a few questions, *monsieur*?" Lerens asked.

"You'll ask them, whether I mind or not." He was surly, Hugo assumed, thanks to too many encounters with the police that ended with him wearing handcuffs.

Lerens ignored the comment. "Where were you on Friday night?"

"Here."

"From when to when?"

Rabin shrugged. "Six to about seven the next morning."

"Anyone with you?"

"Look, I've been going straight for years. Whatever you're trying to pin on me, forget it. The only car I drive these days is the one out front that I paid for."

"Congratulations."

"It's always the same with you people. Someone commits a crime and you have no idea who, so you go bother people who fit your profile and find one who doesn't have an alibi. And then bam, on go the handcuffs."

"That's not what we—"

"And hey, doesn't matter if it's the *right* criminal, does it, because once you're guilty of one thing, no reason why you can't be guilty of something else." He stabbed the trowel into the earth in annoyance. "But I'm off that roulette wheel, like I said. I have a job, and if I want something, I don't steal it. I save up and I buy it."

"You're working?"

"Yes. Construction, electrical, whatever I can get. It's not easy with a criminal record, you know."

"I'm sure it's not," Lerens said. "You have a side business that involves selling art or antiques?"

"Art . . . look if it's about that painting, I don't know anything about it."

"Apparently you do."

"*Merde.*" Rabin looked down and shook his head slowly, knowing he'd given himself away.

Hugo pressed him. "Just to be clear, what painting are *you* talking about?"

"I saw it in the news, that girl who got strangled and the paintings stolen. I assumed that's what you were talking about, but I don't know anything about it."

"You said *that painting* though," Hugo said. "Singular. Which painting were you referring to?"

"I meant *paintings.*"

"Monsieur Rabin," Lerens began. "Your fingerprints were found on the wrapping when two of the paintings were recovered. You want to explain that to me?"

"Actually," Hugo interrupted, "I think I can."

Both Rabin and Lerens looked at him. "Meaning?" the lieutenant asked.

"Well," Hugo said. "When we found the pictures, we thought it was just one. That's what everyone was saying at the château, right?"

"Right," Lerens said.

"Monsieur Rabin here, he just said *painting*, as we noticed. He wouldn't have said that if he'd stolen them, and he wouldn't have said that unless he was there when they were found." Hugo looked at Rabin. "You were part of the fireworks crew, am I right?"

Rabin looked up at him, not speaking for a moment. Then he said, "*Oui*, that's right."

Hugo remembered the scene, the handful of men who stepped back into the darkness when he started asking questions. He must have seen Rabin, but not well enough to recognize him.

"Why didn't you just say so?" Lerens asked.

"Plenty of reasons," Rabin said.

"Such as?"

"I'm on probation. I can't be around explosives."

"That's all?"

"No. The family, the Lambourds, the guy they hired to do the fireworks is a friend of a friend. They told him everyone working at the house had to be clean, no criminal records. If they found out, he'd have lost that job and he did me a favor letting me work it. I need the money."

"When did you touch it?" Hugo asked. "The wrapping around the painting."

"I was the one who found it. Didn't know what it was so I left it there and told my friend. Let him take credit for finding it. I didn't want any attention."

"Did you see who put it there?" Lerens asked.

"No, it was already there, tucked under the bush."

"And if we pull your cell phone records, they will show you were right here at home two nights ago when that girl was attacked?"

"*Oui*. Go ahead and do it, they will."

"Thank you for your time, monsieur," Lerens said. "Happy gardening."

Hugo followed her out through the gate and to the car, where she paused. "Two dead ends in one trip. Not what I was hoping for."

"But we got some answers," Hugo said. "That's always a plus."

Lerens smiled. "Ever the optimist."

"I have to be. I live with Tom."

Hugo had Lerens drop him at the embassy. A cryptic text from the ambassador had requested his presence there immediately. Hugo assumed it had to do with the shooting in the Tuileries, but when he got to Ambassador Taylor's office he saw he was only half right. The other half, he discovered, reflected the truth of his words to Camille Lerens in the car about Tom.

"Sit," Taylor said, switching on a flat-screen television on the wall. "Allow me to present a performance by your best friend."

"What's he done now?" Hugo asked, settling into an armchair beside Taylor. "And what do you mean by *performance*?"

"Apparently some members of the media have been camped outside your apartment hoping for an interview with you."

"Yes, I know. Wait—" Hugo stared at Taylor in disbelief. "He didn't."

"Yes, he most certainly did."

Hugo closed his eyes for a moment, steeling himself, and opened them to look at a television screen showing Tom on the sidewalk outside their building on Rue Jacob. Taylor pressed the play button and they watched in silence as Tom was interviewed in English, French subtitles scrolling beneath his cheery face.

". . . many, many years," Tom was saying. "We roomed together at the FBI. He had some trouble with a few classes, so I helped him out where I could."

"And he was a good shot back then?" the young woman interviewing Tom asked.

"Oh, yes. The best. Well, not actually the best, I was, but he was second best. Very quick on the draw, very accurate."

"So you are not surprised he shot the gun from that man's hand?"

"Not at all," Tom said. "I am surprised he missed three times, but he's been out of the Bureau for a while, let himself go, if you know what I mean."

Twice, Hugo thought. *I missed twice, you bastard.*

"I'm not sure I do . . ."

"I mean, he used to be in great shape, fit, athletic, and deadly with his gun. Not much of a fighter, you know, with fists. Anyway, with this State Department job, he's lost a little of his edge. And gained a few pounds at the same time."

Coming from you . . . Hugo shook his head.

The ambassador chuckled. "He's pretty entertaining, though. Hard to be mad at him sometimes."

"No," Hugo replied. "It really isn't."

"Did you know if the man he shot has a connection to the embassy?" the interviewer asked Tom.

"I do not. You mentioned he was an American?"

"Yes," said the interviewer, who looked more and more to Hugo to be in her late teens. "Is it possible Monsieur Marston knew him?"

Say no, Hugo willed. *For once, do the right thing and say no.*

Tom hesitated at the question, as if intentionally drawing out Hugo's anxiety. "I mean, anything's possible. Hugo meets a lot of people in his job, especially Americans who come into the embassy for one reason or another. He's a friendly guy, what can I say?"

"Some people are saying this is what you Americans call a false-flag operation, that your government set it up to make him a hero."

"That's . . . ridiculous." Tom was shaking his head emphatically. "Why would they do that?"

"To help with Franco-American relations, maybe?"

"No way, that's crazy." Tom was chuckling now. "I'm retired now, but worked for the government for more than twenty years. Getting someone to send a fax at the right time to the right person is a challenge of breathtaking proportions."

"What is a . . . fax?"

"Not the point. The point is, well, first Hugo Marston is the most honest man on the planet, so he'd never do anything like that. But even if the government wanted him to, *ordered* him to, there's no way a bunch of bureaucrats could pull this off logistically, or without someone spilling the beans."

"What beans?" asked the interviewer, confused.

Tom sighed dramatically. "Without someone leaking the plan, telling you, the media. No way."

"And it would involve sacrificing another human being," the interviewer added.

"Precisely! Ridiculous idea."

"Although you people do that all the time."

"Do what?"

"You assassinate foreign leaders, and you sacrifice your own people every day."

"What?" Tom was getting flustered, finally realizing maybe he was being outplayed. For Hugo's part, he wished Tom would just walk away, cut it off before doing even more damage. "We most certainly do not."

"You do. What steps did you people take after all those children got killed by a mad gunman?"

Tom frowned. "Which time?"

"Exactly!" The interviewer was almost giddy with excitement at this point. "People die every day from gun violence. And you make people pay for healthcare they can't afford, so they die."

"Which crazy media outlet are you from?" Tom asked.

"So it would make perfect sense to sacrifice just one man, maybe someone mentally ill, to make a difference in international relations."

"Actually, it makes no sense at all," Tom said. "I mean, it's more probable that some pro-gun group here set this up, that's how—"

The interviewer leaned in. "You have some information about that?"

Hugo groaned. *Just leave. Walk away, Tom. Now!*

"What? No! I'm just saying, your theory is ridiculous."

"Is Monsieur Marston a member of any pro-gun group that you know of?"

"No. I have no idea."

"Either here or in America?"

"Look, I wasn't saying that was a poss—" Tom made a show of looking at his watch. "You know what, I have to go."

"Better late than never," Hugo muttered.

"My thoughts exactly," Taylor said. They watched as Tom strode back into the building, ignoring shouted questions from the interviewer.

"Well then," Hugo said after a moment.

"Yeah. I need to give that guy a job here, just so I can fire him."

"When did this air?"

"Two hours ago. More to the point, it's online."

"Oh, I'm sure it is," Hugo said. He looked down as his phone rang, and then he laughed gently.

"Who is it?" Taylor asked.

"The man himself. You wanna take bets on whether he called to apologize, or to brag?"

CHAPTER TWENTY-SEVEN

"You're an idiot, Tom. A prize-winning, twenty-four-carat, gold-plated, moron-infused idiot."

"Hang on a moment," Tom said, defensively. "I know things went a little off the rails for a moment, but I got that train back on track."

"Is that what you think? Because from where I was sitting it smashed right through the station and exploded into a million pieces."

"With the whole pro-gun lobby thing, you remember that, right?"

"Oh, I do, yes. Very well indeed."

"Stroke of genius," Tom said. "Even if I say so myself."

"Right, because now I'm part of *two* conspiracies, and that's so much better than just one."

"Easy, Mr. Sarcastic. With that little gem, not only did I point out the stupidity of the original conspiracy theory itself, but by introducing the second, even more stupid one, I've pitted them against each other and they will crash head-on and boom, all done."

"Right, that's exactly how conspiracies work."

"There isn't even a pro-gun lobby in France!" Tom was almost yelling.

Hugo sighed. "There is, Tom. They called and want me to speak at their conference in a month."

"Oh. Shit. I didn't know that."

"Well, you do now. They are more oriented toward sporting guns, but are trying to nudge back legislation restricting other firearms."

"Learn something every day, eh?" Tom chuckled. "Well, I hope you told them no. That'd be a terrible idea."

"No kidding, Tom, what do you thi—"

"Well, gotta go, buddy. Oh, and you're welcome for the help."

With that, he was gone.

Ambassador Taylor raised an inquisitive eyebrow.

"If your money was on an apology," Hugo said, "you owe me."

"Oh, it wasn't." Taylor pursed his lips. "We need this figured out before even more shit hits the fan."

"No kidding. And you really can't tell me how it's going?"

"You know I can't."

"Well then, boss," Hugo said. "You'll forgive me if I do a little poking around of my own."

"No, Hugo, I won't." Taylor wagged a disapproving finger. "You have the Lambourd thing on your plate. Not only are you not allowed to investigate yourself, you don't have the time. Solve that and be a hero again."

"Tough to do when I'm not allowed on the property."

"Oh, right, the old lady kicked you out. Well, you'll figure something out," Taylor said. "Apart from that, how is it going?"

"If you must know, I have a nice little pool of suspects, one of whom is missing. A victim who's already lied to me, and a fingerprint that led us to an innocent man."

"Not fantastically, then."

"I hope what your people are doing is progressing a little better." Hugo smiled. "Maybe we should swap investigations."

"You'll get there, Hugo. You always do."

"Although," Hugo said with a smile, "I'd like to have been in the room when you were told the gun from the Tuileries shooting came from here."

The ambassador's face darkened. "No, you wouldn't have. That poor Marchand fellow almost regretted telling me, but I managed to pretend I didn't already know, and he learned a few new swear words in English. I've ordered every single employee of this embassy to fully cooperate with Mari and with the French police on this. On pain of firing. I'm telling you, Hugo, this is very, very bad for me, for us. Every which way."

"I know, boss."

"No, I don't think you do. Look, I know you love Paris and your job, but if things get any hotter around here, you need to know that one of my options is to ship you home and keep you out of sight. And if the people higher up the ladder need a fall guy, well, I will gladly offer to play that role, but they don't like firing ambassadors."

"They'd rather can the RSO?" Hugo asked, his tone grim.

"I imagine it looks better, yes."

"Boss, no, they wouldn't." Hugo shook his head. "I mean, I'm in the middle of an invest—"

"You're not the only detective in Paris, Hugo," Taylor said, his tone firm. "And I didn't say it was going to happen. But just know that it's out of my hands, and so it might."

"I'd go kicking and screaming," Hugo said. "And like you said, you'll figure that part of it out, whoever took the gun."

"I won't, but Mari Harada is on it. She better."

"She's good, so I don't doubt it for a moment. She's working the shooting from this end?"

"Yes, which means she's off limits to you. Anyway, we shouldn't be talking about it at all, so why don't you tell me about your little pool of suspects?"

"Cutting me off, eh?" Hugo gave a wry smile. "Sure, why not? First up is the missing young man, Fabien."

"Grandson of the witch-in-chief."

"Correct," Hugo said. "I've not had a chance to talk to him yet. He disappeared before I had the pleasure. But from what I can gather, he's quite the tearaway. His father's an enabler, Marc Lambourd, probably because they're a lot alike."

"Fabien's your chief suspect?"

"I don't know I'd go that far. It implies I have evidence against him."

"And you don't?"

"Not really. He was having a . . ." Hugo cast around for the right word. "I suppose you could say liaison with our victim, which she lied about."

"But they didn't have a falling out, no reason for him to try and kill her?"

"No. And even if they did, why let her walk down the hallway and do it where he could be caught, instead of just killing her in his room?"

"You're right, that doesn't make sense." Ambassador Taylor frowned. "But he and the paintings both go missing? That seems like an odd coincidence, or something."

"It does, but I also have no reason for him to steal them."

"He might have thought they were valuable?" Taylor suggested.

"I doubt it. Plus they were returned so quickly, whoever took them barely had time to try and sell them."

"What if he had a buyer lined up, and that person changed his mind?"

"No, I don't think so," Hugo said. "If that were the case, he'd have stolen what the buyer wanted. Either a specific piece for a specific reason, or the buyer would've told him which ones were valuable."

"True. Any theories at all?"

"None I'm prepared to share," Hugo said. "Camille has people talking to possible buyers for paintings, stolen and otherwise, but there are so many art shops and underground markets I don't expect her to turn up anything."

"And Fabien himself?"

"A mystery within a mystery. We found a stolen car with his phone inside it, but it all seems very convenient."

"Like he wanted you to find it?"

"Right." *Or someone else did*, Hugo thought. "I just hope he's all right. No one in the family seems too concerned, though, which is somewhat reassuring."

"Anyone in the family with reason to do him harm?"

"Maybe, it's a pretty dysfunctional unit. His aunt, Noelle Manis, had some issues with him. Something happened between her and Fabien, but she's not telling, so I have no idea how serious it was."

"Tight-lipped, eh? So, what about the boy's father, Marc?"

"Very French royalty, that one. Dresses the part, accessorized with shoes I couldn't afford with a year's salary, gold watch, and cologne made from the tears of fairies."

Taylor laughed. "The perfect gentleman."

"Now, yes. He's put his wild days behind him and plays the doting son and loyal family member. Camille did find some gambling losses, which might have meant debt, but it didn't come to much more than $50,000, which doesn't seem too much for a Lambourd."

"Not as much as you thought, huh?"

"No, which means my little kidnapping theory goes away," Hugo said. "I guess he really is selling his house to downsize."

"People do that. Who gets the château when the old lady dies?"

"Under French law, they all do. She can't leave it to just one of them."

"That's right." Taylor snapped his fingers. "I knew that."

"But there's nothing to stop her giving away all the other family treasures before she goes."

"You think Marc is playing a role for loot?"

"Maybe, but I can't see what it has to do with Tammy being attacked or the pictures being stolen."

"And returned," Taylor said, nodding in agreement. "He's cooperative, though?"

"Marc?" Hugo nodded. "In his own way, yes. Like his mother he wants to protect the family name and have us wind things up as soon as possible, but he's been willing to talk to us at least."

"Good. Who else is there?"

"His younger brother, Édouard, who styles himself as an anti-American, asexual, art-loving recluse."

"Interesting. Any reason he'd want to kill Tammy Fotinos?"

"I don't think he hates America quite that much, and otherwise, no."

"Doesn't he have a twin sister?"

"Erika Sipiora. And she's actually Marc's twin, and looks the part."

"Meaning?"

"Dresses well, very educated, polite. Everything you'd expect from French nobility."

"Without the wild past?" Taylor asked.

"Not that I know of. No arrests, not even any wild stories about her. Married well, though, an Italian count who bought them a lovely house in Luxembourg, which she doesn't like to stay in now he's dead."

"Did she kill him?" Taylor winked. "Runs in the family, you know."

"I didn't ask," Hugo said with a chuckle. Then he remembered what she'd told him, and turned serious. "She had a child, you know. Died at age three, kidney disease."

"I'm sorry to hear that."

"It was ten years ago, but she's obviously still very affected by it. The polite but remote façade cracked a little when she talked about it."

"Hardly surprising," Taylor said. "That's not something you ever get over, I'm sure."

"Agreed. Anyway, no reason to think she had a grudge against Tammy, and she's plenty rich by the looks of things so didn't need to steal and sell paintings."

"Who's left, then?"

"Of the household, the youngest sister, Noelle Manis, and Karine Berger." Hugo sat back and crossed his legs at the ankles. "She's the old lady's attendant. Personal servant. Whatever you want to call her, I have no idea."

"And?"

"I did speak to Noelle, who is less than enthusiastic about Marc's fiancée, but I don't think that's more than a touch of jealousy or resentment. Not enough for a motive for murder. And Madame Lambourd still isn't letting us talk to Karine. Too traumatized from finding Tammy at the top of the stairs."

"Too traumatized? Or protecting her for another reason?"

"We'll find out. But Marc confirmed she's got some sort of learning disability so I don't know that she's sophisticated enough to fashion a garrote, attack Tammy, fake finding her, steal four paintings, and then return two of them, all without being found out." Hugo checked his watch. "Still, I do intend to talk to her, or Camille will, more likely. Just to be sure." He stood and stretched his back. "Well, I'm headed to my office, do a couple of things, and then I'm going home."

"Good plan. Let me know of any developments, yes?"

"Of course." Hugo let himself out and made his way down to his office. When he got to Mari Harada's door he knocked, waited for her reply, then opened it and poked his head in. "How's tricks? Investigation going well?"

Harada smiled. "None of your business, as you well know."

"It's okay, the ambassador said you could fill me in."

"Is that so?" She raised an elegant eyebrow. "I'll just double-check with him how much I can share then." She reached slowly for the phone, her eyes never leaving Hugo's.

"Okay, fine, so maybe he didn't use those exact words," Hugo conceded.

"And what words did he use, exactly?'

"Why is everyone around here so insolent?" Hugo asked. "I'm going to my office to pout."

"We get it from you," Harada said, and laughed. Hugo couldn't help but smile, too, and gently closed the office door as he left. Once behind his desk, he dialed Tom's number.

"Hey, pops. Still mad at me?"

"Yes," Hugo said. "I'm calling to cash in a favor."

"Yeah, you have a few of those tucked away. What's up?"

"Your contact within the Paris police. I need something from him."

CHAPTER TWENTY-EIGHT

A
s soon as Hugo had hung up from Tom, his phone buzzed and Lieutenant Lerens's number popped onto the screen.

"Camille, what is it? Does everyone work on Sundays now?"

"Why, where are you?

"At the office. So are the ambassador and Mari."

"It's an American thing, all this working nonstop. I'm in the hot tub with a few friends. Care to join?"

Hugo laughed. "I don't hear any splashing, so where are you really?"

"I might be working," she admitted. "A weird development, too."

"Those are my favorite developments." He felt a rumble in his stomach and remembered the time. "Is this urgent? If not, how about some wine and pizza?"

"That sounds good. I'm in the car, so same as before—pick somewhere close to you and I'll meet you there."

Twenty minutes later an aproned waiter showed them to a small table in the shade of the awning at Le Boissy-d'Anglas on the street of the same name. Couples and families strolled past on the wide sidewalk in front of them, moving at a Sunday evening pace and occasionally throwing glances at the half-dozen occupied tables to see what people were eating and drinking. Lerens ordered them a decent bottle of red wine—like Claudia, she wasn't one to suffer the house offering, although her brand of snobbery did not come from money, like Claudia's. No, hers came from growing up in Bordeaux, where she'd sampled the best wines with her father and brothers from the age of thirteen until she left home at age twenty-five. But, just like Claudia's, it was an affliction she couldn't shake.

They sat quietly as the waiter uncorked the bottle with a few deft movements, and as he directed an American couple to a table in his almost-perfect English. He poured a sample and Lerens poked her nose into the glass, gave a deep inhale, and nodded.

"*Merci*," she said, and the waiter poured a glass for Hugo before recharging Lerens's glass.

"So, what's the news?" Hugo asked, once the waiter had bustled off into the restaurant.

"I got a call from Édouard Lambourd a couple of hours ago. He wanted to meet me."

"A confession by any chance?"

"No, sadly not." Lerens slowly swirled the wine in her glass to let it breathe. "Remember, I said it was weird news. I didn't say it was good news."

"Very true."

"He wanted to meet in a public place, so we got ice cream in the Tuileries."

Hugo smiled. "Nice to know he got over his silly little aversion to the twenty-first century. From not knowing what to call you to inviting you on an ice cream date, that's quite the change of heart."

"Right. But it wasn't exactly a date—he was scared."

"Scared?" Hugo's glass stopped halfway to his mouth. "That's new."

"He said someone was following him all morning."

"Seems unlikely."

"That's what I thought. But he showed me photos, and the same person appears in each one, three different parts of the city."

"Who is it—anyone we know?"

"Look for yourself." Lerens pulled out her phone and opened the photo app. "Last three pictures."

Hugo took the phone and scrolled through the images. One looked to have been taken in Parc Monceau, one on an unidentifiable pedestrian street, and the last in the Tuileries, with the entrance to the Louvre in the distant background. He went back to the first and studied it, and then the others, more closely. It was definitely the same figure in each picture. Hugo squinted, and then enlarged each photo until it blurred, but however he tried to see the person, they were far enough away to remain anonymous.

"A baseball cap, sunglasses, and a beard are about all I can see of his face," Lerens said. "Wearing a blue track suit that you can get anywhere, and from the people and objects around him, I'd say close to six feet."

"Is that a beard, though, or shade?" Hugo squinted again. "Hard to tell."

"My money is on a beard, but who knows if it's even real. I'm having our crime scene people take a look, see if they can enhance the image, but I'm inclined to believe Édouard that the guy was following him. He said he saw him five times, only thought to get photos on the third sighting."

"Yeah," Hugo agreed. "Spotting him twice or even three times might be a coincidence. But not in five different locations."

"Agreed. What do you make of it?"

"No idea," Hugo said truthfully. He finally took a sip of wine and was grateful he'd let Lerens do the choosing. Fresh fruit rolled like velvet on his tongue, and the musty taste of Bordeaux barrels gave the wine a fullness that Hugo relished before swallowing. "Whoever the follower is he's not very good, that much I can tell you."

"Is it possible the family is being targeted by very amateur kidnappers?" Lerens asked. "The finding of Fabien's cell phone after his disappearance, maybe that was clumsy and not intentional. Then this poor example of following . . ."

"It's certainly possible. They have money, have no bodyguards, aren't popular enough to garner much publicity, and therefore police interest, like a movie star would." Hugo eyed the menu and settled on a ham and garlic pizza. "You may be on to something. Objectively speaking they're almost ideal targets for kidnap."

The waiter returned and they ordered, the same thing as it turned out, and then they sat back in silence to watch the world go by for a few minutes, and to let the wheels turn at their own pace in their minds. An old man walked slowly past them, leaning on a knobbled cane with every step, his worn blue beret tipped back on his head. Despite the warmth of the evening he wore a long trench coat, and Hugo watched as the man came to a gradual halt past the restaurant, turn as if in slow motion, and then walk back toward them. He settled behind one of the small tables to Hugo's right, a sigh of relief escaping the man's lips as he got off his feet.

"I know him from somewhere," Lerens said. "He's a World War Two veteran."

"Not many of those left," Hugo said. The man dug into his pants pockets, first the left one, then the right, pulling out loose change and piling it on the table. He counted it with care, a shaky forefinger pulling one coin at a time away from the pile.

"That's not right," Lerens said.

"No, it's not," Hugo agreed. "Split it?"

"Definitely." Lerens gestured to the waiter, who'd been hovering to give the old man time to count his stash. "Monsieur, please tell him his meal is paid for. Anything he wants."

"Including a bottle of wine," Hugo added.

"*Oui, bien sûr,*" the waiter said. *Yes, of course.* "But he drinks Negronis."

"Then a couple of those," Hugo said.

The waiter nodded and walked over to the man, bending to convey the offer. When he'd done so he straightened, and the old man turned slowly in his seat. He lifted a hand in thanks and gave them the slightest of smiles. In unison, Hugo and Lerens lifted their wine glasses and toasted his health: "*Santé, monsieur.*"

Their pizza arrived a few moments later and, as they dragged hot slices onto plates, Hugo spoke. "We need to speak to Karine Berger, whether the old lady likes it or not."

"I know. And I have a plan for that."

"Which is?"

"Madame Lambourd takes a nap at precisely two in the afternoon every day. Karine Berger waits for thirty minutes in case she needs something, and then lies down herself at two-thirty."

"So you're going a-knocking at two-fifteen?"

"I most certainly am."

"You think I'm allowed back in the house?" Hugo asked.

"Good question. Why don't you try talking to Édouard, see if you can get more information from him about his follower? Or reassure him he's not about to be kidnapped, at least."

"Pick me up from the embassy tomorrow?"

"Take an Uber."

"That's not very professional. Plus, the red tape I have to swim through to get reimbursed . . ."

"Fine," Lerens said. "I'll play chauffeur. Just give me a good review."

⚜

The next morning Hugo walked from his apartment on Rue Jacob, crossing Pont du Carrousel with the seven a.m. traffic before making his way to the gardens of the Tuileries, which were quiet this early. His boots crunched on the gravel pathway, and either side of him the grass glistened with dew. He smiled at the trails of paw prints where unleashed dogs had trotted across the manicured lawns earlier that morning. Hugo took this walk nearly every day. It was his commute, a peaceful yet energizing routine on every other day, but somehow not today. A slow anxiety rose in his chest, and instead of enjoying the cool morning air and the emptiness of the park, Hugo felt himself eying those who were there, checking to see what they had in their hands, if they carried backpacks, or whether they were walking alone. Just like he was.

People were watching him, too. The city had upped the police presence in the Tuileries, and groups of three or four *flics* were doing just what he was, checking out the lone walkers, looking casual but on alert for anything out of the ordinary. And for the first time in a long while, Hugo felt the weight of his gun under his armpit, wondered what the policemen would do if they knew he was carrying.

Shoot first and ask questions later? he thought, and tensed a little as two of the uniformed men, about fifty yards ahead, stared at him. He looked down at the pathway but noticed them exchange words and then move toward him. Hugo, dressed in a blue blazer, slacks, and a button-down shirt, didn't have his credentials on display and didn't much want to reach for them.

The cops separated a little as they got close, blocking the pathway, and the one to Hugo's right, the younger one, spoke.

"*Bonjour, monsieur.* Where are you going this morning?"

"*Bonjour.* I'm walking to work."

"And where do you work, monsieur?" The *flic's* tone was friendly enough, but his body language told a different story: feet apart, squared up, his hand hovering close to his holster.

"At the United States embassy. I am head of security there, so you should know I am carrying a gun right now."

The young cop immediately unclipped the strap on his holster and half-drew his gun, stopping only when his older colleague snapped, "Wait!" at him.

"I know who you are," the old *flic* said. "From the television. You're the guy who shot the gunman here, right?"

"That's right. Hugo Marston."

"Well, then, let me shake your hand. I'm Alain Dupont. This is Mathieu Clement. He's a little nervous after that event."

"Understandably," Hugo said. He shook both men's hands.

"Sorry about almost pulling on you," Clement said. "When you said you had a gun, that's about all I heard."

"No problem," Hugo assured him.

"Is it true the gunman was an American?" Dupont asked. "I'm hearing all kinds of crazy rumors about that."

"I'm not part of the investigation," Hugo deflected. "For obvious reasons. But to my knowledge, those things you've been hearing are nothing but crazy bullshit and rumors."

"Glad to hear that," Dupont said, with a nod. "Well, Monsieur Marston, it was an honor to meet you, but we should let you get to work."

Hugo thanked him and shook their hands again, aware that their eyes were on his back as he walked away, aware, too, that if the shooter turned out to be an American after all, even men like Alain Dupont and Matheiu Clement might buy into a conspiracy theory that could spell the end of his time in Paris, and maybe his career with the foreign service.

CHAPTER TWENTY-NINE

When he got to the RSO offices, Hugo was welcomed by the smiling face of his secretary, Emma, and the smell of coffee brewing.

"Good morning. I wasn't sure whether you were on administrative leave or working, so I put on a pot just in case."

"You're an angel," Hugo said. "And as for my status, I'm equally confused, don't worry."

"Well, here you are. I feel like I've not seen much of you lately. Busy dodging the media?"

"Very. Oh, that might be them now . . ." Hugo pulled his buzzing phone from his pocket. "Nope, even worse. Tom."

"I miss him, too."

"I don't." Hugo answered. "Tom, I didn't know you were awake."

"I wasn't, but I got a message just now from my police contact and now have eyes on the reports you asked for."

"Can you send them to me?"

"Nope."

"Tom, don't be difficult." Hugo poured coffee into a mug and stirred in a spoonful of sugar, and then winked at Emma as he retreated into his office.

"I'm not. I gave him my word I wouldn't show it to anyone else, had to. Tell me what you want to know."

"Jeez, Tom, I want to know everything." Hugo pulled a new notepad from a desk drawer and picked up a pen. "Still no ID on the shooter?"

"Correct."

"Then let's start with the names of the people he shot."

"Okay, well, first up is Annabelle Brodeur. She's the only one who died."

"Age and address?"

Tom sighed as if he were divulging state secrets, but gave Hugo what he wanted. "Two people injured, neither of them seriously. Thank God. You want their details, too?"

"Yes, please."

"Okay, they're grouped together so let me take a snap and text it to you."

"That's not sharing?"

"Hush, no, it's not, I'm a man of my word."

"Of course you are." Hugo chuckled. "Any progress on finding out who took the gun from the embassy?"

"Let me check . . . No, doesn't look like it. What else can I tell you?"

Hugo thought for a moment. "I'm curious about the shooter's path of travel. Anything in there about it?"

Hugo heard the rustle of papers, then: "They found some CCTV footage of him right before he entered the Tuileries, southeast corner."

"Interesting. Is there a crime scene diagram showing where his victims were?"

"Of course. Marchand is nothing if not thorough."

"Can you snap that and send it to me?"

"I don't know, Hugo. That's a little too close to showing you the report itself. It's not just names and addresses . . ."

"Tom, come on. My name's being smeared by a bunch of conspiracy theorists, and you certainly didn't help in that regard."

"Fine, fine," Tom said grumpily. "There, sent it to you. But it didn't come from me, got that?"

"Got it. Thank you."

"Welcome. I think," Tom said. "So let me ask you something.

Don't you think it's weird no one has come forward to identify the shooter? No friends, no family, no neighbors. No one."

"It is weird," Hugo agreed. "Normally they'd release a photo, but they don't have one of him alive, and because he is young, well, the police are reluctant to publish the photo of a dead kid."

"Fair enough, although the media's been using shots of him from bystanders, after he was down. Maybe he was a recluse?"

"That'd be my guess. They'll figure it out, that I'm sure of."

"Yeah. So what are you gonna do with the information I just gave you?"

"I was thinking I'd pay a visit to the home of the dead woman, express my condolences. Maybe visit the other victims, too."

"Seriously? You're not supposed to go within a mile of this investigation. Marchand will have kittens if he finds out."

"Then let's hope he doesn't find out."

"What do you hope to gain from that?" Tom pressed. "I mean, seems like you risk getting in trouble for not much reward."

Hugo had put Tom on speaker and was staring at the mapped-out crime scene. "I don't know exactly."

"I recognize that tone," Tom said. "You have an idea but you don't want to share it."

"Something like that. But it's not much of an idea, to be honest."

"Be like that, see if I care. Hey, what's the ambassador doing about the gun thing?"

"He's apoplectic," Hugo said. "He's ordered everyone to cooperate with the French police, and not play the diplomatic immunity card. Anyone who does gets fired."

"Tough but fair, if you ask me."

"My guess is it's one of the locals who work here."

"You think?"

"Why would someone risk their career with the State Department, not to mention a trip to a French prison, to smuggle a gun out of here?"

"No clue, but I bet the conspiracy websites could tell you."

188 THE FRENCH WIDOW

"Probably," Hugo said. "But I'll be steering clear of those for a while. Oh, one more question—do you have the autopsy report there?"

"I do indeed. The shooter is definitely dead, if that's what you're wondering."

"Thanks, Tom, super helpful. I was wondering about the tox report."

"Oh, right. Hang on." Another rustle of papers. "Here it is. Nothing in his blood except ketamine, which would've come from the medics' attempts to save him."

"Yep, sounds right. What about the victim, anything unusual about hers?"

"Yes, Hugo. The three fucking bullet holes in her chest." Hugo heard the rustling of paper. "Seriously, though, other than that, she was hunky dory, pretty much perfect health."

"Okay, thanks, Tom, I appreciate the help."

"Let me know when you can share your bright idea."

"Will do." Hugo hung up and sat back, gesturing Emma to come in when she poked her head around the door. "Everything all right?"

"Yes, just want to be clear that you're not talking to the media. Had three calls this morning already and I've basically been hanging up on them."

"That's perfect, saves me from having to do it. Thank you." He looked down at his phone as a text came in from Camille Lerens. *Meet me at Château Lamb. Urgent.* "Is Cecilee around?"

"I think so. Need a ride somewhere?"

"I do indeed." Hugo got up, texting his subordinate as he moved to the door. "Something's afoot at the Lambourd place."

Twenty minutes later, Hugo stepped out of the car and thanked Cecilee Walker for the ride.

"You need some help in there?" she asked. "Or I can wait if you'll need a ride back."

"Thanks, I'll let you know if I do. And I can get a ride back with Camille. I think."

"Gotcha. Call if you need me."

Hugo nodded and started toward the house, noting the white crime scene unit van parked on the gravel on front of the main doors. As Hugo stepped into the downstairs foyer, a uniformed officer intercepted him and asked for identification.

"Of course." Hugo showed his embassy credentials.

"*Merci*, Monsieur Marston," he said. "Lieutenant Lerens is expecting you in the main living room. You know where that is?"

"I do, thank you." Hugo trotted up the stairs and found Lerens, a couple more uniformed men, and two crime scene techs in white coveralls. They were gathered around a table looking at something, and as he got closer he could see it was a large and opened cardboard box.

"Camille, what's all the excitement about? You said it was urgent."

"Ah, Hugo, *bien*. I wanted you to see the evidence before it went to the lab for testing."

"What evidence?"

"Two things," Lerens said. "First, the other missing paintings."

"Someone returned them?" Hugo heard the surprise in his own voice.

"Yes. With a little addition." Lerens nodded toward the box. "Have a look for yourself."

Hugo stepped up to the table and peered down into the box. "A couple bags of peas? Frozen peas, and . . . Oh. That's not good."

"Not at all."

A plastic sandwich bag was wedged between the two bags of peas, and it contained a single object that the sender had obviously intended to preserve as much as possible: a human finger.

"Tell me what we know," Hugo said.

"The box was left on the sidewalk, in front of the house and not on the property," Lerens said. "A printed note said, *This box belongs at Château Lambourd. Reward for delivery.* Some kids brought it to the front door and Karine Berger gave them a few euros."

"When was this?"

"Not even an hour ago, but we have no idea how long the box was in the street. The peas are still pretty frozen so probably not long."

"No cameras or anything out there?" Hugo asked.

"No, none. I have people canvassing the area, but I'm betting no one noticed anything out of the ordinary."

"Do we think it's . . .?"

"We don't know. The family certainly think it's Fabien's, and to be honest I don't know who else's it would be."

"No distinguishing features?"

"Like what, exactly?" Lerens arched an eyebrow. "It's a finger."

"I don't know. A ring, a wart." Hugo smiled sheepishly. "Yeah, dumb question, sorry."

"No ring and we didn't inspect for warts. I have a better idea."

"His prints are on file from the recent arrest."

"They are, and not just from that one."

"Can you tell if it was removed pre- or postmortem?" Hugo asked.

"No, I'm not even sure the pathologist will be able to say for sure."

"Either way . . ." Hugo shook off the chill that ran down the back of his neck. "So, anything to know about the returned paintings?"

"Nothing obvious. We'll check for prints, but I don't have high hopes." She frowned and stepped away from the table after nodding for the techs to carry on packing up the evidence. "What do you make of it?"

"You go first."

"I'm confused, to be honest," she said. "What is this person trying to achieve?"

"Cutting a finger off is pretty extreme," Hugo conceded. "You don't do that unless you have a damned good reason."

"Like making sure a ransom gets paid."

"Well, that's true." Hugo stroked his chin in thought. "But let me guess, no ransom note?"

"Correct. No ransom note, or any other type of communication."

"Interesting," Hugo said. "Very interesting indeed."

CHAPTER THIRTY

Lieutenant Lerens was right that the package had affected the Lambourd family. When Marc Lambourd walked into the living room he was pale, and the arrogance and bluster had left him. This was no longer a jape involving his son, another scrape with the law that money and the Lambourd name would get him out of. If that finger was Fabien's, this was something entirely different and, unless he was an incredible actor, Hugo could see that realization etched across the man's face.

"We don't know anything for sure," Lerens was assuring him. "You opened the box when it arrived?"

"Yes, Karine brought it into the kitchen while I was there. Since it was addressed to the family and no one in particular, I opened it."

"Did you touch the contents?"

"No, I . . . I reached in but then stopped. I saw what it was, and . . ."

"That's good."

"You can check to see if . . . if it's his?"

"I think so, yes. We'll do what we can."

Lambourd sank into an armchair and sighed. "What does it mean? Who would do this?"

"I don't know," Lerens said.

"Does it mean he's . . . dead?"

"No," Hugo said. "It most definitely doesn't mean that. Let me ask you something. The paintings, did any of them have any special meaning?"

"We've been asked about this before," Lambourd said. "No. Not to me, anyway." He shook his head. "In the first set that got returned my mother said I look like my grandfather, but I couldn't ever see it. So, no is still the answer."

"That's the one that hung over the main fireplace," Hugo said.

"Right. Of no value and questionable quality." He sat back and looked between Hugo and Lerens. "So what happens now? You have to find my son, please. Whatever it takes."

"We'll need your help to begin with," Hugo said.

"Anything, just tell me."

"Your mother was less than thrilled with having me around. I need to have access to the house, the grounds, and everyone here."

"I'll talk to her. This thing . . . it's shaken her up pretty badly."

"She saw it?" Lerens asked.

"She was walking in with Erika as I was opening it. I made sure she didn't see inside, though."

"Good," Hugo said. "The other thing is we need to speak to Karine. Your mother has protected her, kept her from talking to us. We can't do our jobs unless we speak to everyone."

"Yes, of course. I'll make sure she doesn't get in your way. Anything else?"

"Yes," Hugo said. "We're thorough, Monsieur Lambourd, which means we sometimes come across information that is personal and sometimes embarrassing."

"Such as?" Lambourd was immediately defensive.

"We understand you incurred some casino gambling losses."

"What of it?"

"We were wondering if someone has been putting pressure on you to pay the money back."

"Ah, I see." Understanding dawned on Lambourd's face. "And you think it's possible some people took Fabien to pressure me to pay up."

"The thought occurred to us."

"No, that's not possible. Look, the casino I lost money in is owned by some disreputable people. Many of them are. But it's not like it used to be. The owners hire experienced and legally responsible managers.

When someone loses in, for example, an unsanctioned card game, that person negotiates a payment plan. He doesn't get his kneecaps whacked with a bat."

"That's good to know," Hugo said. "So you're saying you've not had any threats made related to those debts."

"I could pay those tomorrow, if I wanted. The delay is not that I can't but that I think someone was cheating." He waved a hand. "None of that stuff is relevant, and you don't need to know about it. But yes, I'm saying no one has threatened me in any way."

"Glad to hear it," Hugo said. "The only other thing is that I'd like a quick word with your gardener."

"Gardener?" Lambourd asked, both he and Lerens looking surprised.

"Yes. It won't take more than two minutes, just a couple of quick questions."

"May I ask why?"

"No, sorry."

"It's just that as a member of the museum's staff—"

"Monsieur Lambourd," Hugo interrupted, working hard to keep his cool. "You just promised me access to every part of this house, including the people who live and work here. I appreciate you feel some responsibility toward them, but the idea that they might somehow be bullied or coerced into saying something detrimental without your guiding presence is a touch insulting to us and them."

Lambourd bristled. "Well, I wasn't suggesting—"

"And as you now know," Hugo went on, "time is of the essence thanks to an unwelcome escalation by whoever is behind this. Which is to say, some of the conventional niceties you would normally enjoy are not appropriate."

"Of course, yes, I'm sorry." Lambourd seemed chastened. "I'll take you to him now. Would you like me to ask Karine to come up now, or later?"

"Why don't I talk to her while you're getting gardening advice?" Lerens said to Hugo.

Hugo nodded his agreement and followed Marc Lambourd out of the living room and down the main stairs. They walked to the French doors at the back of the house that led out onto the garden beside Parc Monceau, and Lambourd pointed out two men snipping at a laurel bush with shears. "The older one has been here twenty years. More. Giles Fremont. I'm sorry I don't know who the younger one is— he's new."

"Thank you, I'll take it from here."

Hugo was true to his word, asking old man Fremont three questions before leaving him alone. Hugo wrote the answers down in his notepad and read them back to the gardener to make sure he'd not misheard, then thanked the old man and headed back into the house. At the foot of the stairs he was accosted by Édouard Lambourd.

"Ah, Monsieur . . . I'm sorry, I'm terrible with names."

"Marston. Hugo Marston."

"Yes, yes. Marston. I suppose you saw the box and its contents?"

"I did. Did you?"

"No, no, I just heard about it. I wouldn't want to see that, not at all. Just horrible. Awful." He held up a hand as Hugo started to move away. "There is something I would like from you, though."

"And what's that?"

"A bodyguard," Lambourd said emphatically.

"Right." Hugo took a deep breath. "I heard about your shadow yesterday, yes."

"Then you'll understand why I need protection."

"I don't mean to downplay your concerns, but I don't think you're in any imminent danger, so a bodyguard would be unnec—"

"Not in danger?" Lambourd's eyes were wide with disbelief. "You just told me you saw what was in that box. My nephew is missing and possibly . . . you know. And now I have someone stalking me, no doubt eying me up as their next victim. How can you possibly say I'm not in danger?"

"Well, from what I heard—"

"That's absurd, ridiculous. Five times I saw him!"

"Yes, I know. Five times you saw him, probably ten he saw you, and not once did he try to do you any harm, isn't that right?"

"Well, he's not going to do anything in public, is he?"

"You think he's going to sneak in here and kidnap you?"

"He did exactly that to Fabien! And almost killed that poor girl while he was at it."

"Possibly," Hugo conceded. "I think if you're out and about in public you're perfectly safe, just as you were yesterday. I can ask Lieutenant Lerens to post a man here overnight, if you're that concerned."

"I already asked her, she said no." He was petulant now, like he was going to one parent after the other had denied him a treat.

"I'll talk to her," Hugo promised. "In the meantime, keep the doors locked and you should be fine. I think if that person had wanted to hurt you, they would have remained hidden and done whatever they were going to do yesterday."

"Then who the hell was it? Why would someone spy on me like that?"

"I don't know yet. We're working on it."

They both turned at the sound of footsteps. Adrien Marchand and another plainclothes detective were crossing the hall toward them. When Marchand reached them, he introduced himself to Édouard Lambourd but left his colleague to hang back and just watch.

"Another detective on the case?" Lambourd said. "And a real one, that's good."

"Real one?" Marchand asked, confusion on his face.

"Well, the one upstairs . . . you know." He looked away, but gestured toward Hugo. "And he's American, so that's not . . . ideal."

"I'm not working on this case," Marchand said stiffly. "I'm here to speak with Monsieur Marston." He turned to Hugo. "If you can spare me a few moments?"

"Certainly, a few." Hugo nodded toward the main doors. "It's a pretty day—shall we go outside?"

Marchand nodded and led the way. Once they were outside, the second detective pulled out a tape recorder, but Marchand shook his head. *Not necessary right now*, was the look on his face.

"Sorry, I know you're busy, but I had a couple of follow-up questions."

"You can call me any time," Hugo said. "I might even answer."

"You've seen my office, right? Small, musty, and no window."

"Any excuse to get out, eh?" Hugo asked.

"Right. And I've heard about this place, wanted to see it for myself."

"I'm sure someone would give you a tour if you asked nicely."

"Adrien, excuse me," Marchand's colleague spoke up, his phone in his hand. "We have to go. Right now."

"What are you talking about?" Marchand asked.

"They identified the shooter. We have his address."

"I'm coming with you," Hugo said, matching Marchand stride for stride to his car. The French detective had huddled with his subordinate out of Hugo's earshot, and then headed quickly to his car.

Now Marchand paused. "What? No, you're not."

"Yes, I am."

They reached the car and Marchand stopped, speaking to Hugo as if to a child. "You are a subject in this investigation—you cannot take part in it. You know that."

"I won't be taking part. I'll just be there, watching."

"No, you'll be here conducting your own investigation into the disappearance of that young man."

"Adrien, listen to me. Half your country thinks I'm a hero, the other half thinks I'm a villain. I can't function properly like this. I need to know who this person was. This person I killed."

"*Exactement.* And it's because you killed him that you can't—"

"Dammit, Adrien, is there any question that I was entitled to pull the trigger? Is there any doubt at all that it was legally justified?"

"*Non.*" Marchand pursed his lips. "Morally justified, too, if you ask me."

"What was his name, and where's he from?"

"Victor Roche, and he lives in a small house on Avenue Lejeune in Drancy."

"That's northeast of Paris?" Hugo associated the name Drancy with the confinement and transportation center set up there by the Nazis in World War Two, but he'd never been there.

"Yes. We have a team headed there now to get eyes on the place. Our intel says it's just him and his mother who live there."

"So he was a kid?" Hugo asked. "How old?"

"Nineteen."

"Shit. So his mother's the one who called in with the identification?"

"No, that was a male voice. Anonymous caller, and the number he used belonged to a prepaid phone, so no way to trace him." Marchand opened the car door. "Sorry, gotta go."

"And I gotta go with you."

"Hugo, you know—"

"You just said I was in the legal and moral right. I'm not going to jeopardize any investigation or prosecution by riding in the car with you. Let me see where he lives. This is what I do, it's what I'm good at. He's dead but I might be able to tell you something about him from how he lived."

"Just watching, I thought you said."

"Well, yes. But I'm always open to questions, should someone have any."

"I'm sure you are." He sighed and jerked a thumb to the back seat. "Get in. But I mean it, Hugo—you stand back and let us do our thing."

"I promise," Hugo said, and hurried to the back of the Renault before Marchand changed his mind. "And thank you."

Once in the car Marchand introduced his colleague. "This is Pierre Laland, just joined us."

"And I thought you were the new kid on the team," Hugo said to Marchand, while shaking Laland's hand.

"Not anymore." Marchand put the car in gear and the wheels spun on the gravel as he accelerated away from the house toward the road. "Thanks in part to your help on the last case, as it happens."

"You're welcome," Hugo said with a smile.

"Yeah, well." Marchand glanced at him in the rearview mirror. "Consider your presence the favor repaid. And buckle up—I'm hitting the lights and sirens."

CHAPTER THIRTY-ONE

The house was one story and built in the 1950s, a brick box that would withstand a hurricane but did little to pretty up the drab street it sat on. By the time they got there, the advance unit had cleared people out of the homes either side of the Roche home, and across the street from it, the yellow crime scene tape that marked the perimeter swayed gently in the breeze. Pretty soon, Hugo knew, the tape would attract curious onlookers like flies, eyes and cameras watching every move.

As he, Laland, and Marchand watched from a safe distance, a remote-controlled robot drove down the ramp of the bomb squad's truck and made its way to the overgrown path that led to the front door.

"Here, look at this." Marchand handed Hugo his cell phone. "It's an app that connects to the two cameras on the robot. There's one stationary one in the front, a stationary one in the back, and one that revolves on the top. The robot operator sees all three and makes one of the screens the main one, and you see it all here."

"Very neat," Hugo said. "The robot is checking for booby traps?"

"Yes. They'll use it to breach the door and then the RAID team will go in. You know what RAID is, yes?"

"Research, assistance, intervention, deterrence. What we would call a SWAT team."

"Right, pretty much. Anyway, they'll make entry and clear the house without disturbing too much, and then we'll go in. I'll go in."

"You got it right the first time with *we*," Hugo said.

"Maybe."

They watched in silence as the robot went up to the front door. A metal voice rang out over the street, identifying the house by number and ordering anyone inside to come out with their hands raised. This went on for fifteen agonizing minutes, but there was no movement.

"Anyone know where the mother is?" Hugo asked.

"No, the neighbors that we moved out haven't seen her in days."

"Not a good sign," Hugo said quietly.

Marchand put a finger to his ear, pressing the earpiece in so he could hear better. "They're about to blow the door."

Hugo would have guessed that from the line of six heavily armed men who were scuttling toward the house. The entry team. The men paused, kneeling at the far end of the pathway to the front door, and ten seconds later the robot joined them, having placed explosives on the door's lock. Five more seconds and the explosives blew, sending debris into the air and imploding the door. The RAID team was through it in a flash, voices at first loud and then muffled as they swept through the house.

In less than two minutes they were filing out, and Marchand had nodded to Hugo that the house was clear.

"No mother?" Hugo asked.

"They didn't see her, but they won't have done an exhaustive search," Marchand said. "That's my job."

The Frenchman started forward with Pierre Laland right behind him. Hugo let them get a few steps ahead, and then followed. As they walked, Marchand pulled three pairs of blue gloves from his pocket and handed two of them to Laland and Hugo.

"These don't mean you get to touch anything. Watching only."

"Got it," Hugo said, relieved that Marchand was even letting him in the house.

At the front door, the smell of smoke and something chemical made Hugo's nose twitch, but inside another odor took over.

"They didn't notice that?" Hugo asked.

"They had masks on." Marchand wrinkled his nose in disgust. "Well, we know she's in here somewhere."

Hugo had seen the floorplan and knew that the front door opened into a large living area, which he now saw included two sagging sofas, a pair of worn armchairs, and a small dining table that had four wooden chairs tucked under it. To their right, there was an opening, which he knew led to a narrow hallway, which in turn led to two bedrooms separated by a relatively large bathroom. The kitchen was at the back left of the house, partly visible through a pair of open glass doors.

"Pierre, check this room and the kitchen," Marchand said. "Hugo, you can watch me check the bedrooms."

They split up, and Hugo followed Marchand down the narrow hallway to the first bedroom. Inside, the walls were covered with wooden crosses, cheap artwork showing Jesus being crucified, and crocheted quotations from the Bible.

"Mother's room," Marchand said. He paused at a small trunk at the foot of the bed, one too small for a person to fit in. He bent and lifted the lid, immediately dropping it closed and staggering backward into Hugo, his forearm across his mouth as he gagged. "My God. Excuse me, I was not expecting that."

"She's inside?" Hugo asked, glancing at the tiny box, and covering his own nose as the stench rolled into him.

"Some of her is. Torso only, from what I saw."

"Monsieur?" It was a female voice from the front door. "Crime Scene Unit. You need us to come in and start photographing?"

"In a minute," Marchand called. "We're taking a quick look first." He glanced at Hugo. "Very quick."

"Agreed." Hugo looked around the room and pointed to the chest of drawers against a wall. "Want me to check these?"

"Yes, I do. But I better do it." Marchand stepped up to the chest and took in a breath through his mouth, and then opened the top drawer. He shook his head, in disgust not disappointment, Hugo thought, and quickly opened and closed the other three drawers. Marchand retreated to the bedroom doorway and gestured for Hugo to follow. "A limb in each drawer."

"Interesting," Hugo said.

"Revolting," Marchand replied. "Now we're just missing the—"

"Monsieur." Laland appeared in the opening to the main living area. His face was pale and his eyes were wide. "*J'ai trouvé la tête.*"

"As you were saying," Hugo said dryly. "Let me guess, the freezer?" Laland nodded.

"You didn't touch it?" Marchand asked.

"Her head? No, no. I shut the door as soon as I saw it."

"Good," Marchand said. "Who the hell kills and cuts up his own mother?"

"You'd be surprised," Hugo said, thinking of two serial killers he'd interviewed who'd done just that. "You mind if we take a peek at his bedroom?"

"We should," Marchand said. He led them to the open door and Hugo and Laland followed him inside.

"This is weird," Laland said.

"A little," Hugo agreed.

The room was spotless, and dominated by a queen-size bed that was perfectly made up, as if an army drill instructor had overseen the operation. The walls were painted white and bare of pictures or other adornments. A bedside table carried a lamp, and when Marchand opened its single drawer Hugo saw a new-looking Bible inside. To Hugo's right was a bookshelf, and he stepped to it to look at the books on it. The complete set of Astérix and Obélix adventures, same for the Tintin comic books. All of the books on the shelves were comic books, Hugo saw. Every single one.

Behind him, Marchand was looking through a large chest of drawers, tutting as he went.

"A nineteen-year-old who folds all of his clothes," he said. "Even his socks and underwear. What's that about?"

"No idea. I don't have kids but my impression of a teenager's bedroom isn't anything like this, so neat and tidy." Hugo glanced at

Laland, who was even paler than before, and seemed to be swaying on his feet. "You okay, Pierre?"

"*Non*. Do you mind if I step outside?" Laland asked. "I think I'm about to puke from the smell."

Marchand waved at him to leave, adding, "We'll be right behind you, unless there's more you need to see, Hugo?"

"Give me just a minute." Hugo was on one knee, peering under the bed. "What have we here?" He reached out and grabbed the handle of a suitcase. He gave it a tug, and it felt at least half full. He turned to Marchand. "You want me to leave it here so crime scene can photo it where he kept it?"

"Yes, please." Marchand looked at Hugo, wariness in his eyes. "You think we need to have it cleared by the bomb squad?"

"Are they here?"

"Yes. I'll have them run a dog over and sniff for explosives. Doesn't seem likely he's that sophisticated, but you never know. With the internet anything's possible."

"Yeah, about that." Hugo stood, leaving the case where it was. "I've not noticed a computer anywhere in the house. It's like it's the seventies in here."

"Controlling religious mother?"

"Could be." Hugo took another look around. "Poor teenage boy missing out on all that porn."

"I'm sorry, what?" Marchand sounded surprised.

"Oh, my mistake." Hugo grimaced. "A joke I should only make to my friend Tom."

"Ah, yes. I've heard you speak of him." Marchand put his hands on his hips. "I think we're about done here, don't you?"

"I don't see anything else here of much interest." Hugo took a final glance around the ordered, clean room and followed Marchand down the hallway and into the welcome fresh air. Hugo walked along the broken pathway deep in thought. He'd hoped to have an idea of who this kid was, more than just his name and where he lived. But his mother wasn't talking, and neither was his bedroom, which would've been Hugo's second-best shot at understanding who Victor Roche was, and why he wanted to kill random people in such a public way. And maybe why he wanted to commit suicide in such a public way, too.

Hugo leaned against Marchand's car and watched the man talking with the three crime scene specialists. One of them would photograph the scene as it was, and then another would put down evidence markers beside anything that could later prove relevant. The third would video record everything the other two were doing to show that they were not changing or tampering with the site.

After a couple of minutes Marchand walked over to Hugo. "What do you think?" he asked.

"What else do we know about those two, mother and son?"

"Not much," Marchand said. "We're still gathering statements from neighbors, but so far the impression is that they were both recluses. She left the house to go to church, usually taking him with her. No one we've talked to liked the mother. We've heard words like *angry, hostile, preachy, unfriendly*. One neighbor said if you went asking for a cup of sugar you'd get a sermon instead."

"School records?"

"Weirdly, no. He didn't attend any of the local schools, so either she homeschooled him or . . . she didn't. A couple of the neighbors said their impression was that he wasn't very bright, and that's putting it kindly."

"So what's your next step?" Hugo asked. "And where's your partner?"

"Laland? Puking somewhere. The first time that smell gets into your nose, it stays for a while."

"Yeah, it does." Hugo agreed. "Second and third times, too."

Marchand nodded. "You asked what my next step is. Probably the first thing is to let the press know that you're not behind some bizarre conspiracy to bring guns to Europe."

"I'd appreciate that."

"But of course." Marchand clapped him on the shoulder. "Now you can go back to being a hero."

"I'll settle for not being the villain." Hugo frowned, unable to put his finger on what was bothering him about the crime scene, other than the obvious violence.

"Why the long face?" Marchand asked. "To be honest, this is about the best we could have hoped for, apart from a chopped-up human being."

"How so?"

"I was afraid this was a religious thing, but there wasn't so much as a prayer rug in that house, let alone in the boy's room."

"Christians can be killers, too."

"Yes, yes, of course. But his room was devoid of anything extreme, in terms of religion or anything else. So we're left with a troubled kid, an oppressive mother who died at his hands, and the Americans off the hook."

"Case closed?"

"I would say so, yes." Marchand looked happy about that.

"What about the gun? Where did he get that?"

"If I had to guess, I'd say someone from your embassy sold it to make money, and he bought it on the streets."

"Guessing is an investigative technique now?" Hugo said it lightly, but Marchand didn't take it that way.

"Hey, don't you dare accuse me of . . . whatever the hell you're suggesting. We identified the shooter and he's dead. His mother is also dead, and whatever loose ends we need to tie up we can do so from follow-up interviews and what we find in that suitcase." He pointed a finger at Hugo's chest. "And considering you people supplied the murder weapon, I'd think it's in your very best interests to agree that for all intents and purposes, this case is closed."

"That's my point," Hugo pressed. "How much time between the guns disappearing from the embassy and him using them? A few days, right?"

"So what?"

"So, much less likely someone just stole them to sell on the street, and they happened to end up with Roche."

"Jesus, Hugo, why can't you—"

"Which means you might still have a coconspirator out there."

"*Might* being the operative word."

"It's too much of a coincidence."

"Look, I agree we need to find out who stole the gun," Marchand said, exasperated. "But that's just the pretty bow on an already-solved investigation."

"I hate to burst your bubble, Adrien." Hugo gave him a sad smile. "But after seeing that house, his room, his mother, we're not just looking for some guy who stole two guns."

Marchand stiffened. "Meaning?"

"We're looking for whoever is behind this." Hugo pointed down the street to the house. "He may have been the gunman, but I'd bet my hat that he was as much a tool in this as the gun was."

"So now there's a mastermind behind everything?" Marchand sounded incredulous.

"Yes, and whoever it is would just love to see you tie that bow on this investigation and walk away from it right now."

"Who?" Marchand demanded.

"That's the part I haven't figured out. But I have an idea or two."

CHAPTER THIRTY-TWO

THE KILLER

One of the biggest myths about people like me, the sociopathic and psychopathic of the world, is that we're all evil geniuses. That we're all highly intelligent and if we're not racking up body counts we're running oil companies and hedge funds.

Not true.

Go to any prison and you'll find a high percentage of psychopaths. And yes, they're in prison because they got caught. Not swindling millions from little old ladies, or plotting to take over the world—no, they got caught robbing banks or stealing cars. The reason for that is, psychopaths tend to be reckless, to repeat the same mistakes and behaviors, and in searching for a thrill, they are not careful. Not clever.

Just plain stupid.

So I want to be clear that while I do share many of the same traits as those prison-bound psychopaths, things like impulsiveness, lack of empathy, and ruthlessness, my intelligence sets me apart from the vast majority of them. It's why my recklessness is calculated, planned. It's the difference between jumping out of a plane (them) and jumping out of a plane wearing a parachute (me). The latter is only slightly less thrilling than the former, but a hell of a lot smarter.

Of course, not everything goes to plan. But my intelligence helps there, too. For instance, I knew about Fabien and that American girl. I don't blame either of them, she's very pretty. But knowing about that, unlike everyone else in the family, let me incorporate her into the plan. That wasn't chance, bad luck, or good luck. I knew she'd be coming my way. I knew her body on the landing would make much more of an impact on people's minds, family and police, than the missing paintings. (And if you've not figured it out yet, they were not an afterthought, they were the point.)

Now, I am intelligent but I'm still (sort of) human, which means I do make mistakes. Not finishing her off was one and had me worried for a while, but I know now she didn't see me because she obviously hasn't given the police my name.

And yes, like everyone I do make mistakes. I'm just clever enough, and plan well enough, to get away with mine. So far, anyway. That damned American Marston still makes me nervous. But as I indicated before, I have a plan for him, too, if need be.

Talking of plans, my master plan progresses well. The finger in the box with the other paintings was fun to do, even though it makes it obvious that the mastermind behind all of this isn't Fabien. In some ways it's a shame to narrow the list of suspects for the police, but it was necessary. Well, I *assume* they'll eliminate Fabien as suspect, because who would do that to themselves? I mean, I freely admit I like to be the center of attention and make a scene, but I'm not cutting off my own finger to create one.

Do you want to know how good I am at this? At reading and manipulating people? I know the one question that everyone wants answered right now. Apart from *Who are you?*, of course. The one thing everyone wants to know after they opened the box and found Fabien's finger.

Does this mean that Fabien is dead?

CHAPTER THIRTY-THREE

Hugo looked at the list of names and addresses confirming he was at the right place. The apartment on Avenue Parmentier took up the top two floors of the five-story building, the ground floor being a high-end wine shop, judging from the prices on the bottles staring out at Hugo. He'd stopped at a café run by an American couple for his once-a-month peanut-butter-and-jelly sandwich, and now finished the last of it before ringing the bell for Arnaud Brodeur's apartment. He waited and a hesitant voice came through the speaker a few seconds later.

"*Oui?*"

Hugo introduced himself and asked if he could come in.

"From the embassy? I don't understand."

"Monsieur Brodeur, I am the man who shot your wife's killer. I have some information about him that's not been released to the public, but the police thought should be shared with you."

"You are not the police?"

"I am working with them, monsieur." *Which is to say, they don't know I'm here but wouldn't be surprised to know I am. Unhappy, but also unsurprised.*

"With Albert Mach . . . I forget his name."

"Adrien Marchand, yes."

A pause. "I have told them what happened, what I saw, and I don't want to relive that."

"I understand. I'm not here to ask any more questions about that."

Another pause, then the front door clicked open. "Take the stairs—the elevator is broken. Again."

Hugo made his way up the wooden stairs, after nodding a greeting at the two men dismantling the elevator on the way in. He knocked on the fourth-floor door and a moment later it was opened by a man in his fifties, sturdier than he'd sounded over the intercom. He was almost six feet tall, with gray hair swept back from a high, intelligent forehead, and he wore a gray sweater over a blue collared shirt, and blue jeans.

"Monsieur Brodeur, pleased to meet you." Hugo extended a hand.

"Technically, it's Doctor Brodeur, but I've not seen patients for a few years so either one will do. Please, come in."

Brodeur led Hugo into the sitting room, which was decorated in a modern style and that caught Hugo by surprise. The sofa, chairs, and side tables looked almost new, but when he sat Hugo appreciated that the furniture had also been built for comfort.

"Can I offer you anything to drink?" Brodeur asked.

"No, thank you."

"So. What can you tell me?"

"That the man's name was Victor Roche, and he was nineteen years old. He lived with his mother, but they were both recluses. The neighbors didn't know them and, to be frank, didn't particularly want to know them."

"Not friendly people?"

"That's putting it mildly," Hugo said. "What's not in the press yet, and I'd be grateful if you kept this to yourself, is that he killed his mother, sometime before committing the shooting."

"Killed his own mother?" Brodeur's eyes opened in surprise. "Who does that?"

"People keep asking me that. Unfortunately, the answer is: quite a lot of people."

"Well, in my line of work I've seen a few things, heard of a few things, so maybe I shouldn't be that surprised. But still." He sighed. "What else?"

"We're still trying to figure out how he got the gun, and what his motivation might have been."

"Not some religious nutcase?"

"His mother was religious, but we've not seen evidence that he was. Certainly nothing pointing to him being an extremist and using that as justification for mass murder."

"But you think . . . my wife, it was random still, yes? That's what the other policeman said—she was just unlucky to be in the wrong place at the wrong time."

"Yes, that seems to be right."

"If you hadn't shot him, he might have shot me, too." He looked up at Hugo. "And God knows how many other people."

"I suppose that just means I was in the right place at the right time."

Brodeur nodded. "I read online some of the conspiracy theories. I never believed them."

"Thank you. They were pretty wild."

"So, if you don't mind me asking, how're you dealing with this?"

"In what sense?" Hugo asked, surprised by the question.

"You killed a teenager. That must weigh on you."

"Of course. But I've had a long career in law enforcement and am very good at compartmentalizing."

"So you have killed others?"

"In the line of duty, yes, I have." Hugo thought for a moment, wondering if there was more information he could or should share with the doctor. He came up empty. "Do you have any questions for me?"

"I don't think so." Brodeur's voice sounded weak again, and a moment later he started to wheeze. "Monsieur, you didn't eat peanuts recently, did you?"

"I had a sandwich with peanut butter half an hour ago. You're allergic?"

"Yes." Brodeur was wheezing harder now, glimmers of panic in his eyes.

"Shoot, I'm so sorry. What can I do?"

"I have an EpiPen, can you . . .?" He pointed to the far end of the sitting room. "Bathroom cabinet."

"Yes, of course." Hugo was on his feet in a flash, moving fast toward the bathroom and he only just heard Brodeur croak out the words, "And wash your hands before you touch it."

Hugo found the bathroom and washed his hands as quickly and thoroughly as he could, then dried them and flung open the cabinet above the sink. His eyes scanned the rows of medicines, ointments, and pill bottles, his curious mind registering some of the labels but his decency trying to prevent him from noticing. He found an EpiPen wedged between a box of Benlysta pills and a large bottle of oxycodone with Arnaud Brodeur's name on it. He rushed back to Brodeur, who sat hunched forward, his hands clasping at the seat cushion either side of him as he gasped for air.

Hugo uncapped the EpiPen as he hurried across the room and handed it to Brodeur, who immediately jammed it into his thigh, pushing down on the auto-ejector and holding it still for three long seconds. When he withdrew it, he sat slowly back and almost immediately his breathing sounded easier to Hugo.

"Do you need me to call an ambulance?" Hugo asked.

"No, no." Brodeur's voice was still a whisper. "I'll be fine now."

"I'm so sorry to have put you in this situation."

"No way for you to know. Would you mind getting me a glass of water?"

"Of course." Hugo had passed the kitchen on his way to the bathroom, and hurried back in that direction. There was a shot glass and two stemless wine glasses in the draining board by the sink, so he quickly filled one of the wine glasses with water from the tap and took it to Brodeur. "Are you feeling better?"

"Yes, thank you. And please, it's not your fault—you had no way to know." His voice was almost back to normal and he managed a smile. "My wife, she used to vet every guest, every visitor. I should be careful like that, but I got so used to her doing it."

"I think that would be very sensible," Hugo said.

The color had returned to Brodeur's face, and he looked at Hugo. "You know, I've never known the police to show up and hand out information without asking for anything in return."

It was Hugo's turn to smile. "You are very astute. If you feel up to it, I do have a couple of questions."

"Please."

"*Merci.*" Hugo took his seat again. "Before he shot your wife, did the gunman say anything?"

"Not that I recall, no."

"He didn't shout at anyone in particular, or randomly at everyone?"

"No, I don't think so. It all happened so fast, it's possible he did and that I didn't hear, or I just don't remember."

"Of course. Do you remember seeing him pull the gun out of his backpack?"

Brodeur thought for a moment. "No. I think I'd just put some trash into a nearby trashcan. That's right, some food that was starting to attract attention from ants and flies. I was about twenty yards, less even, and just saw him standing there with the gun pointed at my wife."

"And I think you've said he didn't try to shoot you."

"No, he just started waving the gun at everyone, me included, then kept walking, firing shots. Then you appeared and stopped it."

"Thank you, and I'm sorry to make you think about those events again."

Brodeur smiled. "Well, I did ask if you had questions, so that's my fault."

"That's the end of them." Hugo stood. "Thank you for your time, I greatly appreciate it. And I'm sorry for your loss, truly."

"And the peanut thing." Brodeur stood and winked to show Hugo he was joking. "You washed your hands?"

"I did. But let's play it safe and not shake."

Arnaud Brodeur nodded in agreement and walked Hugo to the door, locking it behind him as Hugo started down the stairs. His phone rang before he reached the next floor down, and Adrien Marchand's name appeared on the display.

"This is Hugo."

"Marchand here. I said I'd call and let you know what was in Victor Roche's suitcase. The one under his bed."

"Thank you, absolutely," Hugo said.

"Where are you? Are you exercising?"

"Walking down stairs. But I can listen and walk at the same time."

"Quite the treasure trove showing a paranoid and delusional young man, or so one of my colleagues with psychological training tells me."

"Like what?" Hugo paused inside the front doors, where it would be quieter than on the street.

"He had quite a few identification cards. FBI, CIA, and MI6. All poor quality but real enough if you want to believe it. He had a map of the Tuileries, and a manifesto we're going to have to release at some stage."

"Can I see it?"

"When we release it." Marchand paused. "Hugo, we're not even supposed to be having this conversation, so I can't be sending you things we're keeping under wraps."

"Fine, I can wait." Hugo tried to contain his frustration. "Can you tell me what he wrote?"

"In short, no. It's a garbled mess of delusional nonsense. The best I can say is, it was him against the world, and he needed people to see the real him. He talked about a grand gesture, or grand finale. Oh, and a lot about hating his mother, but I think we gathered that much already."

"Yeah, the head in the freezer kinda gives that away," Hugo said. "Any mention of his father, or some kind of father figure from his past?"

"Not that I remember. It might have been in there but I wasn't looking for it. Why?"

"Just curious." Hugo thought for a moment. "The woman who was killed, Annabelle Brodeur. If I can't see the kid's manifesto can I at least see the medical examiner's report on her?"

"No."

"Why not?"

"The better question is *why*?" Marchand said.

"Well, now that you've declared me free and clear of any further investigation . . . you have, right?"

"Look, not officially, but you know we have."

"Please make it official. Anyway, I'd like to see the medical examiner's report and the map in the police report showing the locations of the victims."

"Wait, how do you know the latter even exists?"

Shit, I'm not supposed to know about that, Hugo chided himself, but thought quickly. "It'd be a poor investigation if you hadn't mapped the locations of the victims. How else would you account for all the shots fired and the trajectories of the bullets?"

"Yes, I suppose so. But the answer is no. Case closed."

"Adrien. It really can be if I can just see those documents."

Marchand hesitated, but Hugo knew the policeman's curiosity would get the better of him. It did. "Why do you want to see those things specifically?"

"I've had an idea. I need those to see whether it's a good one."

CHAPTER THIRTY-FOUR

Hugo took a taxi back to the embassy, enjoying the peace and quiet on the ride there. Some months earlier he'd decided to err on the side of caution and told his staff not to use ride-share transportation, despite its ease and convenience—what was safe for most people was a potential security threat for embassy staffers. There, Hugo was immediately summoned to Ambassador Taylor's office.

His face was dark with anger. "I thought I made myself very clear about your involvement in the shooter investigation."

"Boss, I was just—"

"Ignoring explicit orders is what you were doing!" Taylor thundered. "Look at this." He held up his tablet, which showed a photo of Hugo exiting the Roche house under a headline that read, *Mastermind Caught Meddling?*

"Oh, for God's sake."

"Precisely my thought. What the hell were you doing there?"

Hugo had thought the conspiracy angle was dead, along with Victor Roche, who was clearly *not* an American.

"Marchand seemed to think I could help. Plus, as far as he's concerned this conspiracy nonsense is dead and buried, so he was fine with me being there."

"That tells me a little about his judgment," Taylor snapped. "And yours is well under review."

"Boss, it's his investigation. We can't pander to the crazies out there, and if I can help him wrap up that investigation sooner rather than later, that's good, right?"

"Did you?"

"Not there and then," Hugo admitted.

"Well, what did you find out?" Taylor was calming down, like a kettle coming off the boil.

"That before he went on his rampage he killed his mother."

Taylor paused, clearly surprised. "Is that unusual?"

"Not for a mass shooter, no. It's pretty common for them to kill someone close to them, especially if they feel like there's unfinished business between them."

"You think there was in this case?"

"I'm gonna have to say yes to that. A big fat yes."

"How so?"

"He chopped her into several pieces." Hugo grimaced. "Head in the freezer, which scared the crap out of Marchand's partner when he came across it."

"Jeez, I bet."

"That's unusual, if you ask me, the dismemberment."

"What do you make of it?"

"Too soon to tell."

"Come on, Hugo, you must have some thoughts."

"I do, but I need to get my mind back on the Lambourd case. The boy Fabien is still missing, and whoever's behind this is now taunting us."

"The finger in the box," Taylor said.

"Precisely. And I have to confess, it doesn't make sense to me."

"Explain that."

"Okay, sure." Hugo took a deep breath. "For one thing, it brings added heat to the case. We're now a hundred percent sure that whoever did this has committed one, and maybe more, acts of violence. That means more police, more scrutiny, and more chance of being caught. So why do it?"

"Good point. But I assume for the same reason every criminal taunts the police. He thinks he's smarter than them and he likes to see a reaction."

"I'm sure that's part of it. But why return the paintings, too? They would have been a taunt if sent by themselves, but along with the finger they don't do much in terms of provocation."

"Why, then?"

"I don't . . ." A thought hit him. "Hang on a sec, boss." He pulled out his phone and dialed Lieutenant Lerens. When she picked up, he spoke hurriedly. "Camille, it's Hugo."

"Oh, the amazing disappearing Hugo?" Her tone was sarcastic, not joking, and Hugo remembered that he'd left her in the lurch. "Look, I'm sorry about earlier. But you probably saw in the news they identified the Tuileries shooter."

"I did. Some French kid. But the news didn't explain why my investigative partner disappeared on me without a word."

"Oh, right," Hugo said. "Sorry about that, a rush of blood to the head."

"I assumed something like that." Her voice softened. "Just don't do it again."

"No, indeed."

"Anyway, the news also said nothing about what you found in the house, or the kid's motive. Religious whacko, I presume?"

"No real evidence of that," Hugo said. "It appears his mother was extremely religious, but of the going-to-church and praying-all-day kind, not the violent kind."

"The kid too?"

"Less so, if anything."

"Then what?"

"We're still working on it," Hugo said.

"We? The ambassador has pulled you off my case for that one now?"

"Oh, no, nothing like—"

"Some warning would've been welcome, Hugo. And polite."

"Camille, no. Lambourd is still my priority, that's why I'm calling. Where are the four paintings?"

"Still being processed."

"Good. When they are, what's the plan?"

"I don't know, I hadn't really thought about it. If we don't find anything, return them, I guess."

"That's what you'd normally do?"

"Yes. If they have no evidentiary value there's no point keeping them. Obviously we'll take photos in case they're needed for any kind of court case, but the pictures themselves can go back. Why do you ask?"

"Just an idea that they are more important to this little mystery than we've previously thought."

"In what way?"

"Still working on that."

"Care to share?"

"Yes, let's talk in person at the Lambourd place. And make sure the family is there. I have something to say to them."

"So do I. We'll know who owns that finger by then, and I'll need to share that information. Nine o'clock tomorrow morning work for you?"

"What about . . .?" Hugo checked his watch and was surprised to see that the working day was at an end. "That'll do just fine."

The next morning, the family gathered in the living room, and Hugo watched from one side while pretending to be on his phone. The lady of the house, Charlotte Lambourd, sat in a chintz armchair reading the morning newspaper, apparently oblivious to the presence of anyone else, including her caretaker, Karine Berger, who fluttered about her like an anxious butterfly.

Édouard Lambourd sat on one end of the long sofa in the room, slowly stirring a cup of coffee that perched on a delicate saucer. He threw occasional glances toward his mother, as if wishing he'd thought to bring something to read, too. He was dressed in a cream cricket sweater and gray slacks, and was studiously ignoring both Hugo and Camille Lerens. The other end of the sofa was occupied by Erika Sipiora, wearing a flowing white summer dress and matching white sandals. Her attention was on her twin brother, Marc, who was pacing in front of the fireplace. All of them had been affected by the finger in the box—it was clear from their faces—but Marc appeared shaken to his core. He'd gone from thinking this was another Fabien jape to fearing that his only son might now be dead.

"Can we get started?" Marc Lambourd asked, stopping to look at Lerens and then Hugo.

"Your sister Noelle isn't here," Lerens pointed out.

"She's not feeling well, again." There was something in the elder brother's voice that gave Hugo pause.

"I guess you could say the real Lambourd family is here," Edward said quietly. Isn't that what you wanted?"

"Adopted as a baby doesn't qualify her?" Hugo made an effort to hide the disdain in his voice, but only because of the news they were about to deliver.

"She's part of the family." Charlotte Lambourd spoke up, and her tone was firm. "My son has a strange sense of humor—ignore him."

"*Alors*, that's fine, we can begin." Lerens cleared her throat. "The first thing is not good news, I'm afraid. The finger in the box definitely belongs to Fabien."

Marc Lambourd closed his eyes for a moment and paled even more, steadying himself with a hand on the mantle. "You're absolutely sure?" he asked quietly.

"Yes, I'm so very sorry," Lerens said. "His print was a definite match. I had three different fingerprint analysts do the work, and they all reached the same conclusion."

"What does this mean exactly?" Marc Lambourd asked.

"I wouldn't want to speculate," Lerens answered. "I don't think that would do any good at all."

Lambourd shook his head and muttered something under his breath. It was clear the family was giving him this moment to gather himself or to take the lead on asking questions. When he remained quiet for a minute, Erika Sipiora spoke up.

"Are you any closer to finding him?" she asked.

"We're doing everything we can, I promise," Lerens said.

"That's not very specific," Sipiora replied.

"When I know something, when I have something I can share, I promise I will."

"Which means that right now . . ." She glanced at her twin brother and didn't finish the sentence.

Hugo knew how the rest of that sentence was about to go: *Which means that right now, you're NOT closer to finding him*. He was glad Sipiora had the decency to cut herself off. Marc didn't need a reminder of that particular truth.

Lerens looked over at Hugo. "Monsieur Marston had something for you all, I believe."

"Oh, yes," Hugo started. "It's not much but I wanted to let you know about the paintings." He held up an apologetic hand. "I know that may not seem like the most important thing right now, but we like to keep you informed of even the smaller things."

Lerens had picked him up from his apartment that morning, and he'd laid out what he was about to tell the Lambourd family. He'd not told her why, which had irritated her, but she knew how he worked, and it was a personal rule that he didn't share a theory until it had taken on a more solid form. He'd seen too many times on the job an investigator come up with or be told a theory of the case, and have that theory drive the investigation rather than the facts. *Theories are easier to come up with than facts, most of the time, and a whole helluva lot easier to use as fuel for a case.* He couldn't even recall who'd told him that, but it was true, and as much as Tom, the ambassador, Lerens, and even Claudia could push him to share an embryonic theory, he wouldn't do it.

"We'll take any news we can get," Édouard Lambourd said, still staring into his coffee cup.

"Two of the four paintings have been processed, the first two that were returned. I'm afraid nothing came of those tests, no DNA or fingerprints that help us." *Just ones that didn't*, Hugo thought.

"So you're returning them," Édouard said matter-of-factly.

"No. Not yet. Same for the other two once testing is complete."

"Why not?" Erika Sipiora asked. "If they're not evidence why can't we have them back?"

"Technically, they *are* still evidence," Hugo assured her. "They were the items stolen. Just because they didn't produce usable evidence, that doesn't change anything."

"So how long will you keep them?" Sipiora gestured to the empty spaces on the walls. "They may not be valuable or great works of art, but they have sentimental value to us and give the room balance."

"I'm afraid we'll need to keep them in the police evidence locker until the case is resolved," Hugo said.

"Resolved?" Sipiora asked. "What does that mean exactly?"

"It means they stay with the police until the perpetrator is caught and prosecuted."

Édouard shook his head with disappointment, but his sister wasn't about to let it go. "That's ridiculous," she said. "You're punishing us for the sins of some stranger. How is it even legal for you to keep property like that?"

"I'm afraid that—" Hugo began.

"What if you never figure out who did this?" Sipiora pressed. "You'll keep the paintings forever?"

"I'm sure after a few years maybe the police would relinquish them, right, Lieutenant?" Hugo turned to her for help.

"That's possible." Lerens frowned. "But I've never seen that done. Evidence is evidence, whether it's a gun or a painting."

Hugo noticed Charlotte Lambourd watching the interaction over the top of her folded newspaper, her eyes on Édouard and then Erika, and occasional glances toward her oldest child, and—it was obvious to Hugo from the way her eyes softened—her favorite child. As Erika fumed at the information she'd just received, the old lady finally spoke.

"My suggestion, detectives," she said, her voice firm. "Is that for the sake of my son and grandson, you stop dithering here, find the person responsible for this outrage, bring Fabien home, and return our property to us the moment that's done."

CHAPTER THIRTY-FIVE

They were walking out of the Lambourd house when Édouard scurried up behind them.

"*Excusez-moi*," he said. "Have you found the person who was following me?"

"Not yet," Lieutenant Lerens said. "But we're hard at work, I promise you. Have you seen that person again?"

"*Non*, are you joking?" Lambourd seemed incensed by the question. "I haven't left the house since that happened, and don't plan to. So I would very much appreciate it if you finished your investigation and caught that person. Soon."

"We will do our best, Monsieur Lambourd. And as I told you before, if you do go out into the city and you see him, call the police immediately."

"As I just said, I have no desire to hang myself out as bait, so will remain here."

"As you wish, monsieur." Lerens turned and walked to the car, Hugo close on her heels. They got in and Lerens asked him, "Where to?"

"I wish I knew. What else do you want to do on the case?"

"I'll head back to the unit. We have the call detail records for all the family's phones. I'm meeting with our analyst to see who's been where over the past week. She's a genius at spotting not just where people's phones hit cell towers but also this new thing called call pattern analysis."

"I read about that," Hugo said. "Something about looking at a person's pattern of how and when they use their phone, and spotting anomalies."

"Right. Like in this case, if someone's phone was turned off around the time Fabien disappeared, when it looks like it normally wouldn't be."

"Sounds useful, if not determinative," Hugo said. "And probably doesn't make for enthralling meetings. If you don't mind, can you drop me at the embassy and I'll do some work there? I want to call our victim Tammy and see how she's doing, whether she remembers anything more." He grimaced. "I should probably tell her about Fabien, too."

"The finger? I'd prefer that not get out right now."

"Your investigation," Hugo said. "I'll hold off on giving her that information, just a general update."

"*Merci bien*, I'd appreciate that."

Back in his office, Hugo dialed Tammy Fotinos to check in on her. She was recovering well, she said, and remembered nothing more that was helpful. She was worried about Fabien, though, and made Hugo promise to call her the moment he found out anything, and he felt a pang of guilt at withholding the fact he was most likely dead.

That responsibility complete, he wandered over to Mari Harada's door and knocked.

"How goes it?" she asked him. "I heard about the finger in the box. What's that about?"

"No clue just yet, but seems likely it's a taunt of some sort. So, a question for you."

"Fire away," she said.

"On the Tuileries shooter, do you—"

"Lemme stop you right there, Hugo." She held up a hand to cut him off. "You know you can't be in on that investigation."

"Oh, you didn't hear? Marchand let me tag along for the raid."

"I heard all right," she said with a chuckle. "And I saw the headlines. But I take my orders from the ambassador, not any of your French police buddies, and last I heard, his orders were that you're walled off." She cocked her head. "By the way, how did the ambassador respond?"

"Not well at first, as you might imagine. It's more about the optics for him than any real concern about me being involved in the investigation, the politics rather than the practicalities. But I get that.

Anyway, we talked and he agrees that now we know the shooter wasn't an American I'm pretty much in the clear."

"Maybe so, but I'm still not sure I need to be telling you anything from my end of things," Harada said.

"Then I'll keep my question general. If I wanted to observe the grounds of the embassy and surrounding streets, would I be able to easily access video surveillance footage from my computer?"

"No."

"We stopped recording our surroundings?" Hugo asked, surprised. "Who ordered that? Last I heard—"

"Hugo, take a breath," Harada said, amusement in her eyes. "You used the word 'easily' and given your technological deficiencies, the answer is no. But it can be done, and I can make it easier. What are you looking for?"

"Not what, but who. Or whom. I can never get those straight."

"No one cares. Who or whom are you looking for?"

Hugo winked. "Let's just say I'll know them when I see them."

"One of your famous hunches, eh?"

"Something like that. Two other questions—do you have a list of suspects for stealing the gun? And do you know when it was stolen, a time frame?"

"Yes, and yes." She wagged a finger. "And that's all I'm telling you."

"I could solve this for you, you know."

"This is where I make a comment about an able-bodied white guy riding in on his white horse and playing the hero, and then roll my eyes so hard my head falls off."

"Fine, don't tell me then. Wait, don't you work for me?"

"We both work for the man upstairs," Harada reminded him.

Hugo turned at the sound of Emma's voice behind him.

"Let me guess," she said. "You left your phone in your office."

"For two minutes," Hugo said. "To discuss important matters with a colleague."

Harada leaned around him to smile at Emma. "And we're all done. You can remove him from my presence."

"We are not done," Hugo said. "I need—"

"To answer your office phone," Emma interrupted. She pointed down the hallway. "And right now, young man!"

Harada grinned and rubbed her hands together. "If there's gonna be a spanking, I wanna watch!"

"That's unprofessional," Hugo protested weakly, trying not to smile.

"Seriously, though," Emma said. "Hurry. Camille Lerens is trying to reach you. Something's happened to one of the Lambourds."

"Which one?" Hugo asked, starting down the short hallway.

"Here's an idea," Emma said. "Answer your phone and find out for yourself."

Hugo strode into his office and grabbed the receiver from his desktop. "Camille, this is Hugo. What's going on?"

"We've had another little twist with our friends the Lambourds."

"What is it?" Hugo asked. "Or should I say, who is it?"

"Our princess has been assaulted."

"Erika Sipiora? What happened?"

"In Parc Monceau, attacked from behind, she didn't see who did it."

"Is she all right?" Hugo asked.

"You've met her, right? Tough lady, and so yeah, she's all right."

Hugo sank into his chair. "Was it a robbery?"

"Looks like it," Lerens said. "Obviously I'm headed back to the Lambourd house now. I can swing by the embassy if you're free to go with me."

"At this rate, we should just set up an office there to work out of."

"I know—all this driving is giving me a bad back."

"That's age," Hugo joked. "And I am free. I'll wait in the usual spot. Try not to run me over."

"Maybe. I'll be there in ten minutes."

Hugo grabbed his jacket and walked to Emma's desk. "I'm going out, and don't worry—I'll keep my phone on and with me at all times."

"As you should," Emma said without looking up.

"Don't you want to know where I'm going?" he asked, and began to walk away.

"I can track your phone, Hugo. I'll figure it out."

"Wait, you can do what?" He pulled up short. "You're joking, right?"

"Me?" Emma gave him her most innocent look. "You know I never joke. Now, off you go."

Hugo set off again and called over his shoulder. "You better be joking—that'd be a violation of my privacy!"

In Lieutenant Lerens's car, Hugo texted Tom to ask if he could use his police sources to find out who the embassy suspects were.

I've worked that favor off, Tom replied.

That's my call. And not quite.

Jerk. You want names or more?

Just one name, actually, but . . .

What? Which one?

I don't know.

Jesus.

Gimme all names and dates of birth. That'll tell me who's guilty.

Just that????

Thank you.

How can you tell from that?????????

Gotta go. With Camille.

Jerk.

Twenty minutes later he was sitting on a sofa in the Lambourds' living room, with Erika Sipiora in a chair opposite them. The left side of her face was slightly swollen, and the makeup she'd applied to the black eye was barely disguising it.

"You didn't make a police report?" Lerens was asking.

"No. There's no point."

"Why not?"

"There were no witnesses, I didn't see his face, and I'm pretty sure there are no cameras in the middle of Parc Monceau, right?"

"That's true."

"And, to be honest," Sipiora said, giving Lerens a doleful look, "my confidence in the Paris police is not at an all-time high right now."

"Given everything that's happened, I would have thought it even more important to report this," Hugo said.

"I thought you should know, yes." Sipiora turned to him. "For this investigation maybe, but there's no need for you or your men to get sidetracked on some completely unrelated and most likely unsolvable crime."

"Did the person take anything from you?" Lerens pressed.

"A broach and my wallet, so he got some cash."

"Credit cards? And how much was the broach worth, do you know?"

"I keep my credit cards in a separate wallet," Sipiora said. "And if I had to guess, the broach is worth very little."

"Do you have a photo, or can you describe it for me?"

"No, I can't," she said, frustration in her voice. "Look, can you please focus on what happened to Fabien? My brother is going out of his mind with worry and no one cares about a stupid broach."

Lerens nodded that she understood, and when she spoke her voice was calm and reassuring. "I promise, looking for whoever attacked you won't detract from this investigation, but on the off-chance it's related, we need to pursue it."

"I wasn't even hurt really," Sipiora protested, weakly this time. "Fine, it's a Georgian design, with a square faceted rock crystal in silver bezel, with scrolled black enamel band with my daughter's name on it."

"It's the one you wore to the party?" Hugo asked. "Gold, right?"

"Yes, that's the one." Sipiora raised an eyebrow. "I'm impressed, Monsieur Marston, there's about one man in a million who would notice, let alone remember something like that."

"Very true," Lerens said, smiling. "But Hugo is special that way, trust me."

"Sentimental value rather than monetary," Hugo said, ignoring the gentle jibe.

"Yes. But I can have another one made. As I keep saying, the important thing is finding Fabien."

"Agreed," Hugo said. "But if it takes no extra resources the police should look into your assault. If nothing else, because we don't want it happening to anyone else."

The three of them turned to the living room doors as a voice reached them from upstairs, the muffled word repeated over and over.

"No! . . . No! . . . No!"

Lerens and Hugo glanced at each other and at the same time leapt to their feet and hurried to the doors. Hugo followed Lerens out to the landing and up the stairs, taking them two at a time to the top floor. They looked to their left, where the voice had come from, and hurried down the long, wide hallway to an open bedroom door. Inside, Marc Lambourd knelt on the floor at the end of an enormous and antique four-poster bed. Stretched out on the floor, with her head in his lap, was his sister Noelle Manis.

Marc Lambourd turned as he heard them enter, his face pale and streaked with tears. When he spoke his voice was thick and disbelieving.

"She's dead. My God, she's dead."

CHAPTER THIRTY-SIX

L erens moved quickly into the room and to Marc Lambourd's side, knelt down, and put her fingertips on the motionless woman's wrist. She glanced back at Hugo and he saw in her eyes that Lambourd was right.

Noelle Manis was dead.

Hugo stepped out of the bedroom at the sound of approaching footsteps. Édouard Lambourd and Erika Sipiora were approaching, worry on their faces.

"What's going on?" Édouard asked. "I heard Marc cry out."

"Please, don't come any closer," Hugo said. "If you can wait for me down in the living room, we'll be right there." They didn't move. "Please, go get your mother and I'll be right down to talk to you."

"Is everyone all right?" Sipiora asked. "Just tell us that."

"No, everyone's not all right." Hugo stepped further out into the hallway to block any view they might have. "Please. I'll be there in a moment."

The siblings glanced at each other, then made a slow U-turn and headed back down the long hallway. Hugo watched until they started down the stairs, and then moved back into the bedroom, where Lerens had a hand on Lambourd's shoulder.

"Monsieur, we need to step outside for a moment, can you do that?"

"Outside?" Confusion wracked Lambourd's face.

"Yes. Leave Noelle here just for a moment while we attend to . . . things we have to do." Her voice was still soft, and Hugo was

233

impressed with how calm, and calming, she was. "Just for a moment, please."

Lambourd stayed where he was, and he looked down at his sister. "*Ma chérie*," he whispered. *My darling.* "What happened? What happened? Please, come back to us."

Lerens stood, keeping a hand on his shoulder. "Just for a minute or two, Monsieur Lambourd, come with me." Her voice and grip were strong enough to persuade him, and Hugo hurried to an armchair, picked up a cushion, and handed it to Lambourd to place under Manis's head. He stood, and Lerens steered him out of the bedroom.

"Find someone to be with him," she said quietly to Hugo. "I'll get a team in here."

"Of course, but I want to look around first," Hugo said.

"Then find someone to take care of him fast."

Hugo nodded and led a catatonic Marc Lambourd down the stairs to the living room. When they entered, his brother and sister moved quickly to his side and guided him to a large, wingback leather chair.

"Thank you," Hugo said. "Where is your mother?

"Probably in the kitchen or maybe her bedroom," Sipiora said. "I texted her but she's not responded, which is normal. What the hell is going on?"

"I'm really sorry," Hugo said. "There's no easy way to tell you this, but your sister Noelle is dead."

Silence filled the room for a moment, and then Édouard said, his voice cracking, "Dead? How is that possible? What happened?"

"I don't know yet," Hugo said.

Marc Lambourd turned his head slowly and looked up at Hugo. "What's going on here? Why is all this happening?"

"I don't know yet," Hugo said. "But I will find out."

"Please." Lambourd sank back in the large chair, defeated and deflated, his eyes staring at the floor in front of him, his face as white as a ghost. Hugo glanced back at him as he left the room, and then hurried downstairs to find the widow who ran this household. The only person he found, though, was Karine Berger, who was in the huge kitchen preparing a tea tray. He introduced himself and she nodded a friendly, if somewhat reserved, greeting.

"Is that for Madame Lambourd?" he asked.

"*Oui, monsieur*, it is." Berger picked up a knife and sliced the crusts off some thin sandwiches, her movements nimble and deft. "She spent a lot of time in England and likes their tradition of tea and sandwiches. Cucumber in particular."

"Not something I ever got used to," Hugo said. "All that bread and cake before dinner. Do you know where she is?"

"She doesn't eat much at night, not anymore. So this is good for her."

Hugo was surprised by Berger, whom he'd not met before. Family members talked of her as if she were someone delicate and emotionally fragile, and maybe she was, but the woman Hugo was talking to seemed at ease, capable, and not in the least in need of protection from a few questions.

"I see. Where is she right now?"

"*Dans sa chambre*, or she should be," Berger said. *In her bedroom.* "Sometimes it's hard to know in this place."

"Well, would you have time to make an extra cup of tea and take it to Monsieur Marc?"

She stopped what she was doing and looked at Hugo. "Normally, if he wants something he will text me."

"I see. He's in the living room right now, and I think he could use some tea. Maybe for everyone."

"Yes, well. I suppose I can do that. He's been good to me, Marc, especially lately. And with all that's going on with him."

"You mean with his son?"

"*Oui, bien sûr.* And his fiancée breaking it off yesterday."

"Right, of course, very sad," Hugo said, but his mind was racing. *When, why, and how did that happen? And of course no one in the family thought to tell us!* "How did you come to find out about that?" Hugo asked gently.

She shrugged. "This family, they talk when I'm there because sometimes they don't see me. It's not that I'm one of them, not in that way, no. That would be impossible."

"Was Noelle one of them?"

Berger's eyes narrowed. "Was?"

Hugo gave her his most disarming smile. She didn't need to know the news about Noelle just yet. "I'm sorry, I meant *is*."

Berger seemed to consider the question, staring at the teapot on the tray. "I suppose, yes. She doesn't always think so, if you ask me. But Madame Charlotte does, I know that much."

Hugo very much wanted to ask about the adoption, find out how and why someone as unmaternal as Charlotte Lambourd would take on another child. But he wanted to inspect the room where Noelle had died before the crime scene team got there.

"I heard Noelle wasn't well this morning?" he asked.

"I don't know anything about that," Berger said. "I didn't see or hear from her." Behind her the kettle bubbled and steamed wildly. "The best tea is made from water that is just about to boil, but hasn't yet. Did you know that?"

"I don't think so, no."

"Well, it is." She turned and poured the scorching water into a mug. "I'll take some to the family. They like the way I make tea."

"Thank you," Hugo said. "And please, would you wake Madame Lambourd and have her join everyone in the living room? I promise, it's very important."

She hesitated again. "*Oui, monsieur, absolument.*"

Hugo thanked her and hurried out of the kitchen, and up two flights of stairs to the top floor. The crime scene unit hadn't arrived but Lerens had retrieved her "go-bag" containing gloves, booties, and face masks, and she handed one set of each to Hugo.

"Put these on," she said. "Then a quick look, but no touching."

"I've done this once or twice before, you know." But he did as he was told and followed Lerens back into the bedroom. To their right a velvet-covered straight-backed chair was tucked neatly under an ornate desk, upon which sat a Gucci handbag, and an open but dark-screened laptop. Beside it was a wicker basket for trash, with what looked like a solitary crumpled piece of paper in it.

Directly in front of them, Noelle Manis lay on her back, dressed in a white nightgown that covered her down to her knees. Her face was pale and waxy, her hands and bare feet, too. Her long, brown hair poured down the sides of the cushion that Marc Lambourd had placed under her head, and her eyes were closed. A line of deep redness looked to circle her neck, somewhere between a bruise and a rash.

"Strangled?" Lerens was obviously looking at the same thing he was.

"Looks like it. Our garroter back again?" He bent to look more closely at the marks on Manis's neck.

"If so, he's learned from his mistakes," Lerens said, her tone grim.

"These aren't . . . something not right about that."

"Meaning?" Lerens stooped beside him. "Ah. Looks less severe than the injuries to Tammy Fotinos."

"Right, which doesn't make sense since Noelle is dead and Tammy isn't."

"Marc didn't mention how he found her, did he?" Lerens asked.

"No, and I didn't ask." Hugo straightened and looked around the room, and then went to the desk. The computer was cold under his gloved fingertips and he couldn't see inside the zipped purse, so he looked across the room, not seeing anything obviously out of place except a pillowcase lying on the floor to the left side of the bed. The pillow itself was partially stuffed under the bed. He moved toward them, and looked at the huge armoire that sat at the back of the large room. One of the doors was slightly ajar.

"Look, don't touch, remember." Lerens was watching him.

"Right, of course." He moved to the armoire, careful not to step on the pillowcase or touch the pillow with his feet. When he got to it he peered inside. "Ah, I see."

"See what?"

He got out his phone and flicked the flashlight app on, and then aimed it at the opening. He shone it up and down, then turned off the app and retreated to the more open area where Lerens stood.

"A rope," he said. "Looks like it's attached to a rail inside, at the top of the armoire."

"And the other end?"

"I couldn't see it, but am guessing it was around her neck."

"Suicide?" Lerens asked, disbelief in her voice.

"Possibly." He looked down at Manis's body. "Doesn't seem very probable, though, does it?"

"*Merde.* We're supposed to be solving this crime, not finding more bodies."

"*Excusez-moi.*" The voice came from the doorway, where a crime scene specialist stood, dressed in white coveralls, booties, and a mask, and with a camera in her hand.

"*Bien*, we're ready for you." Lerens gestured toward the door. "After you, Hugo."

Hugo watched the crime scene tech from the doorway. In years gone by, the photographers were more circumspect about what they took pictures of and how many. They were thorough, sure, but they were the ones who had to develop the pictures, so wasteful and unnecessary shots were extra work. Nowadays, with digital cameras and simple downloads, photographers took hundreds of pictures, which, while more thorough, actually meant more work for the investigators to have to comb through them. And sure enough, this tech was moving through the room, capturing everything from multiple angles and at different ranges at a pace that Hugo found frustrating. He wanted to see inside that armoire.

The tech got there eventually, photographing it from the back of the bedroom, moving closer with more shots, and then close up, cutting it into segments. She moved to get an angle through the cracked-open door. Then she lowered her camera and said, "That's the whole room. I'm going to open this and get what's inside."

"Good," said Hugo. He still had his surgical gloves on and his hands were sweaty now, but he didn't want to remove them in case there was something in there he wanted to inspect for himself.

The tech opened the armoire doors and took another dozen

photographs. That done, she reached in and then held up for Hugo and Lerens to see a length of rope with a noose at one end. She untied the other end from the rail inside the armoire, placed the rope in a plastic bag, and walked across the room to the desk and pointed to the laptop.

"Do you want me to me to try and fire this up?" she asked.

"Yes, please," Lerens said. "If there's a password then just shut it down again and we'll hand it over to our digital forensics people."

"Will do." The tech pressed the power button, and they all waited, watching in silence and not moving as the screen flickered into life. Ten seconds later, she stepped back, took five more photographs, and looked back at Hugo and Lerens.

"You guys might want to come look at this," she said.

A moment later Hugo and Lerens were looking down on an electronic document that had been created and left up on the screen, with five lines of writing on it.

I killed Fabien. He did more to me than you know. I could barely live with myself,
and I couldn't stand him being in the family, seeing him. I couldn't take it.
And now I can't live with myself.
I'm sorry.
I never did belong, anyway.

"Well, well," Hugo said. "The classic suicide note in unclassic format. How . . . helpful?"

"You're not buying it," Lerens said. "Aren't you the guy who talks about following the evidence and not prejudging?"

"I am." He turned to the lieutenant. "I don't suppose it's relevant, but I just found out that Marc and his fiancée split up last night. I saw Karine Berger in the kitchen, and she happened to mention it."

"Doesn't seem like something his sister would kill herself over."

"No, of course not." Hugo waved a hand dismissively. "I just didn't want to forget to mention it."

"Interesting coincidence, though," Lerens mused.

"It sure is."

"And you don't like coincidences, if I remember rightly."

"They happen, which is why someone invented a word for them," Hugo said, deep in thought. "They just don't happen as often as some people would like you to believe."

CHAPTER THIRTY-SEVEN

Hugo and Lerens left the crime scene folks to do their thing—video the scene, photograph it, then place numbered yellow "tents" beside pieces of possible evidence and rephotograph everything, and finally collect and bag physical evidence. Hugo was glad the tech had bagged the rope already. If there were to be telltale forensics here, they'd be on that piece of evidence for sure.

Hugo and Lerens headed down the long hallway to the stairs, their first order of business to talk to Marc Lambourd and the other family members to see if anyone knew anything. As they approached the double doors of the living room, Hugo saw that the entire family was now assembled there. Lerens stopped, seeing the same thing.

"We need to talk to Marc alone," she said.

"We do."

"I feel like if we walk in there and make that request we'll be devoured alive on the spot." She gave Hugo a small smile. "Then again, we're the police and they're just incredibly rich and well connected. Let's go."

Hugo followed her into the room and immediately heads swiveled their way, but Hugo didn't particularly like the looks they were getting. Édouard Lambourd and Erika Sipiora stood by the large fireplace, as if drawn by the absent paintings to fill the gaps on the walls with their own visages. Marc sat on the sofa with his head in his hands and an empty teacup on a low table in front of him. Charlotte Lambourd sat in a comfortable armchair closest to him, and when she turned to look at Hugo and Lerens, her eyes glittered and her jaw clenched.

"Good afternoon," Lerens said. "First of all, I am very sorry for your loss. Please know that we are working diligently to find out precisely what happened and what is going on."

"Not for long," Charlotte Lambourd said.

"Excuse me?" Lerens cocked her head, clearly not understanding.

"I called the *préfet de police*. You will be replaced, due to your intrusive and ineffective techniques and investigation."

"No one has mentioned that to me," Lerens said stiffly. "And until they do, I will carry on with my duties."

"And I don't work for the *préfet de police*," Hugo said. He turned to Marc Lambourd. "Monsieur, may we speak with you in private for just a moment?"

"Why in private?" Charlotte demanded. She was still in charge, but Hugo could see how the news about Noelle had rattled her. And Marc Lambourd, for once in his life, looked unsure. He glanced at each member of his family, none of whom seemed to give him any visual cues. He stood slowly and sighed, then nodded and walked toward Hugo and Lerens.

"There's a small study, not open to the public—we can use that," he said. He led them out of the living room, turned right, and passed the top of the staircase and then stopped in front of a wooden door that had a discreet keypad beside it. He punched in a code and pushed the door open and beckoned them to enter.

Small? Hugo thought, amused. It was at least three times the size of his office back at the embassy. A large walnut desk sat to their left with a solid oak chair behind it. Opposite them, with its back to a window, was a chesterfield suite—a deep-buttoned three-person sofa and matching armchairs in a rich brown, and well-used, leather. The room smelled a little musty, and Hugo soon understood why—bookshelves filled with leather-bound books, maybe law books, filled the wall space to his right.

"This was my father's study," Marc Lambourd explained. "We'd only come in here to get yelled at, or when he wasn't here to find his secret stash of postcards. I wonder if all fathers are so obliv—." He stopped himself midword, realizing the import of what he was saying. "Jesus. I guess we are." He sank into one of the chairs, and Hugo and Lerens perched on the sofa across from him. "My God, my poor boy." Lambourd looked up. "What's going on here?"

"We're close to finding out," Hugo said, ignoring a look from Lerens.

"I mean, first Fabien, then Noelle. Am I next, am I on someone's hit list?"

"Monsieur, when did you last see Noelle?" Lerens asked.

"Yesterday evening." He shook his head. "She had a migraine this morning, so I didn't see her."

"That happens often?" Hugo asked.

"I'm afraid so." Lambourd looked pale, exhausted. "She's seen every specialist there is, but the only thing she can do is lie in the dark and wait for it to pass. We all know not to bother her, there's nothing we can do, and trying to help just makes it worse."

"You two were close?" Lerens asked.

"We were. The closest of all the siblings, I'd say." A hitch in his voice reminded Hugo what he'd heard before.

"Until Noelle made those accusations."

"They weren't accusations, not really." Lambourd's tone was firm, absolutely certain, but he didn't look at either Hugo or Lerens. "Just a misunderstanding. We all got past it."

Unless you all didn't, Hugo thought. *Was it bad enough to give Noelle a reason to hurt Fabien, or Marc to hurt Noelle maybe?*

"May I ask why your engagement ended?" Lerens asked. Lambourd looked up in surprise, and she said in a kind voice, "Yes, we know."

"Of course you do. This family has the darkest of secrets but can't keep that one for more than an hour."

"Why was it a secret?" Hugo asked.

"Because it was no one's business but ours," Lambourd said. "Who told you?"

"Can you tell us," Hugo said, ignoring the question, "did you break it off, or did she?"

"How is this relevant to anything? I mean really?" Lambourd stared at him for a moment, and when Hugo didn't reply Lambourd seemed to give in. "I'm not even sure. I think she was starting to, then I got angry and finished breaking it off."

"Why did she start to?" Hugo asked, his tone gentle.

"Many reasons. We'd had problems, she and Fabien hadn't been getting along. And no, nothing like with him and Noelle. Then my mother . . . she's been making comments throughout the engagement and I suppose they finally got to her. She said she didn't want to be part of such a, excuse me for repeating her words, a fucked-up family."

"How was she not getting along with Fabien?" Hugo asked.

"I told you, not like that. And it doesn't matter. My mother was the main problem, if you ask me."

"Why didn't she like your fiancée?" Lerens asked.

"She never got to know her," Lambourd said, his tone bitter. "Took one look at her lineage, or lack of it, saw she had olive skin, and concluded she wasn't good enough for her son. No matter what her grown son himself thought."

"And she made her feelings known, obviously," Lerens said.

"It's one of the reasons she called the *préfet* about you," Lambourd said. "She's a racist old woman. God knows what she thinks of the whole gender-swapping thing."

Hugo bristled at the words, which in his mind intentionally were thrown like darts, but Lerens ignored them.

"You said it didn't matter about what happened between Noelle and Fabien," she said. "But no one has said exactly what it was, and it might matter. Can you tell us, please?"

He stared at her for a long moment, and then snorted. "If I don't, I'm sure a member of the family will be happy to. Édouard, most likely—he does love a salacious story whether it's true or not." He sighed and sat back. "About six months ago, Noelle said Fabien had been peeking at her."

"Peeking?" Hugo asked.

"Like in the shower. Once there, and once in the bedroom."

Lambourd waved a hand. "I talked to him about it. Both times it was accidental."

"How so?"

"The first time he was wanting to borrow a book from her, the second time . . . I don't even remember. But she'd not locked the door either time, she admitted that."

"I see. So basically no big deal, as far as you were concerned," Lerens said.

"Not at all. To her, I guess it was. We talked about it, but she never really believed him—not because he was lying, but she just . . ." He shook his head. "I don't know, sometimes I get the feeling she resented him for coming between her and me."

"Monsieur." Lerens cleared her throat. "Can you describe as precisely as possible how you found Noelle? And why you went in?"

"Huh?" Lambourd looked up, as if remembering that Noelle was the reason he was in there with two investigators. "Yes. Of course. I went in because no one had seen her all day. I thought maybe she'd recovered and gone out. She'll go for a walk in the park sometimes after it clears up. But she'd be gone so long. That was unusual so I wanted to check in case . . . I don't know, in case she was still in there and needed help."

"And where was she exactly?" Hugo asked.

"I saw her as soon as I came through the door." Lambourd's eyes glazed over as he remembered the scene, and his voice became a monotone. "It didn't make sense at first. Like, why she'd be there, in front of the armoire. I could see her head but it was too high for her to be sitting on the floor. I knew something was wrong so I ran over and she was just . . . dangling on the end of that rope." He shivered and took a deep breath. "I held her up with one arm and managed to get the rope off with the other. It was so tight, I had to really . . . it was hard to get it off. And you arrived soon after. How did you know to come?"

"You cried out, monsieur," Lerens said. "We heard you and came immediately."

"I don't recall doing that," Lambourd said.

"That's normal," Hugo assured him. "Let me ask you this, if I may be blunt. You said earlier, first Fabien and now Noelle. Do you doubt that she committed suicide?"

"Of course I have doubts. Why would she do that?"

Lerens shrugged. "Her role within the family, perhaps? Did she have depression? Any other mental health issues?"

"She seemed sad sometimes, bitter maybe, but that's the Lambourd family motto. And if there was any depression it was very mild," Lambourd said. "She certainly hasn't tried to hurt herself before, nothing like that. Not that I know about, anyway."

"How long did you know your fiancée?" Hugo asked.

"Eighteen months. We've been engaged for the last six."

"When were you planning to get married?" Lerens asked.

"We were supposed to discuss that with the family this weekend. We never got around to it, obviously."

"No, of course not."

"She had a joke about us." Lambourd closed his eyes for a moment, then reopened them and went on. "It was no secret that she had trouble fitting in, anyone would. But she'd say that maybe if she hung around the family long enough then she'd get Stockholm syndrome and live with our craziness."

"That's one way to do it," Lerens said, with a sympathetic smile. She glanced at Hugo. "Hey, what's with you?" Hugo had fixated on a space somewhere over Marc Lambourd's right shoulder. "Hugo. Anyone in there?"

"That's it." Hugo turned his head and looked at her. "That might just be the answer."

"Stockholm syndrome? The answer to what? This case? How?"

"Enough with the questions." Hugo stood. "But not exactly."

"*Not exactly* to which one?" Lerens asked him, exasperated.

"It's the only thing that makes sense—it must be. Not exactly Stockholm syndrome, of course, but some variation of it."

"Hugo, you're rambling like a lunatic. What are you talking about?"

Hugo turned to Marc Lambourd. "Odd question, but do you

know if Noelle ever locked her computer with a password, and if so do you know what it was?"

"She didn't, no," Lambourd said. "She barely used it so had nothing to protect. Why do you ask? And what is this about Stockholm syndrome?"

"Hmm?" Hugo was still lost in thought. "It's when a captive becomes desensitized to their situation and starts to sympathize or have positive feelings toward his or her captors. Sometimes even come over to their cause, if they have one."

"No, no." Lambourd waved away his answer. "I know what it is. I want to know how—"

"Not this case, something else," Hugo said. "Monsieur, may we have your permission to look at its contents—her computer, I mean?"

"I . . . suppose so, yes."

"Thank you." Lerens stood and gestured to the door. "Why don't you rejoin your family? And, of course, if you can think of anything else please let us know."

"Yes, of course." Marc Lambourd stood and walked to the door. He paused, his hand on the knob. "Why is this happening to us? To our family? And where is my son?"

"I hope we'll have answers for you soon, monsieur," Lerens said.

Lambourd said nothing in reply, just opened the door and left it open as he walked slowly back to the living room. Lerens turned to Hugo.

"What do we tell the rest of the family?" she asked. "That they managed to drive their sister to suicide because she was adopted as a baby?"

"No, not that."

"Then what?"

"Oh, no, I didn't mean . . ." Hugo looked up at her. "I meant it wasn't suicide."

CHAPTER THIRTY-EIGHT

Lerens hurried after Hugo as he trotted down the stairs, phone in hand.

"Where are you, Tom?" he muttered as it rang. "Hey, there you are. Did you find out the suspects?"

"Easy, tiger. How about a *Hi, Tom, how're you?* Or maybe, *I miss you, Tom, I don't see you enough these days?*"

"Yeah, yeah, miss you," Hugo said. "The suspects?"

"You're an insensitive monster. I don't know how Claudia puts up with you. By the way, I saw her out with another guy last night. Real handsome fellow."

"Good for her," Hugo said, impatient. "We're not dating exclusively, Tom, so stop trying to snitch on her."

"Okay, well, it was a lie to see if you had feelings. You don't."

"I do, just not for you." Hugo couldn't help but smile as he said it. "Now, the names?"

"Yes, yes, you want me to list them? There's five people at this point, and Hugo, there's something you need to know."

"What?"

"They haven't said anything officially, not even to the ambassador," Tom said. "But the investigation is basically out of string."

"Meaning?"

"The five people are all administrators. They share log-in information for the system that keeps track of and catalogues the weapons."

"So?"

"So, all five have been grilled and all deny it. Without an

admission, a confession, there's no way to tell which one made the false entry."

"Sounds like the system needs to be changed," Hugo said mildly.

"Oh, once Taylor hears about this little flaw, I'm betting it gets changed in a hurry." Tom paused, and then said, "Wait, you don't care that it can't be narrowed down. Ahh. You've already done that."

"I think so."

"Dude, you haven't even seen the list of administrators. How can you narrow them down without even—"

"By their ages," Hugo interrupted. "And just the women."

"It was a chick who stole the gun?" The surprise in Tom's voice was clear. "Wow. Didn't see that coming."

"Tom, focus."

"Right, yes. The women. Let's see, there are three on the list and all are French. Sixty-three, thirty, and twenty-two."

"Do you have marital statuses for them?"

"Err, looking . . . yep."

"I'm betting the thirty-year-old is unmarried," Hugo said.

"Was that a question?"

"Tom."

"Yes, she's unmarried. But so is the twenty-two-year-old."

"Too young."

"For what? And how did you know the thirty-year-old would be unmarried?"

"Thanks, Tom. When this is all over I'll buy you dinner and explain."

"When will that be, exactly? I'm pretty hungry right now."

"Not tonight, sorry," Hugo said. "But very soon, if I'm right. Send me her name, will you? The thirty-year-old."

"This isn't some bizarre new way of finding dates, is it? Because if so, I want no part of it."

"Very funny. The sooner you send the name, the sooner you get a free dinner."

"Already did. Now go do your solving thing."

Hugo hung up and wandered into the kitchen, his nose leading him in there once it caught the rich scent of something baking in the oven. At the far end, Édouard Lambourd was pouring a bottle into what looked like a coffee filter that sat atop a crystal decanter.

"Port?" Hugo asked.

"*Non*, but a good Bordeaux."

"I tasted a 1963 Cockburns port once. It'd been decanted, of course, and I tried it alongside a younger port."

"That so?"

"I was stationed in England, years ago. I told my host I wouldn't be able to tell the difference since I'd never drunk the stuff."

"Ah, I see." Édouard Lambourd smiled. "With a '63 Cockburns, I'm betting you could."

"No comparison—they were almost two different drinks." Hugo inspected the label. "You always drink wine this good for dinner?"

"Normally, no. We're trying to do something nice for Marc." He finished pouring the last of the wine into the filter, and Hugo watched as the red liquid dribbled down the inside of the decanter. "He lived in England for a while, liked it very much. So we're preparing a nice, traditional meal for him. Comfort food, I suppose."

"I've heard he's a big believer in food feeding the soul as well as the body."

"Yes, he most definitely is." Lambourd rolled his eyes. "And I suspect that came from his fiancée's influence, so I think tonight we can indulge him."

"That is nice. What are you making?"

"Erika and I are sharing the duties, but she's a better cook than me. I take care of the wine, and bought the most expensive *foie gras*. She's making a steak and kidney pie with mashed potatoes."

"That's what I'm smelling," Hugo said, his mouth almost watering. "Delicious."

"It's all a little heavy for my palate, but I grant you it smells heavenly."

"For dessert?" Hugo asked.

"Ah, for dessert she's making bread pudding." He grimaced a little. "Sticking with the theme of heavy food, it seems."

"And yet, still delicious."

"Perhaps. Of course, the *foie gras* and the wine had to be French. English pâté is . . . lumps of meat, no better than dog food, and their wine is worse than vinegar. And we can hardly drink beer for dinner."

Hugo smiled. "Hardly."

"You Americans drink beer with dinner, *n'est-ce pas*?"

"Americans don't discriminate. They drink beer with lunch, dinner, snacks, whenever they want. We are less bound by tradition, perhaps."

"Or taste, perhaps."

Asshole, perhaps, Hugo thought, but just smiled, and asked, "Your mother, how does she feel about English food?"

"Unless it's high tea, then not much."

"I would imagine she's not going to eat the pie or the pudding."

"Probably not." Lambourd smirked. "But then again, neither will I. I think I told you, I'm a vegetarian, so just Erika and Marc will have that pleasure. After all it's for him, *n'est-ce pas*? Mother will enjoy the *foie gras*, I'll have a salad and maybe some pudding, and everyone will appreciate the wine."

"That seems like a confusing way to prepare a dinner, all around one person." Hugo checked his watch. "Late dinner, too."

"We are accustomed to that." Lambourd peered at the oven timer. "I'd guess ten o'clock, which is fine. Also, he's our brother and while we've suffered one tragedy, he's suffered two. It's not such a great sacrifice."

A thought nudged at Hugo, like the first large wave of an incoming tide, and it almost shocked him with its cold touch, with the sense that there was another surge coming. Not of salty water, of course, but a second revelation that was inevitable and devastating, another blow to this noble if horribly flawed family.

"If you'll excuse me, I should get back to work," Hugo said.

Lambourd looked surprised. "*Non*, it's late. Have a glass of wine, relax for a moment."

"I'd love to, but right now there's something I need to take care of." He ignored Édouard Lambourd's suspicious look and hurried from the kitchen. Camille Lerens was headed down the stairs, her face like thunder. "Camille, I wondered where you'd—"

Lerens glanced over her shoulder to make sure she wasn't being followed by anyone. "The old lady. A witch. Not enough that she wants me removed from this case, but she had to list all my failings one by one, while making very obvious allusions to my gender and sexuality, heavily dosed with racism and—"

"She's awful," Hugo agreed. "But I need a couple of things. I think I have an idea what's going on."

Lerens stopped three stairs from the bottom. "You do?"

"I do."

"What do you need?"

"An autopsy report, if it exists, which I doubt, and some medical records."

"I heard you ask for one earlier. You need me to get the same one?"

"No. That was for the Tuileries case, this is for ours. Two different people—autopsy report and medical records for one, just medical records for another."

"But who . . ." Lerens frowned in thought. "I assume the medical records are for Tammy Fotinos for some reason. But the autopsy report . . . we've only had one person dead and there's not been an autopsy performed. Yet."

"Wrong on both counts," Hugo said with a smile.

"*Merde*. I hate it when you're like this, so smug."

"Sorry. But you like it when I'm right, don't you?"

"Of course. Fine, tell me what you need and I'll get it."

"Thanks," Hugo said. His phone buzzed and when he checked the screen he saw Mari Harada's name. "I need to take this."

"But who do you need those records for?" Lerens asked, exasperated.

"Hi, Mari. Hold on just a second." He had the phone to his ear but looked back at Lerens. "Camille, if you don't mind can you head back to the prefecture and start drafting the search warrants, or whatever you use to get that medical information. We need them as soon as possible. I'll text you the names once I know both of them."

"How can you know you need medical records, but not know the names?" Lerens asked, incredulous. "You know what, never mind, I'll just do as I'm told, but it's late so we won't get anything until tomorrow, probably in the afternoon."

"That's fine," Hugo said. "I can have a relaxing dinner with Tom, maybe Claudia, and sleep late tomorrow."

Hugo smiled and gave her a friendly wave as Lieutenant Camille Lerens stomped out of Château Lambourd toward her car, muttering to herself but, Hugo hoped, with hope in her heart that they were close to catching their killer.

CHAPTER THIRTY-NINE

Hugo stepped outside of Château Lambourd barely a minute after Camille Lerens did, his boots crunching on the same gravel that her tires had kicked up as she sped from the property. The sun had drifted downward in the western sky, and was now floating behind the trees that separated the château's manicured lawns and the public lands of Parc Monceau, casting long shadows over the grass and the driveway in front of Hugo.

He started walking toward the exit that would lead through a private gate, down a small alley, and then onto the Boulevard Malesherbes, which was busy at this time of night with people looking for somewhere to grab a late bite to eat, or a nightcap if they'd already dined. The smell of grilled lamb drifted over to him, quickly overtaken by a closer and familiar odor of freshly baked pizza.

He decided to eat alone, not wanting to wait for however long it might take Claudia or Tom to get to him and, in any case, he'd been around people all day and welcomed the idea of a few minutes to indulge himself, by himself. He might even eschew the house wine for something more sumptuous. Not anything the Lambourds would drink, no doubt, but something that would linger on the tongue rather than just wash the day from the back of his throat.

He walked with one eye on the sidewalk cafés and restaurants, not caring about the type of food or name on the awning, looking instead for just the right seat—one looking out onto the sidewalk, with his back to the wall (not window), and preferably away from any heavy smokers. A quarter mile from the Parc, he spotted the perfect dining spot and slid quickly through several rows of happy eaters and squeezed himself behind the small round pedestal that bistros and cafés used as tables.

To his left, six old men had pulled tables close to sit together and were ordering, some in broken French but some fluently, which intrigued Hugo. He listened. It was a new mystery to solve, how these men of different nationalities knew each other, were eating together.

It turned out to be not much of a mystery. They were comrades from the Second World War, a mix of French and English survivors whose paths had crossed seven decades previously in the worst possible way. Here they were, together again, to share as many bottles of wine as they wanted instead of sipping stale water from mud-spattered canteens. To enjoy plates of *escargots* and duck confit instead of chewing on stale bread and scooping franks and beans from a can. The waitress brought him a basket of bread, and Hugo pointed to a mid-range-priced bottle on the menu for himself, more interested in the conversation to his left than whether he'd ordered a Bordeaux or a Burgundy. From what he could tell, two of the men knew each other well, one Frenchman with a fine, white mustache and the American who sat beside him. The American seemed to know the other four, but he'd introduced them to the Frenchman as if they were strangers, swapping not just names but also regiment details from their war service.

Hugo was distracted for a moment when a waiter slid between the close tables in front of him with a large pizza dripping over the edge of a plate, the scent of blue cheese and caramelized onions reminding him to order, and order fast. But his ears tuned back into the old boys' chatter, mostly because they were telling literal war stories, and Hugo had long been fascinated with both world wars. He was almost annoyed when his phone rang, but when he saw it was Claudia he gladly answered.

"It's a sad day when I get news about my lover, the great American cowboy, from the internet before I get it from him," she chided.

"What now? Did I mastermind the heist of the Mona Lisa or something?"

"Quite the opposite. That Marchand character was saying nice things about you, how the Tuileries shootings case is closed, and you're a hero after all."

"Closed? I never said it was closed, not at all."

"Hugo, it's his case, not yours. He gets to decide that."

"Yes, but—"

"Are you outside? You're not on a date, are you?"

Hugo smiled. "Would you mind if I was?"

"I'd dash over there and murder the bitch," Claudia said, with a giggle.

"I'm having a bite at a bistro before heading home."

"With Tom?"

"No."

"Camille?" Claudia guessed.

"With Hugo, and only Hugo."

"Are you serious?" She sounded genuinely outraged this time. "Hugo, you should've called me. I have nothing to do tonight and haven't seen you for months. Or it feels like months."

"Days, technically. But I know what you mean." Beside him, one of the old Americans had launched into a tale about being stuck in a burning church in the middle of nowhere with a sniper just waiting for them to come out. He tried listening to both the old man and Claudia, but he missed her question. "I'm sorry, what did you ask? A little noisy here."

"About how the case is going. But call me when you get home, if you're not too tired. You can tell me from the comfort of your couch."

"I could do that," Hugo said. "Or, if you want to meet me there in an hour, I can tell you in person from the comfort of my bed."

"I like the sound of that. Want me to bring anything?"

"If you have a decent bottle lying around, you can bring that," Hugo said. "And maybe that French maid costume."

"We just call them maids here, Hugo." She laughed again. "And you must be thinking of one of your other girlfriends. I have no such thing."

"I'll take you how you are, my dear, costume or not."

"Same. But maybe greet me at the door in a double-breasted suit and that fedora I like."

"We'll see. Make it ninety minutes. I haven't ordered yet and need to get back home somehow."

"And find that suit."

Hugo chuckled. "Yes, and find that suit."

The waitress appeared as Hugo hung up, and he ordered the same pizza that had wafted past his nose. It would be too big for just him, of course, but leftovers were always a good idea. That done, he sat back, took a large mouthful of wine, and tuned back into the war stories flowing over the table next to him. The Frenchman with the white mustache had a hand on his American friend's shoulder, and they were taking turns with their story about the sniper.

"There was one way out," the Frenchman was saying, and in impressively good English. "And George, he finds three twigs for the three of us. Breaks one in half and holds them so we can't see the broken one."

George guffawed, and spoke to the other four men. "Arnaud here looked at me like I was crazy. Like I'd lost it. He had no idea about drawing the short straw!"

All six men laughed, and the one furthest from Hugo, a tiny old man wearing a blue baseball cap, asked, "So, what happened? Who got the short straw?"

The two comrades looked at each other and then down at their drinks. Eventually, George spoke. "The man who's not here. His name was JJ. Good man, could make you laugh on your worst day."

"He went out first, huh?" the hat man said quietly.

"*Mais*, non," Arnaud said, a look of surprise on his face. "You were never in that situation, my friend, that much is clear."

"He drove tanks, remember?" George said, nudging his French comrade.

"Ahh, *oui*. Of course." He took a slow sip of what looked like whisky. "First out, no, that's not how it works." He looked up at the man with the cap. "There was one way out. The building was on fire. That bastard knew we had to come out at some point, and soon. He was waiting, watching. And one thing he knew, we wouldn't come out until we had to." He waved an arm. "Maybe reinforcements would come, drive him away, and save us. Maybe it would rain and the fire would stop. No, he knew we'd only come out when we had to. And I could picture him looking down the barrel, the sights of his gun on the front door of that damned church, his finger on the trigger." He took another sip. "George here went first. That bastard got a shot off but was well behind. This old man used to be fast!"

"A donkey is fast when it's being shot at," George said. "Bet your ass I was."

"I went second. The shots were closer to me but I ran until I got to where George was. Safe." He sighed and shook his head. "By then, the sniper had his eye trained, his reflexes. JJ was faster than us, but not fast enough. One shot, his brains in the dust."

"We told him to wait," George said quietly. "We said we'd find the sniper and kill him, but the fire was too fast, too hot, there wasn't time. So we tried to distract the sniper. We knew JJ was making the most difficult run, was in the most danger. We didn't have enough bullets to shoot so we started throwing things, that barrel, you remember?"

"Yes." Arnaud nodded. "But it was obvious what we were doing. It was too loud, so clear to the bastard sniper it was just a distraction. And told him where we were, which made him feel safe. And so all we can do is occasionally meet on the anniversary of that day, apologize to JJ for failing him, and drink ourselves closer to joining him, wherever he is." He raised his glass and the other five did the same. "To *mon ami*, JJ Hensley."

"Wait a minute." The man with the blue cap sat with his drink in the air, staring at George. "Your last name is Hensley."

"Yep," George said. "JJ was my little brother. He was my only brother, and I couldn't save him."

There were murmurs of sympathy around the table, but Hugo didn't hear. Didn't see the waitress arrive with his pizza, and a flirtatious smile. Didn't see or hear anything except the interior of Château Lambourd, and the rushing sound in his ears. It happened like it always happened, the kaleidoscope of facts jumbled and spinning in his head, colorful and confusing, jigsaw pieces tumbling around each other to show visions of what happened but no coherent picture.

Until they did.

In these moments, Hugo found it hard to breathe, his whole body focusing as the pieces fell into place and the picture formed. Where gaps remained his mind reached for the things he understood the least and tried them, one by one, until the edges matched up and their meaning became clear. And as exciting as these seconds were, there was always a tinge of regret that it'd taken him so long. He looked down at his phone, which he'd pulled out without realizing, and dialed Camille Lerens.

"I know what happened," Hugo said. "And I know why."

"Seriously? How? I mean who, and what?"

"Ironically, some old men nearby. They were a distraction for me, and they were talking about a distraction that didn't work. It was too obvious. The distractions, I knew there was something off. I knew it but I couldn't figure out what it was until now."

"The paintings, you mean?"

"No, they weren't a distraction at all. They were the point."

"Then what are you talking about?" Hugo didn't respond, a new thought swelling inside his mind. "Hugo, answer me. And how sure are you? Do we need to get over there tonight?"

"Oh, my God." Hugo rose slowly to his feet as he realized what was about to happen. "Not just tonight, Camille. We need to get over there right now. Hurry!"

CHAPTER FORTY

Hugo scrambled in his jacket pocket for his wallet and felt a wash of relief at the stack of euro notes. He threw two twenties on the table and ran. It took him five minutes to get back to the château, but it felt like an age, his fingers clumsy and fat on the keypad that let him through the private gate, his boots slipping on the gravel as he charged toward the front door. He was prepared to kick it down, but the family hadn't locked it for the night yet, a security failure that otherwise would've annoyed him given what the Lambourds had suffered recently. But the threat wasn't from any outsider, from some kidnapper or debt-collector—no, the threat was from within and was far more insidious, far more evil, than any outside danger could have been.

Hugo raced into the main hallway but slowed to a walk to give himself a moment to catch his breath. He was sure he was right about who was behind it all, he *knew* he was right, but he was dismayed by how cold and vindictive this killer was.

He heard voices coming from the large kitchen and strode in to find the family gathered around the long wooden table, which had been covered with a tablecloth and decorated with candles and two small bouquets of daisies. Karine Berger was at the stove and stared as he came in. The room was full of the smell of cooked pastry, meat, and garlic, but Hugo almost gagged at the rich aroma.

"Monsieur Marston, what are you doing here?" Marc Lambourd asked.

"Monsieur, you were not invited to dinner," his mother snapped.

"You can't just come in whenever you want. I don't care who you think you are."

Hugo looked at the table and was relieved to see they'd just finished the first course of *foie gras*. The steak and kidney pie, Erika Sipiora's creation, sat on a wooden cutting board on a counter in front of Karine Berger, who drifted over to them, her eyes on Hugo.

"Should I get another plate?" she asked Charlotte.

"*Non*, he is leaving. Is the pie ready?" She waved a hand over the table. "Clear these and bring it over. The American will show himself out."

"No, he won't," Hugo said firmly.

"Why are you here?" Édouard Lambourd asked.

"Because I know what happened. I know what happened to Tammy Fotinos, why the paintings were taken." He turned to Marc Lambourd. "I know pretty much everything."

Lambourd's voice was quiet. "So you know what happened to Fabien, too."

"Not all of it. I was hoping for some enlightenment here."

Charlotte Lambourd pointed her knife at Hugo. "Are you accusing someone in this household? Because if you are, you better be very careful about what you say."

"I agree with my mother," Erika Sipiora said. "And if you know who is behind this, why are you here without the police?"

"They are on the way, trust me."

Charlotte banged a tiny fist on the table with surprising force, and the silverware and plates on the table rattled. "We will not say another word until the real police are here."

Hugo thought quickly. He knew it would be best if at least Camille Lerens was there. He didn't want to tip his hand, and even though he was armed, and presumed none of them were, he was still outnumbered. And he had no doubt at all that, given the chance, his quarry would slit his throat and sip fine wine as he bled out.

And this crazy family might even help bury my body, he thought.

"If you won't leave, then stand over there," Charlotte Lambourd said, pointing to the far corner of the kitchen.

"With all due respect, Madame, I'll stay where I am," Hugo said. "And I'd ask you all to do the same."

"We can eat, surely," Marc Lambourd said.

"No, you can't," Hugo said, and moved to the table. He picked up two bottles of wine and put them on a sideboard behind him.

"Nonsense, how dare you?" Charlotte Lambourd said. "Let us have our meal, for God's sake. This is an outrage."

Karine Berger was clearly more intent on obeying her mistress than listening to Hugo, and she carried the pie on the cutting board and put it in front of Marc Lambourd.

"Here you are," she said. "You serve those who are eating it. I will get the mashed potatoes."

"Don't touch that," Hugo warned. "I mean it."

"For heaven's sake, this is ridiculous." Marc Lambourd picked up a large serving spoon and was about to plunge it through the crust when Hugo barked at him.

"I said no!" Hugo pulled his Glock from his shoulder holster and pointed it at Lambourd, who stared back at him in apparent disbelief. Charlotte Lambourd and Karine Berger gasped, while Édouard and Erika Sipiora froze in their seats, mouths gaping.

"Are you insane?" Marc Lambourd finally asked.

"No, but I'm very serious," Hugo said.

The sound of approaching sirens grabbed everyone's attention, and gave Hugo the time he needed to holster his gun, step forward, and scoop up the pie from in front of Lambourd. He put it behind him, beside the wine.

"What the—?" Lambourd started to protest, a large serving spoon in his hand.

"No alcohol, and definitely no English pie," Hugo said.

Moments later they heard the sound of tires skidding in gravel, and then footsteps running into the house and through the grand hall.

"In here, the kitchen!" Hugo shouted, and two *flics* followed by a hard-breathing Camille Lerens ran into the room and came to an immediate halt. The policemen had their weapons drawn and held in the *sul* position, clutched close to the chest with the barrel pointing to the ground.

"What's going on, Hugo?" Lerens demanded. She scanned the room for the apparent danger, the emergency Hugo had transmitted over the phone, but all she saw was a family sitting down to a late supper.

"We have a killer at the table," Hugo said, his tone mild.

"This is outrageous," Charlotte Lambourd stuttered. She rose to her feet. "You two . . . you are maniacs set on destroying this family, and I will see to it that it's you who are ruined. Your careers, your lives, how dare you come in here—"

"That's enough," Lerens snapped, and the old widow glared at the lieutenant for a moment before sinking back into her chair, a thin arm reaching for her water glass.

"Hugo, with me," Lerens said, not any more kindly. She looked at the police officers. "No one leaves. No one so much as moves."

"And no one gets any goddam pie," Hugo said quietly, ignoring the inquisitive looks from the *flics*.

They moved out of the kitchen into the large hall, and Hugo could see Lerens was unhappy. Not just at being yelled at but also at Hugo for putting her in a position where she didn't know exactly what was happening.

"Camille, listen," he started, knowing he owed her an explanation. "I would have explained everything on the phone but there wasn't time. I had to get back here and stop that." He waved a hand toward the kitchen.

"The family meal?"

"Actually yes. Okay, here's the story as I see it." He looked around and, not seeing any chairs, steered her to the wide steps, which creaked gently under their weight as they sat. "Like I said on the phone, this was about the paintings after all. And before we do anything else, you need to get someone to retrieve them from the evidence locker and strip them down, take the frames off, the backing if there is any. Every part that can come off needs to."

"We'll need a search warrant."

"Then get one," Hugo said. "Until that happens, we won't have any hard proof of what I think happened."

Lerens looked at him for a moment. "Fine, I can get the process started, but not until you've laid out your case. A magistrate is going to want new facts, supportable facts, before essentially ordering the destruction of Lambourd family heirlooms."

"Understood," Hugo said.

"And even if we get a signature tonight, we won't be doing anything until the morning."

"But you can still make an arrest tonight?" Hugo asked.

"If you convince me, yes."

"Good," Hugo said. "Which takes us back to the theft of those paintings not being a distraction."

"You mean, because if it was a distraction, it was too obviously one?" Lerens ventured.

"Exactly. But our killer jumped on the fact we thought it was and provided several other distractions, the more the merrier to lead us down all the wrong paths."

"Such as?"

"Edouard being followed and Erika Sipiora being assaulted."

"I see." Lerens sighed. "You're not going to tell me who the killer is right away, are you?"

"You need to see how I got there. I don't want to start with the conclusion and explain my reasoning, Camille. I want to show you my calculations and see if you agree with the answer."

"I don't see why," she said.

"Because we can't get the proof until the morning, at the earliest. And even then, it will support my theory and maybe not point to the actual killer."

"Are you saying Fabien is definitely dead?"

"I'm afraid so."

"Are you a hundred percent sure about that?"

"Yes, I am."

"Hugo, listen." Her eyes narrowed and she looked hard at him.

"These people. They can destroy careers, just like the old lady said. Unless you have enough for me to walk out of here with a suspect in handcuffs, enough that they stay in handcuffs, you've put me in a very difficult position indeed."

"I know, Camille." He swallowed, suddenly worried she might not see it the way he did. He was right, he *knew* he was right. But would she? "So listen very carefully to what I have to say. If you think I'm wrong, I'll do everything I can to take the fall for this evening. I promise."

"Oh, I'll listen." Lerens nodded her head slowly. "But it better be good."

"It's not." Hugo smiled grimly. "It's absolutely abominable."

CHAPTER FORTY-ONE
THE KILLER

There we were. Sitting around the table like the happiest family in the world instead of the most dysfunctional. Two cops with their hands on their holsters looking for an excuse to shoot the overstuffed, overfed, and overrich family that their own lower-middle-class upbringings had taught them to despise.

I don't know if anyone had been suspecting poor Noelle of being the killer. Obviously not, at this point. The suicide note was a slightly obvious touch, but I needed finality, I needed the case to be closed, and she was more expendable than anyone else. I mean, the lumbering oaf Karine Berger maybe, but if she's not around to take care of Mother, who's going to do it? Not me, nor the other siblings. Plus, poor Karine is a few IQ points shy of a mongoose, and I may have underestimated the American and his trans sidekick, but I never thought they'd buy into Karine being a criminal mastermind.

And that leaves three.

The American seems very sure of himself, which is consistent with every American I've ever met, but the policewoman, Lerens, she's not. I'm guessing she's smart enough to know that her career is riding on what happens in the next few minutes because my mother isn't joking about ruining careers, lives even. I think she's where my ruthless streak comes from. Of course, I enjoy it more than she does, or maybe she just hides her pleasure as well as I do.

We're starting to look at one another, around the table. We're not allowed to move and no one knows what to say, so here we are with our thoughts. With our doubts and suspicions.

Even my mother. I think part of her would be proud of the cold-blooded machinations of one of her kids, but I also think she'd be very angry. Mostly that she'd not figured it out, that she'd raised a monster in her own image without realizing.

And yes, that means she killed her husbands, of course it does. I don't have any proof that would stand up in court, but I know the facts and circumstances of their deaths. And I know her. Know that just as I am her, she is me. And in her situation, I know exactly what I would have done.

There's a test for psychopaths, developed by some doctor named Robert Hare in the 1970s. Seriously, it's a test—you answer twenty questions and you can score zero, one, or two for each. If you end up with thirty or more points, congratulations—you made the cut. I diagnosed myself, by the way. I didn't need that in some doctor's notes or computer, waiting to be spotted by someone ready to blackmail me.

Here's where I scored two out of two, to get me to my final score: lack of empathy, lack of remorse, superficial charm, glibness, impulsive, don't learn from mistakes, need for stimulation, cunning and manipulative, a frequent liar, a shallow affect, living a parasitic lifestyle (although who in my family doesn't?), sexual promiscuity, early behavioral problems, irresponsible, no long-term goals, failure to accept responsibility, and many short-term marital-like relationships.

I was at a thirty-four, which was disappointing—I don't like others scoring higher than me. I want the maximum. I'm competitive that way.

In that vein, I would also love to know if that American has really figured out the extent of what I was doing. I actually think maybe he has.

CHAPTER FORTY-TWO

Camille Lerens held up both hands, letting Hugo know that if he wasn't prepared to name the killer just yet, she was going to direct the flow of information.

"How do you know it's someone inside the family?" she asked. "Let's start with that."

"Lots of reasons," Hugo said. "The superficial ones, like no signs of a break-in or intruder, no obvious reason anyone would want those paintings, and no real motive to harm either Tammy or Fabien from outside the family. Plus, burglars don't usually carry garrotes."

"True. And the gambling thing didn't go anywhere," Lerens conceded. "Not to mention, Fabien might have been a difficult kid, but we couldn't find any real enemies."

"Right, with no ransom note, kidnapping was never the likely answer. And then there were the signs that pointed toward the family."

"Like what?"

"The paintings. They were returned to a place where they'd be found, where they wouldn't be harmed, and at a time when whoever returned them wouldn't be seen."

Lerens nodded her agreement. "Only the family would be able to find out the gardeners' schedule and have access to the return site."

"And no one would bat an eyelid at a member of the family taking a stroll through the garden. And remember, I talked to the head guy about when the edging was done. That told me the rough time the paintings were stashed and again suggested someone in or very close to the household put them there."

"Hang on," Lerens said. "What was the motive, money?"

"Revenge. Pure and simple."

"That surprises me with this family," Lerens said. "I thought everything was about money and status. And who was it that said, *a man who desires revenge should dig two graves?*"

"I don't know," Hugo said. "But in this case it's not a man, it's a woman."

"Seriously? You mean . . ."

"Erika Sipiora."

"I said it before, Hugo, and I'll say it again. You better be damn sure about this before accusing her of murder. No, not just sure. You better be *right*."

"Ten years ago Erika had a daughter called Alice, named after the little girl's great-grandmother. She'd have been three years old. Ten years ago to this very day, that daughter died. I wanted the medical records because I think that Erika found someone who . . ." He stopped himself and thought for a second. "Look, I don't have any proof yet. I think we need to have this discussion in the kitchen. There are some secrets those people have been keeping from each other and I think you need to put on your camera phone, the video, and we need to go in there and confront them. That's the only proof you're going to get right now, and without it Erika may well go free tonight. And with her resources, maybe we never see her again."

"I need more than that, Hugo. What possible motive could she have to kill her nephew and her sister, and basically destroy the family forever?"

"Revenge, pure and simple."

"Explain," Lerens insisted.

"You remember we couldn't figure out why the paintings and the finger were in the box. We knew they were a taunt, but we were wrong about who was being taunted."

"Not the police?"

"Not the police," Hugo said. "She was taunting Marc. Including the paintings was another distraction, and a successful one for a while. We bought into it. But the finger, that was for Marc and only Marc. Until he saw that, he was barely concerned about his son's disappearance. He and everyone else figured it was the usual Fabien mischief."

"But the finger changed that," Lerens agreed. "What else?"

"Come on, Camille, we're wasting time out here." Hugo was impatient, the pieces were assembled in his mind, and he knew a confrontation was necessary to getting Lerens on board.

"Almost. A little more to make me believe."

"Look," Hugo said, leaning forward. "Erika was the one who immediately pointed to Fabien as the one sleeping with Tammy Fotinos, making him our number one suspect, or so she hoped. And I don't know if you noticed, but she was the one who pressed hardest for the paintings to be returned."

"So what?"

"They were key to her plan. The point of it, which I'll get to."

"What else?"

"It was nothing at the time, but I overheard a conversation, an argument, between her and Marc, and part of it had to do with her having a printer delivered here."

"For the suicide note."

"And the note on the box that had Fabien's finger on it. Only she didn't need the suicide note in the end. She got lucky with Noelle's unlocked computer. Maybe if you scour the house you'll find it. Look in every trashcan and recycling container, if these people even believe in that."

"So she's seeking revenge against Marc. Why?"

"She blames him for her daughter's death." Hugo stood. "I'll explain more when we're in there, but let's get on with it."

"*Merde*, Hugo. And you get mad at Tom for pushing the envelope." She threw her hands in the air in exasperation. "It's on you if this goes wrong."

"Agreed."

"No, I mean it. If this fails, it'll be you I lead out in handcuffs. I may take them off in the driveway but not before I've introduced your delicate areas to the tips of my boots."

"Duly noted." Hugo took a deep breath. "Let's do this."

Camille Lerens stood and led the way back into the kitchen, and when they entered, all eyes fell on them. Hugo admired her in that moment, the way she commanded the room and held herself like the strong policewoman she was, speaking only when she was ready to. When she did, everyone in the room hung on her words.

"Hugo Marston is the most intelligent man and finest investigator I have ever known. He has made some allegations to me in private about one of you, and he expects me to arrest that person. I will do so, unless the person has an explanation for some of the evidence that, at this moment, seems very incriminating indeed." She glanced at Hugo, and he knew he was the only one to see the twinkle in her eye. "And I have assured him that if there *are* valid answers to his questions, I will arrest him for trespassing. I will take him out of here in handcuffs myself."

"That would make us all very happy," Charlotte Lambourd said. But the venom had gone from her words, drained away by tiredness and, perhaps, the knowledge that one of her children was to be revealed as being as cold-blooded as she was.

"Princess Erika, am I right that today is the ten-year anniversary of your daughter's death?"

Sipiora sat stiffly in her chair, watching him closely, only her lips moving. "It is."

"And am I right in thinking that her death was not necessary, not inevitable?"

"She had kidney disease," Sipiora said. "Incurable kidney disease."

"You're not answering the question." Hugo's voice was gentle. He didn't need tempers flaring right now. "She could have been saved, right? Ten years ago today, she could have been saved."

"This is ridiculous," Marc Lambourd said. "What are you doing?"

"And monsieur." He turned to Marc Lambourd. "Am I right in thinking that you're the one who could have saved her?"

"How?" Édouard Lambourd spoke up for the first time. "What is he talking about?"

"I wondered if you knew," Hugo said. "I assumed the whole family was tested to look for a match, but I have no idea who had access to the results."

"Well, yes, I was," Édouard said. "And yes, we were tested, but no one matched."

"Not true," Hugo said, looking at Marc Lambourd.

"Wait, Marc." Édouard managed to look both confused and outraged at the same time. "You were a match for Alice?"

"No," Marc Lambourd said, his eyes down. "I was not."

"Not him," Hugo said. "Fabien was a match, right?" Hugo chanced a bluff. "I mean, that's what the medical records indicate."

"Only in theory. He was too young to donate," Marc Lambourd said hurriedly. "The law did not allow it."

"The law," Erika Sipiora snorted with derision. "Wasn't that the year you off-loaded two yachts and an apartment in Dubai to avoid paying taxes? The same year your girlfriend permanently disabled a man because she was driving drunk, I believe. Are you still paying for that one, or did the poor wretch die finally? I do know that she never saw the inside of a jail cell."

"So, I was right, it was Fabien, not Marc," Hugo said.

Sipiora's head snapped around. "You said you had the medical records that showed that."

"Tomorrow," Hugo said mildly. "I'll have those tomorrow. I was going with my theory. Shall I continue?"

Charlotte Lambourd was looking around the table as if she were in the wrong house, tired and confused, and mumbling something no one could hear.

"You had the means and ability to have Fabien donate a kidney to save Alice," Hugo went on. "You chose not to."

"For God's sake," Marc Lambourd sputtered. "He was a small boy. How could I make him do that?"

"I didn't know about this," Édouard said, almost as lost as his mother. "But you could have saved Alice? No one needs two kidneys. He'd have been fine."

"I wasn't going to risk it," Marc Lambourd said emphatically. "I'd lost my wife, his mother, and there was no way I was going to lose him, too. Not for something that wasn't my fault. And by doing something that was against the law. It was too risky."

"It wasn't risky at all," Sipiora said. "I had the surgeon, the hospital, all of it ready and you were told how low the risks were. You chose your son over my little girl. No, you chose a tiny piece of your son's flesh, one he didn't even need, over my daughter."

"It wasn't my fault, or his, that Alice had kidney disease," Marc Lambourd said, indignant.

"It's your fault she died of it, though." Sipiora's voice was cold and hard. "And for what? Fabien was a selfish, craven, even more cowardly version of you. He was a worthless human being who did nothing for anyone except himself. For someone like that, my daughter dies." She glanced at Hugo. "This isn't a confession, by the way. Everything I've said is true, and none of it means I did anything wrong."

"It's a pretty good motive," Hugo said. "The ten-year anniversary."

"And nothing happened on the previous nine, so what's your point?" Sipiora said.

"Ah, but this one's different, isn't it?" Hugo stared at her. "This is the first time your little brother started playing happily families, the first time he'd managed to hold together what you could never have."

"He's my older brother." Sipiora's eyes narrowed. "Which you already know, so—"

"Another thing I realized." Hugo held her gaze still. "Another resentment. His special treatment as the firstborn when you were actually Baby A, weren't you?"

"What does that even mean?" Édouard Lambourd asked.

"When someone has twins, they designate Baby A and Baby B. Baby A is always the firstborn, but Charlotte had complications during the Cesarean section and Marc was taken out first." Hugo had wondered more than once whether, as traditional in mindset and controlling in nature as Charlotte Lambourd was, she'd decided in advance there would be this "complication." He went on. "Another reason to resent him, especially as you found out about all those trinkets and heirlooms going his way. Ending up with Fabien, no doubt."

"So, all you have is this silly motive," Sipiora said. "You said you wanted me to answer some questions, and so far I've not heard any."

"Ah, yes." Hugo noted how cool she was still. Impressive. And scary. "The robbery in the Parc. One thing was stolen, right?"

"A broach, I already described it to you."

"What you described was a mourning broach. One you'd worn since the death of Alice." Hugo pointed to the ceiling. "Almost every photo of you in the living room has you wearing it, which made me wonder when you said it didn't mean anything."

"You're saying I wasn't assaulted?" It was Sipiora's turn to be indignant. "You saw the injuries!"

"I did. I would bet you paid someone, a beggar or someone in need, to rough you up. Their reward was cash and a broach to pawn. A broach you no longer needed, because you were closing your account on Alice's death by taking out Fabien."

"I'm still not hearing any questions," Sipiora said.

"Where is he?" Hugo asked.

"I don't know."

"Bullshit. Where is he?"

"I told you, I don't know."

"Why did you do this?" Marc Lambourd's voice was a whisper, but it drifted across the table, chilling everyone in the room like a ghost. "Did you hurt Fabien?"

Sipiora didn't reply, but Hugo spoke up. "I'm sorry to tell you this, Monsieur Lambourd. But it wasn't Fabien she was out to hurt. It was you."

"Me?"

"He was the tool she used to do that. To her, he was expendable, a means to an end."

"By killing him?"

"You were supposed to wonder. To not know. I think she wanted to torture you by having you live every day hoping for his return, wondering if he was alive somewhere out there." Hugo took a steadying breath, because what he had to say next was perhaps the most horrific accusation he'd ever made. But, so far, Erika Sipiora hadn't cracked and he had to give Lieutenant Lerens a reason, or maybe just the confidence even, to put handcuffs on the woman and put her in jail until more proof arrived. "Tomorrow we will take apart the pictures that we're keeping in evidence, and I think behind the canvas we'll find photographic evidence of your son's death."

"What?" Édouard Lambourd was as white as a sheet, and his eyes were wide with confusion. "That doesn't make any sense."

"It does to her, I'm afraid," Hugo said calmly. "With those pictures hanging in the family home, your son would be looking down at you every second you were in the room, and you'd have no idea. He'd see you, but you wouldn't see him."

"Oh, my God." Marc Lambourd slumped forward over the table and his face was ashen. "I can't believe that would be true."

Hugo looked at Sipiora. "You made a comment to me that struck me as odd at the time. About looking at something but not really seeing it." Sipiora inclined her head as if to acknowledge, even appreciate, Hugo's perceptiveness, but she said nothing. "I'm afraid there's something more," Hugo continued. He felt sick himself, unwilling to say the words but needing Sipiora to give some indication of guilt. Anything. "Something even worse."

"What?" Édouard and Marc Lambourd asked at the same time.

"I'm sorry to have to tell you this, but you need to know. It'll come out at the trial, if there is one. I think that your sister wanted to make you commit the ultimate sin against your son, do something that if you found out about it later could never be undone."

"What? What are you saying?"

"There's a reason she offered to cook for you tonight, and it had nothing to do with sympathy. And there's a specific reason she chose this dish."

Lambourd stared at Hugo and stammered. "You mean, steak and—"

At the same moment, Marc Lambourd made a choking sound and then slumped sideways out of his chair and onto the tile floor. His brother, Édouard, leapt up, threw his napkin onto the table, and strode to the door. Hugo nodded to the policeman to let him pass. Charlotte Lambourd also rose to her feet, but immediately sank back into her chair where she sat, catatonic beside her caretaker, Karine Berger, who rocked gently back and forth in her own seat, repeating a prayer in a terrified whisper, her eyes fixed on the plate in front of her, seemingly oblivious to anything or anyone else in the room.

Erika Sipiora watched it all happen with a smile that spread slowly across her face, a smile of derision and amusement, a smile that never reached her eyes, which she finally turned on Hugo. She said nothing, just held the smile in place and then extended her arms, a polite invitation for Camille Lerens to adorn them with handcuffs.

Lerens did so, handing her off to the two *flics* in the room, and Hugo watched as Princess Erika Sipiora was led from the family kitchen, her head high, her eyes staring straight ahead, and that ghastly smile still playing on her lips.

CHAPTER FORTY-THREE

It was almost midnight when Hugo finally called Claudia to explain exactly what happened. He'd found a moment to text her, to call off their rendezvous, but didn't get to explain until they talked on the phone.

"Hugo, that's just monstrous," she'd said. "How do you explain something like that?"

"I could try," he said, and then yawned. "But can it wait until the morning?"

"Don't you have to go to the prefecture for the execution of the search warrant, for the paintings?"

"Not before breakfast, no. If you want to meet early, we can eat something before I head over."

"I'd love that." She paused and he heard the humor in her voice. "Unless you're gonna cancel on me again."

"If something happens overnight, I may. Assuming I even hear my phone ring, which I won't."

"How about I get Jean to drive me, and we pick you up? Then he can drop you at the prefecture afterward."

"I'm not going to argue with that plan."

"Are you still doing something on the Tuileries shooter?"

"Claudia, I need to sleep. But yes, that's not quite a closed book just yet."

"I don't know how that can be, with the shooter dead, his mother dead, and nothing to indicate another person involved."

Hugo yawned again. "I never said that last bit."

"Seriously?"

"At breakfast. Good night, beautiful lady."

Jean's Mercedes was idling in front of his apartment building at seven the next morning, with Claudia looking beautiful and alert despite the early hour. She threw open the back door and patted the seat beside her.

"You're full of energy," he said, sleep still blurring his vision despite the hot shower he'd taken.

"I get to have breakfast with my lover, why wouldn't I be?"

"Fair enough. Where are we going?"

Six minutes later they pulled up in front of a café Hugo had never been into on the long and narrow Rue Saint-André-des-Arts, and when they went inside two of the waiters recognized Claudia, waving for her to take her pick of tables.

She chose one against the window and they settled in, watching each other and then the people wandering by on their way to work. Hugo ordered orange juice, two croissants, and coffee, and Claudia said she'd have the same. Their waiter, an older gentleman who greeted Claudia by name, bowed after taking their order and said *sotto voce* that their breakfast would be free, in gratitude for Hugo's saving lives in the Tuileries.

Once they had their food, Claudia pressed him for details about the Lambourd case.

"Are you going to write about it?" Hugo asked.

"No, someone else has that assignment," she said. "But I'm so curious—they're such a well-respected family."

"Psychopaths pop up in all walks of life," Hugo said. "Rich or poor, it doesn't much matter."

"But to try and serve her own brother his son in a pie, I mean . . ." Her eyes were wide, almost imploring Hugo to explain something so monstrous.

"Don't think of it as one act by her against him." Hugo sipped his coffee. "Look, ever since she was a child, since she was born, basically, she's resented him. And you have to understand that psychopaths not only have a limited range of emotions, but all those emotions are about them. Everything in their world is looked at through the prism of how it affects them. It didn't matter that Marc loved Fabien, that he was family, that he was a slightly wild but basically normal teenage kid. All that mattered was that Erika's daughter had been taken away by the one person she resented the most. Logic, law, reason . . . none of those things mattered."

"But to go so far." Claudia nibbled the end of a croissant. "It's unthinkable."

"Yeah, to normal people it is. It's sickening. But she doesn't think of Fabien as a human being, nor her brother really. And I don't even think she'd have seen her own daughter as anything but an extension of herself. She would have been a terrible, awful mother, which is part of the irony of all this."

"Yeah, I suppose if she's capable of this she wasn't likely to be nurturing, was she?"

"Not at all. But the one thing she had in common with humanity was that she wanted closure, or the closest thing to it she could achieve. And that meant maximum revenge."

"Something worse than killing Marc Lambourd?"

"Yes. Then she'd have no target for her anger, no outlet for the evil. I'm guessing that she took photos of Fabien, either dead or dying, and somehow put them in the paintings. I think that's something she would never have revealed, maybe on her deathbed, but otherwise, never." He took another sip of coffee. "But the kidney in the pie, I suspect that at some point she'd have let him know, or hinted at it. Nothing he could allege that could be proven, and of course there'd be no evidence left at that point."

"That's so . . . horrific."

"And would have been utterly devastating to him. I mean, that's not something you can tell a therapist and have them make you feel better."

They ate in silence for a minute, and then Claudia looked up. "Wait, what about the sister? She killed her, too? It wasn't suicide?"

"Yes, I'm certain of it."

"Why did she do that? Because she and Marc were close, so to make him more lonely and miserable?"

"Actually no, I think for her that was just a happy by-product of that murder." Hugo wiped his buttery fingers on a napkin. It was a question he felt able to answer, but one that caused him considerable pain. The moment he'd realized *why* Erika Sipiora killed Noelle Manis, he knew it was partly his fault. He was logical and dispassionate enough to know that, in truth, only Sipiora was responsible for Noelle's death. But it was something Hugo had said that triggered Sipiora's awful plan.

"Hugo," Claudia said. "Are you all right?"

"Yeah. I will be, anyway. Sometimes this job puts you close to bad people, and sometimes they're bad enough that you start to blame yourself for things. And sometimes you're right to, just a little."

"Hugo, no!" She leaned forward. "What are you talking about, you've not done anything . . . how on earth could you be responsible for any of this?"

"I get blinders sometimes, when I'm chasing someone. I don't see what the collateral consequences might be because I'm so focused on what I'm doing."

"What are you talking about?" Her voice was firm, and he knew he had to tell her.

"When Camille and I were with the family, after I'd realized that the pictures were at the heart of this, I said something. I said it because I knew it'd provoke a response from whoever the killer was. The trouble is, I didn't know who it was or what they'd do."

"What did you say?"

"I told the family that the paintings were evidence. That, because of that, they wouldn't be returned until the case was solved. That the pictures could stay in our custody for years." He sighed. "I knew that the person wanted the paintings back in the house. And I was right. Erika wanted them there looking over her devastated brother. I just didn't predict how far she'd go to get us to close the case."

"She hung her own sister?" Claudia seemed incredulous. "How does someone even do that?"

"No, I think she used the garrote. It was hard to tell, and may be hard to prove, but I think she used a pillow case to make the mark around Noelle's neck look more consistent with a hanging suicide."

"My God, she's evil." Claudia had tears in her eyes, and Hugo knew they were for him and not for any member of the Lambourd family.

"Evil presupposes some moral direction, albeit a bad one. She doesn't have that. She just cares about survival and her own immediate needs. She's a reptile. Nothing more than a calculating, cold-blooded reptile."

"That's kind of how I thought of the mother, Charlotte." Claudia smiled. "Horrible thing to say, but she does seem a little like that, no?"

"Oh, I agree. I wondered for a long time if she had a hand in this, given her history." Hugo grimaced. "Turns out I was focused on the wrong widow."

Claudia signaled for two more coffees, and they sat and watched out of the window. Eventually, she spoke. "You don't want to go to the prefecture, do you?"

"Wow." He smiled, for the first time since they'd sat down. "That's very perceptive of you."

"I know you, Hugo. You have a huge capacity for dealing with this awful stuff, for putting it in one compartment or other in your brain." She tilted her head and looked at him with kindness in her eyes. "But sometimes even you have had enough. Of someone, or something. And that's totally fine, Hugo. If you've had enough of this awful woman, don't go."

"I've had more than enough. I don't want to be around anything to do with her. But it's my job."

"It's your job?"

"Yes."

"No. You've done your job on this case. You identified the murderer and she's in jail, right?" When he nodded, she went on. "Let me ask you this. Whatever is happening at the prefecture, will your absence affect that?"

"What do you mean?"

"I mean, can they physically achieve what they need to achieve without you there?"

"Well, I don't know." He sat back and thought for a moment. "They're taking apart those paintings, and if they find something, *when* they find something, they'll keep it as evidence."

"You'd just be watching."

"Correct."

"And subjecting yourself to seeing more terrible shit that this woman has done."

"Again, correct."

"Good, then I'll call Camille and let her know you won't be there." Claudia pulled out her phone, and then paused. "I should give her a good reason, though."

"I've got one for you: I'm busy."

"Yeah, she might need more than that. Busy doing what?"

"You asked me about it last night. The Tuileries shooter."

"Right, of course. You have something to do on that case. I'll tell her that."

"Thank you." He drained his coffee. "And it has the added benefit of being true. And since we've finally gotten to see each other, would you care to join me in catching another conniving murderer?"

Claudia looked over the top of her phone at him, and then smiled. "Oh, Hugo. You're such an old-fashioned romantic. Why not?"

CHAPTER FORTY-FOUR

Emma gave Claudia a big hug when they walked into the RSO offices at the embassy, following it with a wink to Hugo, which he ignored.

"You'll be needing coffee, my dears?" Emma asked.

"Not for an hour or two," Hugo said. "And then your strongest brew." He turned to Claudia. "Come meet the new kid on the block."

He led her to Mari Harada's office and knocked on the door. "She keeps it closed so she can control the temperature. Cooler than we have the rest of the office is better for her condition."

Claudia nodded, and when Harada opened the door and beckoned them inside, Claudia quickly closed it behind them. Hugo made the introductions, and while Claudia went to shake her hand, Harada winced.

"Oh, I'm so sorry," Claudia said.

"Not you," Harada said through gritted teeth. "We call it an MS hug. A cute name for a steel band closing around my chest and making breathing painful. Like calling a broken foot a toe tickle."

"Anything we can do?" Claudia asked, exchanging worried glances with Hugo.

"Nope, it'll pass." Harada let out a hiss of air and dabbed at her eyes with the back of her hand. "Hurts like hell but see, all gone. The bastard of it is, there's nothing wrong in the chest, it's the wiring in my brain and spinal cord mixing up signals and making it happen."

"I'm sorry," Claudia said. "How awful for you."

"Well, life can be awful," Harada said, matter-of-factly. She jerked a thumb at Hugo. "I mean, you have to put up with him without being paid, so my sympathies for that."

Hugo smiled. "How do you know she's not getting paid?"

They laughed and then Harada retreated behind her large desk. "You're here for the video files, I assume. And nice idea to bring some backup."

"I was told we were catching a killer," Claudia said. "Not watching videos."

"Same thing," Hugo assured her. "Assuming I'm right, of course. Otherwise a massive waste of time."

"In which case," Claudia said with her sweetest smile, "the murderer will be me."

"I was actually planning to offer my assistance, too," Harada said. "Knocking on doors is a little beyond me these days, but my eyes are working well, as of right now."

"The more the merrier," Hugo said.

Harada's office had space for a second desk, which had a pair of monitors and another computer on it, and a pair of plain swivel chairs that she offered to Claudia and Hugo. "I've set it up for just the two of us, Hugo, but if you each take one screen and I use my laptop every angle will be covered. It's all ready to go—you just need to hit play."

"Wait, I don't even know what I'm looking for," Claudia said.

Harada rolled her eyes. "Nice work, boss. Bring in an unpaid intern and give her no direction or guidance."

"She's a volunteer, not an intern," Hugo said. "And enough of your cheek."

Harada ignored the remark and opened her desk drawer. She pulled out a photo and handed it to Claudia. "It's not a *what* that you're looking for—it's a who. Whom. Whichever. This guy."

"He's a killer?" Claudia studied the photo. "He looks like everyone's fifty-year-old neighbor."

"You're still fooled by appearances?" Hugo asked. "That's cute."

"Hush, you know what I mean."

"We have a twelve-hour period, so play it double-speed but don't take your eyes off the screen," he said. "Or if you do, pause it first."

"Yes, sir." Claudia sat down opposite the double monitors, each of which showed the view from four different cameras high up on the embassy's outer walls. Hugo took the chair beside her, and she put the photo on the desk in between them, for reference. "Probably not the worse date we've been on," she said quietly, trying not to smile.

"You're very welcome," Hugo replied, before Mari Harada hushed them both with a strict look over the top of her reading glasses.

Hugo spent a moment looking at the screen, familiarizing himself with the views he'd be scanning. Two of them looked out over the quiet Rue Boissy-d'Anglas, a narrow street running north-south on the embassy's east side. It was quiet thanks to gendarmes stationed along it, keeping vehicular traffic out, and foot traffic to a minimum. The other two screens looked out over Avenue Gabriel, a much busier street separating the embassy from the popular Jardin des Champs-Élysées. Heavily trafficked by tourists and Parisians alike, spotting their man would be much harder, but Hugo was relying on that common downfall of so many criminals—a combination of laziness and overconfidence. The cameras had actually been placed in the line of trees that sat along the broad sidewalk in front of the embassy, trees that would have blocked any view of the street had the cameras been on the building itself. This wasn't something Hugo knew about, or had even thought about, and he briefly wondered if the local government knew the Americans had security cameras in their trees. But he had more important things to worry about.

He looked at the controls on the screen, and played with them for a moment, zooming in and out as the footage rolled. He glanced at Claudia's large screen and saw she was doing the same.

"Mind some music while we work?" Harada asked. When Hugo and Claudia nodded assent she picked up her phone, hit a few buttons, and Handel's Water Music began to play.

"I expected something more exotic," Hugo said.

"That's because you're a closet racist," Harada said, unable to conceal her smile.

They sat in silence, eyes roaming their screens, looking for the man in the picture. After thirty minutes Hugo groaned and stood up, stretching his back as he watched.

"Maybe we should rotate," he suggested. "That way we won't stagnate."

"You two can," Harada said. "My chair is too expensive for your butt, and my butt is too delicate for those chairs."

"Playing the sympathy card, are we?" Hugo rolled his eyes.

"Damn straight."

Hugo and Claudia swapped places, and did so again after the next thirty, fruitless minutes. Soon after, Emma tapped lightly on the door and brought in a tray of coffee mugs, a much-needed jolt of focus for Hugo. Fifteen minutes later, Claudia sat upright in her seat, then grabbed the photo, and held it up beside the screen.

"You got him?" Hugo asked.

"I believe so. What do you think?"

Hugo leaned over. "That's him, all right. Keep watching. If I'm right about this then in the next five or . . ." Hugo clapped his hands. "Right on cue. There she is."

"Who is that?" Claudia asked.

"Her name is Michelle Hallee," Harada said. "One of the local admin staff, she was on the shortlist of suspects."

"A *rendezvous*," Claudia said. "Prompt people, I like that about them. What's she handing him, the guns?"

"That's what my money is on." Hugo watched intently, and then pointed to the screen as another figure appeared. "Holy shit. There you have it, proof positive."

"Isn't that . . ." Claudia shook her head in disbelief. "That's him. He's the Tuileries shooter, right?"

"It most certainly is," Hugo said. "Victor Roche himself."

"Give me the camera number and the date and time," Harada said.

"I wanna look. I'll also burn that clip to a thumb drive so you can take it to the real police."

Hugo shot her a look. "Oh, you heard about what the old lady said, eh?"

"I did," Harada said. "But don't worry, hon, I'm sure she meant Camille Lerens and not you."

"Probably not," Hugo said mildly. "But they've not been *real* enough to solve this part of the puzzle, have they? So yes, they'll need probably a good five or ten minutes either side of the handover. It increases the tension."

"Aye-aye, cap'n," Harada said.

Claudia read out the date, time, and camera number and, with a few clicks of her mouse, the footage was on a thumb drive that Harada handed to Hugo.

"Here you go, guard it with your life," she said. "And if you agree, I'll have Michelle Hallee watched until Marchand buys in, and then he can have her picked up and questioned."

"I do agree." Hugo shook his head slowly. "Well then, Doctor Brodeur. It seems your moment for the spotlight has come, you murderous bastard."

⚜

Adrien Marchand's office was even smaller than Hugo's, with just enough room for a cheap desk, an expensive office chair behind it, and two wooden chairs opposite it for visitors.

"You buy that chair yourself?" Hugo asked.

"Excellent deduction," Marchand said, his eyes wary.

"Not really. Doesn't go with the state-provided décor."

"I'm a relatively young and somewhat athletic man, Hugo. But someone forgot to tell my back." Behind Marchand hung a print of soccer star Kylian Mbappé celebrating a goal in the national jersey, with the words in French: "I find the harder I work, the more luck I seem to have—Thomas Jefferson."

"You're an admirer of Thomas Jefferson?" Hugo asked.

"I'm an admirer of Mbappé." He paused for a moment. "Is this about my closed case?"

"Yes, your almost closed case that needs one more arrest."

"Yours, for wasting my time?"

"If I am, then feel free." Hugo leaned forward and put the thumb drive on the desk in front of Marchand. "On that, you will find video footage of Arnaud Brodeur meeting with Michelle Hallee, one of just three women who had access to the firearms and the paperwork. Less than a week before the shooting in the Tuileries, she hands him a shoebox."

"On the same day the gun went missing?"

"The very same day." Hugo smiled, saving the best for last, or in case Marchand resisted what he was hearing. The detective digested the news for a moment, and then rubbed a hand over his face as the meaning of this dawned on him. "*Merde.* The husband of the only woman to die in the shooting had possession of the gun that killed her. It wasn't a random shooting at all."

"No, it wasn't."

"You've connected Brodeur with the shooter?"

"Normally I'd say that's your job," Hugo said. "But they made it easy for us. Victor Roche showed up at the handoff."

Marchand held up the disk. "It was caught on this, too?"

"Yep, he steps up just moments after Brodeur takes the box."

"*Incroyable,*" Marchand said. "How the hell . . .?"

"Those writings we found stashed under his bed about being a CIA agent, needing to bring chaos to Paris, sacrifice for the greater good . . ." Hugo grimaced at the thought of that twisted treasure trove. "Turns out Doctor Brodeur wasn't a medical doctor but a psychiatrist. And he wasn't retired—he lost his license two years ago for improper relations with a patient."

"Michelle Hallee?"

"That'd be my guess. I couldn't get that information because it violates patient confidentiality." Hugo smiled. "But I imagine you have your ways. Anyway, I'd put money on Victor Roche having been a patient of Brodeur's at the time he lost his license. From what I know from the investigation, the kid wasn't very bright, was desperate for a father figure, and was extremely suggestible. I think Brodeur got inside his head and convinced the kid he was working with the CIA on some incredible mission. And think about that. As far as I know, the kid had no friends, no family, and not even an internet connection. So it had to be a person filling his head with these ideas. With one specific mission, one that required Victor to shoot people. Or shoot one person and aim randomly at anyone else nearby. Roche was brainwashed into living with some sick form of Stockholm syndrome, you might say."

Marchand shook his head slowly. "If that's true, what a monster."

"A lot of that going around lately."

"So I hear." Marchand picked up a pen and made some notes on a pad in front of him. "What made you look into Brodeur?"

"Two things got my attention initially. I went to talk to him, at his apartment, and while I was there I looked into his medicine cabinet and, among other medications, I noticed Benlysta in it."

"What is that?" Marchand asked.

"It's an immunosuppressant, designed and most commonly used to treat lupus. We knew from the autopsy report that his wife had healthy joints, skin, and organs, which means she didn't have it."

"What about Brodeur himself?"

"Nine out of ten lupus sufferers are women so while that's possible, it's less likely and he didn't seem to be having any issues when I was there. Anyway, it suggested the possibility to me that he had a lover."

"That's quite a leap."

"Not really. I mean, there were also two wine glasses in his sink. Think it through. I knew he didn't have kids, so the meds weren't theirs. Most likely a woman's, and who would keep important medication like that in a mere friend's medicine cabinet? And there was a second bathroom, but it was in *his*. Also, this is just days after the shooting—no way he's on the dating trail already, and even if he was, no way someone with lupus would store her meds in his apartment days after meeting him for the first time."

"So he had a lover before the shooting. Michelle Hallee."

"And she's moved in since."

"That's an elaborate plan to kill your own wife, though." Marchand looked dubious.

"It is. People can be devious, and smart people realize the best way to carry out nefarious acts is to get other people to do them. I mean, yes, complex, but clever and effective. The killer gets killed and why would anyone look further afield?"

"Jesus, he couldn't just leave his wife?"

"Actually no. Since he lost his license she was the sole breadwinner. If he left her, he'd leave with nothing."

"Makes sense. If you're a twisted bastard," Marchand added. "You said there was a second thing."

"The diagram of the scene I asked you for. It shows Victor Roche entering the park more than two hundred meters from where he started shooting. That told me he had a reason to wait, to start shooting at the time and place he did. So, what was the reason? The first person he shot, perhaps?"

"Madame Brodeur."

"Right. And the specific, close-up killing of her, three shots in fact, was then followed by random single shots at people further away. I remember seeing people much closer, easier targets, but he didn't aim for them. Why not?"

"Because his only intended victim was already dead," Marchand said. "The others he shot, they were just out of pure luck. Good for him, maybe, but bad for them."

Hugo nodded. "I think if you search his place you'll find more evidence of the affair, and also something linking him to Victor Roche. And, more likely than not, a fairly recent and impressive life insurance policy."

CHAPTER FORTY-FIVE

The next morning, Hugo was woken by a ray of sunshine slanting through the bedroom window. He rolled over, away from it, and looked at the face of his sometime-lover, Claudia. A wisp of hair lay across her cheek, and he brushed it lightly back into place with his fingertips. Behind him, his phone buzzed on the bedside table and he sat up as carefully as he could to answer it. Claudia stirred and opened her eyes.

"Morning, handsome," she mumbled.

"It is." Hugo looked at his phone, which showed a text message from Lieutenant-Intern Adrien Marchand: *Call me*. Hugo would, but not yet. "Coffee?"

"Not if you're making it."

"Want me to kick you out of bed so you can?"

"No, I want a cuddle before this day starts. Get back in here."

Hugo slid back under the covers and Claudia draped an arm and a leg over him, and then nuzzled her face into his neck.

"Sleep well?" he asked, caressing her arm.

"Like a baby. You?"

"Same, for once."

"I worried the case would keep you up."

Hugo laughed softly. "Which one?"

"Either one. But I'm glad they didn't." She gave him a squeeze. "Was that someone trying to get hold of you already?"

"Marchand. Hopefully letting me know they picked up Arnaud Brodeur."

"You need to call him back?"

"At some point. Keep cuddling for now, though."

"With pleasure."

They lay in silence for a while, and then Claudia gave him one big squeeze before sitting up. "How about I make the coffee while you call Marchand? I'm kind of curious myself."

"Deal." Hugo watched her climb out of bed, still naked, and head to the door, where she paused.

"Is Tom here?" she asked.

"I have no idea. He comes and goes like a specter."

"Better safe than sorry," she said, and grabbed Hugo's robe from the back of the door. She slipped it on, blew him a kiss, and let herself out, closing the door behind her. Hugo took a deep breath, then picked up his phone and called Adrien Marchand.

"Oh, you found my cherry jam," Hugo said. "Where was it?"

Claudia sipped her coffee, and then said, "In the fridge. At eye level."

"Ah. No wonder I missed it."

She'd made coffee but also put three croissants into the oven for a few minutes to heat away the burgeoning staleness from them, and then served up the humble spread on the coffee table, forcing Hugo to get out of bed, put on some clothes, and shuffle into the living room.

"So, what happened?" Claudia asked, before taking a bite.

"Well, they got him." Hugo spread a dollop of jam onto the bitten end of his croissant. "And then he faked a heart attack and tried to escape from the hospital."

"Seriously?"

"He actually managed to unlock his handcuffs, the one attaching him to the rail of the hospital bed."

"Impressive."

"That's what I said." Hugo took a bite and chewed for a moment. "Marchand didn't seem to find it as amusing."

"He wouldn't."

"Anyway, they spotted him sneaking down the hallway, so he didn't get far."

"Did he confess?"

"No, not yet. But the fake heart attack and escape attempt say plenty by themselves."

"For sure," Claudia agreed. "What else did Marchand have to say?"

"Apparently someone who was in the park that evening turned in video footage from their phone that caught the shooting, specifically of his wife. Brodeur just happened to have left her alone and was standing by a trash can looking at his phone when the shooting started. An overflowing trash can that no one in their right mind would want to be standing beside."

"Unless they were making sure they were out of the line of fire," Claudia prompted.

"Exactly. Not exactly a smoking gun, but I think we have that with the handover from Michelle Hallee. Who, by the way, is singing like a bird to save her skin."

"But not a peep from Brodeur?"

"Marchand says Brodeur thinks he's smarter than everyone else and is talking but not giving them anything useful. No admissions, that is."

"Maybe he is smarter than them."

"Maybe." Hugo nudged her with his elbow. "I'd sure love a crack at him—then we'd see how smart he is."

"You'd tie him in knots," Claudia said. "Be fun to watch."

"It'd also be against every rule in the book."

"I'm sure. I'd love to interrogate Erika Sipiora, too, but they found photos of Fabien, dead or dying, behind each canvas, as I knew they would, and per her lawyers she's not talking to anyone. Anyway, talking of books, you should write one now you're an internationally famous hero."

"Me?" Hugo was surprised at the suggestion, partly because it was something he'd thought about a lot, but never mentioned to anyone.

"Not one of the mysteries that you like to read. Although I guess you could. I was meaning about your cases."

"Maybe I will." Hugo polished off his first croissant and tore the remaining one in half.

"You have it," Claudia said. "One's my limit."

"Well, thanks." Hugo ladled more jam onto the pastry. "What about you?"

"What about me?"

"Your writing. Book? Articles?"

"I don't know—nothing worth talking about right now." She got up from the couch. "More coffee?"

They both started at the sound of a crash from the spare bedroom, otherwise known as Tom's room.

"I guess he *is* here," Hugo said. He got up and went to the bedroom door. "Tom, you okay?"

"Yeah, yeah, fine," said a muffled voice. "But what the fuck is this?"

"No clue, I can't see through doors. You want coffee?"

"Hell yes. Hang on . . ."

Hugo stayed by the closed door, but put a hand on the knob when he heard what sounded like wood splitting.

"Tom, what are you doing in there?"

A moment later the door opened and a bedraggled Tom stepped out into the living room. Behind him, Hugo saw a two-foot-long piece of floorboard sticking up into the air.

"Check this out." Tom headed straight for the sofa and plonked himself down on it, grabbing the last half of the remaining croissant and stuffing into his mouth as he sat. Next to the empty plate he put down an object wrapped in a worn and very dirty rag.

"What is it?" Hugo sat down opposite Tom, in an armchair, and leaned over the table. Claudia appeared behind him, putting three mugs of coffee on the table.

"So I lost my balance as I was getting up," Tom began.

"Hungover?" Claudia asked.

"Of course, stupid question," Tom said. He reached for a mug and took a slurp of coffee. "Fuck, that's hot. Anyway, I fell into the tall lamp that you stupidly put too close to the bed. The lamp then fell over and hit the floor, and right where it hit a piece of the board popped loose. I was trying to fix it when I noticed this rag stuffed under the board. Look for yourself."

Hugo reached out and opened the rag. Wrapped inside it was a square, silver case, about the thickness of a smart phone. It was dull and needed a good polish but it looked to be expensive, with intricate patterns engraved on it. Hugo picked it up and rubbed his thumb against what he thought might be an emblem or symbol of some sort.

"Can you read it?" Claudia asked, leaning over.

"It looks like someone's initials. Yeah, it is. *HVL*." Hugo turned it over gently. "It's a cigarette case. Heavy, probably silver." He found a small release button and the case popped open when he pushed it. A tight row of cigarettes lined the inside, their once-white paper slightly yellowed with age. "Complete with antique smokes."

"Why would they be under a floorboard?" Claudia asked.

"No clue." Hugo studied the cigarettes. "But that's odd."

"What is?" Tom asked.

"They're Lucky Strikes. American cigarettes, stashed in a Paris apartment."

"Can you tell how old?" Claudia asked.

"No, but if there's other stuff hidden under the floor that might give us a clue." Hugo stood, and Tom did too. "And a fun mystery to solve."

"Yeah, so let me clean up a little in there first, if you don't mind." Tom ran a hand through his mussy hair. "And make sure my screens are all off. Don't want to frighten the lady."

Claudia rolled her eyes. "It's not 1950, Tom. I've seen whatever you're watching before."

"I doubt it." Tom rounded the coffee table and went into his room, closing the door behind him.

"He's so old-fashioned," Claudia said. "And not in a cute way." She took the cigarette case from Hugo. "So, what do you make of this?"

"I don't really know. But funny to think it's been hiding under the floor the entire time I've been here."

"I wonder who HVL was."

"You're a pretty decent journalist. I bet you could find out."

"Why thank you, handsome." She planted a kiss on his cheek and handed the case back. "I bet I could. And if there's anything else under there, maybe I'll have something to write about."

"Like a body?"

"That might be a little much," she said. "Unless it's a thousand years old. Now that'd be a story."

They laughed, and then turned as Tom opened his bedroom door.

"All safe," he said cheerily. "Grab a flashlight and let's see if there are any other goodies to be found."

"Will do." Hugo turned to Claudia. "Just to be clear, after this last week I'm all tapped out on the clue-solving front. Whether it's just the cigarette case or more treasure, this little mystery is all yours."

ACKNOWLEDGMENTS

A s usual, the help and support of many people made this book possible. I would like to thank the slew of friends and readers who offered up their names for use in the book, you all know who you are! Much gratitude, also, to Jacquie Wiesner for her assistance with French corrections and other edits. Thanks again to James Ziskin, not just a good friend and fabulous author, but the creator of the family tree graphic in the book. Appreciation to Rachel Miner who inspired me to continue to represent the people of the world in my books, especially those who don't normally get a look-in. And thanks to my newest editor, Nicola, who spotted typos and helped me translate from English into American.

And, as always, I am indebted to my fantastic agent Ann Collette, and my long-time and best ever editor, Dan Mayer. Finally, to my long-suffering family, who give me the support, encouragement, time, and love that allows me to stay calm and carry on writing.